From the Heart of a Prairie Farm Wife

by

Maurine Becotte

Bloomington, IN Milton Keynes, UK

authorHOUSE

AuthorHouse™
1663 Liberty Drive, Suite 200
Bloomington, IN 47403
www.authorhouse.com
Phone: 1-800-839-8640

AuthorHouse™ UK Ltd.
500 Avebury Boulevard
Central Milton Keynes, MK9 2BE
www.authorhouse.co.uk
Phone: 08001974150

First published by AuthorHouse 1/23/2009

ISBN: 978-1-4259-2197-2 (sc)

Library of Congress Control Number: 2006903101

Printed in the United States of America
Bloomington, Indiana

This book is printed on acid-free paper.

Dedication

This book is dedicated to all of Maurine's children, grandchildren and also to the great-grandchildren she never had the opportunity to know. Maurine loved each and everyone for who they were "Her Family".

Appreciation

*I would like to express my thanks to those who helped me
make this book possible.
Thank you to -
Rhonda Boxall for her typing skills,
Karen Bullerwell for helping me with Mom's Biography,
Grace Pollock for proof reading for me.
My children Paul, Robbie and Carrie and
my brother David and family,
who encouraged me in this endeavor.
Thank you also to all the
STAFF at AuthorHouse Publishing.
Without their patient guidance this book would not have
been possible.*

*Thanks Mom for leaving us this wonderful legacy.
And last but not least. Thanks Dad,
for the many times you were an
inspiration to us all and for the encouragement
that kept Mon writing.
Mom, Dad, you were the best,
that is why I felt I should share this book
with anyone who wishes to read it.*

Your Loving Daughter, Elaine

TABLE OF CONTENTS

FRANCE 1940

Death and destruction on every hand,
As we fought each other in No-Man's Land;
The Poles were with us; the Czechs were for us,
All of us guided by one commend,
All were trying to stop that German Band.

We thought of our homes, our loved ones dear,
We laughed at danger, we scoffed at fear;
Our only goal was to rid the land,
Of that cruel, destructive, unmerciful band.

Bombs fell like rain from the planes o'er head,
The R.A.F. to our aid they sped;
The trouble was it came too late,
For Adolph Hitler had written our fate.

'Twas a well fought battle and hard to lose,
Between death and defeat we had to choose;
We stood up well, we faced our foe,
But one or the other had to go.

We had to retreat from that Nazi band,
Letting them o'er run our dear homeland;
But someday, God willing, we'll cross the Rhine,
And re-establish the Maginot Line.

- 1940 -

TO A CROW

Oh, noble bird of glistening black,
We see the sun shining on your back.

We watch for you in your ebony coat;
As you fight the weather to keep afloat.

We anxiously listen for your plaintive cry;
As you soar about in the prairie sky.

Some think you silly to come so soon;
But on the prairie we welcome your tune,

You walk, you strut, you know your worth;
The sign of spring, the land's rebirth.

We hear your caw tho you cannot sing;
When you appear, 'tis Spring, 'tis Spring.

- February 1973 -

FRANCE OF FORTY-FOUR

The sky is now so dark with planes,
The channel white with foam;
The allied forces swooping o'er,
The land we once called home.

Those little Boats of Britain are,
A crossin' o'er the lea;
While ships of allied nations ply,
Back across the sea.

It will not now be long,
Until we're free again,
To show this whole wide world,
That we are not insane.

They drove us from our dear homeland,
Forced us to do their will;
With threats of death and bondage,
They weren't ashamed to kill.

But now that German army,
Are having such a time;
That if God is only willing,
They'll loose our Maginot Line.

We'll drive the Huns before us,
Back to old No-Man's-Land;
And we'll help the Allies free the world,
Of this cruel, destructive band.

We've suffered now for four long years,
This reign of murder and hate,
For our defenses were ill prepared,
And the Allies came to late.

We thought that our release had come,
At the Battle of Dunkirk;
But Adolph knew the answer to,
That little Allied quirk.

But now they're safe at Cherbourg,
Across from good old Dover;
We'll show that German Reichstag,
That this old war ain't over.

The Jersies thought themselves so smart,
With many new inventions;
But as yet our Allied boys,
Have spoilt their intentions.

Their paratroops have landed safe,
Their Dough boys are alright;
And with the close of Forty-four,
We'll see old England's might.

The losses have been many,
But with a definite trend;
We now depend on Churchill,
To lead us to the end.

And with the help of Eisenhower,
As all the Russian brave;
Before this war is over,
We'll build a German grave.

We'll build a mammoth tombstone,
Unequaled in its kind;
And on its broad and gray expanse,
This epitaph you'll find.

"They died but for a foolish whim,
Led by a man insane;
Let God forgive the innocent,
And all the guilty blame."

- June 22, 1944

THATCHERIZATION

Now "fast time" has hit Saskatchewan,
It's caused an awful fuss;
The farmers' wives are frantic,
And the farmers start to cuss.

When your talking to your neighbor,
Or planning on a spree;
Your always have to set the time,
As we're Thatcherized you see.

We used to rise at five o'clock,
And put in quite a day;
But now we have to rise at four,
Since Thatcher's had his say.

He has robbed us of an hour's sleep,
When it feels the best to us;
He knows the farmer will work till dark,
It's the nature of the cuss.

For the farmer is a useful soul,
And don't defend his rights;
Sixteen hours a day he'll work and toil,
And slave from morn till night.

Let Mr. Thatcher bleed us dry,
Of even our ambition;
Or should we farmers all unite,
To send him to Perdition.

Now school it starts at nine-fast time,
Yet in our minds, it's only eight;
But the Unit says we must attend,
And of course we can't be late.

An hour may not mean much to him,
But to stir up a family of nine;
It takes a lot of coaxing,
To have them rise and shine.

Now he may say that to bed they go,
An hour earlier is fine;
But when the sun is shining bright,
How can one confine all nine.

It may be nice for the city guy,
But it makes the farmer bark;
He can't take off at five o'clock,
But much work on till dark.

Perhaps he thinks we'll make the extra,
To pay the raise in taxes;
But what I'd like to see take place,
Is the farmers on their _____.

And when you raise those taxes,
And increase the pension plan;
Up, up go our expenses,
We're against you to a man.

Let's hope that when October has rolled around again,
That our Government officials have become a little sane;
And put us back on standard time, I'm sure we won't complain,
And may we on this good old time, forever more remain.

For the trouble and the turmoil drives the housewife mad,
And upon talking to your neighbor, they think it's just as bad;
So Mr. Thatacher will you listen to a busy housewife's plea,
"Please stick to good old Standard Time or no more votes from me."

- Summer 1966 -

HOMEWARD BOUND

I'm heading for Saskatchewan,
Where the air is pure and free;
I'm tired of city turmoil,
So it's Saskatchewan for me.

They can have their oil derricks,
Where the mountains hem you in;
But I'll take the clear sky;
And the whistling prairie wind.

You can take your fish and fruit trees,
Your sunshine and your rain;
But I'll take Saskatchewan,
With its fields of golden grain.

You can take all Canada,
Inland, lakes and sea;
But I'll stick to Saskatchewan,
Despite its heavy freeze.

They sing about Alberta,
B.C., and all the rest;
But when it comes to freedom,
Saskatchewan stands the test.

So I'm heading for Saskatchewan,
Land of the brave and free;
The friendliest nest, out in the West,
It is the home for me.

- January 1973 -

WE SALUTE YOU PIONEERS

Here's to the Dufferin District,
To those who have come and gone;
Here's to the early settlers,
From nineteen hundred on.

Here's to the early pioneers,
The hardiest and the best;
Coming from the East and the South,
To settle in the West.

Freight in they must from Battleford,
Which was the end of rail;
Slowly, surely the oxen plod,
Along the dusty trail.

Here's to their grit and stamina,
And their belief in God;
As they suffered many hardships,
While they broke the prairie sod.

Suffering from the prairie wind,
Flies, heat and bitter cold;
Prairie fire and lack of feed,
Until some their homesteads sold.

Others slowly worked with oxen,
While some had horses too;
But walk they must to turn the sod,
And stones were quite a few.

Logs and wood came from the river,
To be used for house and fire;
But the spirit of the homesteader,
Never seemed to lag or tire.

The Indians were a friendly lot,
Helpful, kind and good;
Letting white men stay with them,
While cutting logs and wood.

Houses built of lumber,
Were scarce I really fear;
Brought out from the East,
To be reassembled here.

There were many little babies,
Who arrived in a log shack;
But of large and healthy families,
There wasn't any lack.

Almost ninety miles,
The mail team had to go;
In the heat of summer,
Thru the cold and snow.

But the Royal Mail it must go thru,
Regardless of the weather;
For contact with the outside world,
Was a boon to the homesteader.

Fancy clothes were hard to get,
But they did the best they could;
Whether it faintly showed of Quaker,
Or perhaps it was Robin Hood.

Times were hard in those old days,
And money mighty scare;
"Survival of the fittest" was,
The law that was in force.

In 1908 the school was built,
By local talent as you know;
Receiving the name of Dufferin,
From a County in Ontario.

By 1911 Cut Knife started,
When the railway came to town;
Two years later times improved,
And the track was extended on.

They had hauled their grain to Adanac,
With horses and ox team;
When the rail line came to Cut Knife,
It was the farmer's dream

Thrashing grain was quite a chore,
The housewife's task supreme;
They had a crew of twenty men,
And a big engine run by steam.

In the year of ten and four,
Travel was extended far;
A few of the early pioneers,
Bought for themselves a car.

Now the children and the children's children,
Generations one to four;
Have spread across our fair domain,
And also on to foreign shores.

The "Old Folks" too are mostly gone,
But a few are with us still;
Some have moved to warmer climes,
And some to "Heavenly Hills".

So let's salute our pioneers,
For developing a dream;
If it had not been for them,
Where might "you and I" have been.

January 10 -15, 1971

EASTER

Atiskit, Ataskit,
A bunny with a basket;
Hopping here, hopping there,
Goodies, goodies, everywhere.

Chocolate eggs with a hollow sound,
Other candies small and round;
Easter rabbits long and slim,
Easter chickens neat and trim.

But oh, where are the eggs,
With the chicks inside;
With tiny toothpick legs,
And eyes bright and wide.

Where are all the hard boiled eggs,
That the children made with glee;
Now everything's got at the local store,
At a large price you see.

A lot of effort and planning,
Has been put aside I feel;
It has become commercialized,
A great big financial deal.

But it's holiday time for the children,
A sacred time for the old;
A time of religious blessing,
When tales of the Lord are told.

But the part that's most important,
Is the season of the year;
It's time to renew our faith in life,
For spring is almost here.

March 25 - 30, 1972

HOUSEWIFE'S PLEA

A little bit of time for loving and living;
A little bit of time for getting and giving;
A little bit of time, a little bit of time.

A little bit of time for hurrying and scurrying;
A little bit of time for fretting and worrying;
A little bit of time, a little bit of time.

A little bit of time for gardening and growing;
A little bit of time for weeding and sowing;
A little bit of time, a little bit of time.

A little bit of time for dancing and singing;
A little bit of time for working and playing;
A little bit of time, a little bit of time.

A little bit of time for washing and drying;
A little bit of time for cooking and frying;
A little bit of time, a little bit of time.

A little bit of time for milking and churning;
A little bit of time for reading and learning;
A little bit of time, a little bit of time.

A little bit of time for walking and sitting;
A little bit of time for sleeping and dreaming;
A little bit of time, a little of time.

A little bit of time for resting and sighing;
A little bit of time for laughing and crying;
A little bit of time, a little bit of time.

A little bit of time but time's running out;
A little more time we need no doubt;
Is always the housewife's plea.

September 1970

DEPENDENCE

Oh the farmer is a stubborn cuss,
This I will avow;
But I believe it is the weather,
That makes him so, somehow.

For when the spring has rolled around,
And it's time to plow and sow;
The weather man gets ornery,
And surely starts to snow.

But then the sun shines brightly,
And this quickly melts away;
But he must delay his planting,
For yet another day.

The weed seeds are already there,
They really start full force;
But eradicate the blessed things,
The farmer must of course.

So its work the soil, plant the grain,
And harrow it but fast;
Hoping the weather man helps out,
With a shower at the last.

But usually the shower fails.
And the grain it doesn't sprout;
But the weed seeds keep on coming,
So spray we must no doubt.

Next we think we'll summer fallow,
According to tradition;
But those big stones keep popping up,
To spoil our ambition.

A few delays with broken parts,
And the weeds have gone to seed;
And so we turn the cattle in,
To let them have the feed.

Our crops become a bumper,
And our hopes are running high;
But the weather man, he changes this,
By turning very dry.

So first we see it wilt and wither,
And then the bugs appear;
Now again we pray for moisture,
But the Good Lord doesn't hear.

Thus the early crop has had it,
And the late is failing fast;
Then one afternoon at tea time,
The rain clouds roll in fast.

But when the storm is over,
We wish it had stayed away;
For hail the size of golf balls,
Fell on our fields that day.

We look things over carefully,
And decide to leave it stand;
If it does not make a paying crop,
It will at least improve the land.

The weather man co-operates,
With sunshine and with rain;
Our hopes start rising higher,
Only to be dashed again.

As one morning very early,
From out a cloudy sky;
Snow flakes are gently falling,
As the dark grey clouds roll by.

And when a week had passed away,
The summer sun returned;
The crop is badly leaning,
And the farmer's quite concerned.

But the farmer is a saving soul,
As he always needs must be;
So he pulls in with the swather,
And cuts it tenderly.

Now all he has to do is wait,
Until the grain tests dry;
He hopes the wind blows briskly,
With a clear and sunny sky.

He's in a state of mental turmoil,
By the time ten days have past;
Then he pulls in with the combine,
He's underway at last.

But you must hurry Mr. Farmer,
There's always plenty yet to do;
So be an early riser,
And work the whole night thru.

The grain is slowly pouring,
From out the auger spout;
You cuss a little and pray a little,
That the machinery will hold out.

Of course the weather changes,
It could not last for long;
This is the very reason,
The farmer's so stubborn and strong.

So with one more dry spell,
This job is off the books;
But he has several others waiting,
No matter which way he looks.

But the farmer never worries much,
He seldom gets in a stew;
But if the weather only holds,
He can always find lots to do.

So clasp your hands oh farmer man,
And offer up a prayer;
That when you get to heaven,
The weather will suit you there.

October 1970

ASKING MY MIRROR

Fifty years have come and gone,
Since the day that I was born;
Have I justified the end,
For to this world, God did me send.

Have I accomplished what I should?
Have I done the best I could?
Have I led a fruitful life,
Tho somewhat full of toil and strife?

Have I aided those in need?
Have I done my good will deed?
Have I extended a helping hand,
To those worse off than what I am?

Have I been to others, kind and good,
Done as the "Good Lord" thought I should.
Look on my neighbor as a friend,
And tried my erring ways to mend?

Have I walked the narrow line,
Keeping upright, strong and fine;
Set an example for the young,
Yet remaining unknown and unsung?

Now think you well my fellow man,
Examine your life while yet you can;
If you have not held your self on high,
There still is time to have a try.

January 1973

NOW AND THEN

Farming in Saskatchewan has changed a lot you see;
Or have you ever stopped and thought how it used to be.

We used to be small farmers with neighbors close at hand;
But now we live unto ourselves with acres and acres of land.

We used to call upon our friends to pass the time of day;
But now as far as neighbors go you're a hundred miles away.

No matter what you want or do, its always rush to town;
But when you cannot make ends meet, it really gets you down.

We used to farm with horses - four, six or eight a span;
But now they're mechanized and dieselized almost to a man.

Your future power, a little colt, playing happily, you would find;
But did you ever see a tractor with a tractorette behind.

Regardless if it's gas or diesel this you'll never see;
And if you must replace a part, it's as expensive as can be.

We used to get our milk and cream from a bovine with four feet;
But now it comes in box or can, marked dried, condensed or sweet.

It used to be we grew our grain and sold it in the fall;
Now we grow a great deal more but can't sell it at all.

It used to be we had a garden, some chickens and a sow;
We had time for work, time for rest and time for fun somehow.

But no matter what we buy its at the price the others set;
And when we come to sell our stuff, we must take what we can get.

Expenses keep on rising, our income has gone flat;
But no matter what we do, we cannot alter that.

But now its work and worry from morning until night;
If we're to prolong existence, we cannot alter that.

But both ends are fighting, to reach a central goal;
And the farmer's in the middle away down in the hole.

March 1970

CHRISTMAS

When it's Christmas in the prairie and it's twenty-nine below;
The wind is blowing briskly and it's started into snow.

The kids are real excited but a little frightened too;
For fear the storm will heighten and Old Santa won't get thru.

The household's in a dither and mother's in a state;
For fear she cannot chase the kids to bed before too late.

There's streamers hanging crooked and scattered on the floor;
While sister's fighting brother to decorate the door.

The Christmas tree is standing at an angle all awry;
The star on top is pointing anywhere but towards the sky.

With lights and balls and tinsel lying everywhere;
Mother takes a look about and sighs in deep despair.

So rush around "Dear Mother" and put all things to right;
Chase the wee ones off to bed and kiss them all goodnight.

Now place the much desired gifts beneath the honored tree;
Cross your weary hands and pray on slowly bended knee.

For hope and health and happiness in the coming year;
And absence of misfortune that would bring a falling tear.

Now off to bed you trundle in a sentimental frame;
All too soon to realize that morning's come again.

A holler from the staircase, a yell that Santa's here;
A clatter of ten little feet and then a rousing cheer.

You'll never know if Uncle Joe or maybe Aunt Louise;
Had given little Johnny that great big pair of skis.

Or whether cousin Mona or perhaps Old Uncle Jed;
Had really robbed their pocketbook to produce that giant sled.

Now wouldn't it be terrible, when the thank you notes were read;
If you thanked cousin for the skis and auntie for the sled.

So rise and shine "Dear Mother", commotion's underway;
Do you really think that you'll survive another Christmas day?

You'll have to stuff the turkey and put it in to cook;
While reading little Johnny his brand new story book.

Now feed the kids some staples before they start to stuff;
Or else before the day is out; their tummies will feel rough.

The boys are quarreling over who will go out to ski;
While the girls are yelling loudly, "Mommy, look at me".

You turn to see the painted faces supplied by Auntie Jean;
And think your little daughters look like Shiba's so-called Queen.

In the meantime Dad's been taking a lovely beauty sleep;
So you rouse him very firmly with - "You know it's time to eat".

At last the breakfast's over and its getting very late;
The kiddies start on goodies as tho they never ate.

You pacify the quarrels and mend the broken toys;
You sympathize with sorrows and recommend the joys.

So Mother's trotting here and there and tidying up a bit;
Wondering if she'll last the day or really take a fit.

And when the evening hour has drawn to a close;
You tuck each tired child away in deep and sweet repose.

You offer up another prayer of thankfulness and joy;
And wish a "Merry Christmas" to each sleepy girl and boy.

- January 1966 -

THE LITTLE WHITE FOAL

The little white foal stood trembling,
On the hill at the break of day;
Little dreaming of what the future held,
On the glory and strife far away.

He struggled to stand and gain balance,
While the gray mare watched with concern;
She waited and watched with patience,
As the fog rolled in from the burn.

She listened with ears held erect,
For the herd on the crest over there'
Tending her foal with mother-love,
In born in the little gray mare.

The big white Arabian stallion,
Grazed as he watched his band;
Little dreaming that human captors,
Would drive them from this land.

But the little gray mare and her tiny foal,
Were hidden well that day;
They escaped the noisy roundup,
And alone were allowed to stay.

With spindly legs and curly tail,
He struggled again to his feet;
With a frightened eye and pink little nose,
He snuggled his mother's teat.

His little white coat and pointed ears,
Twitched as he took his fill;
'Twas a picture of maternal love,
As the world around was still.

By leaps and bounds he grew and grew,
And with his size grew speed;
The endurance of the little foal,
Was never to leave him in need.

But the savagery of this wild land,
Where nature reigned supreme;
Where the natural law was to kill to eat,
And to live was only a dream.

But two tough years have come and gone,
And we still see the pair alive;
They have run and raced and fought the foe,
And managed to survive.

But now we see a whirlybird,
Take up the chase full fair;
For far and wide have reached the tale,
Of the milk-white colt and racing mare.

They chased them thru the sage brush,
They chased them across the plain;
They cornered them in a canyon,
From which escape was in vain.

Little he knew of his future home,
Or the money he'd make his master;
Nothing he knew of the life he'd lead,
Or how he'd meet disaster.

After many hours of coaxing,
Training and tender care;
They were loaded aboard an airplane,
And shipped to a millionaire.

'Twas he that established a stable,
And set the world on fire;
By breeding a line of racing stock,
Led by the milk-white sire.

He lived the life of Riley,
In luxury and style;
He showed them all that he could run,
The fastest measured mile.

One day as the race was ending,
And the bets were running high;
The snow white stallion led the field,
His feet just seem to fly.

There issued from the crowd a groan,
The great white horse was down;
The other horses passed him by,
We knew he'd lost his crown.

We little counted on the fate,
That befell the King that day;
His heart was broke the vet had said,
That's how he passed away.

Endurance and speed he had to give,
And he gave the best that he had;
He lived and died doing his utmost,
This thoroughbred-Arab lad.

The little gray mare was aged and gone,
The Arab stallion was sold,
And this is the tale of the little white foal,
As to me, it was told.

- March 1969 -

PAST, PRESENT AND FUTURE

Here's to the drink I'm going to drink,
Here's to the one I had;
Here's to the way it will make me feel,
And I hope its not too bad.

Here's to the man I used to be,
And the one I might have been;
Here's to the life I should have led,
And the sights I might have seen.

Here's to the health and happiness,
Although it can't be mine;
Here's to the ones I dearly miss,
The ones I left behind.

Here's to the money I have spent,
That which I couldn't afford;
Here's to the drifting life I've led,
With a drink as a burning sword.

Here's to the parents that I had,
Who are lost and gone from me;
Here's to the son I could have been,
If liquor hadn't got to me.

Here's to the wife I had and lost,
Here's to the children three;
Here's to the bum I have become,
All for the love of THEE.

Here's to the future tho it be grim,
Here's to a past the same;
Here's to the last damn drink I'll take,
And I'll never drink again.

For life has become a weary grind,
And I cannot carry on;
From bar to bar, both near and far,
They call me the lonesome one.

I crave to be like the other guy,
Repent I will and I can;
I'll cure the craze for the cursed drink,
God willing, I'll be a MAN.

- February 1970 -

23

FEMALE AMBITION

The little black calf stood grazing,
By the side of its dam one day;
It began to dream of the future,
And its life in the far away.

It strolled to a slight depression,
Laid down with a deepening sigh;
And while the sun shone brightly,
It dozed as it closed its eyes.

It dreamed of the far off highlands,
Where the blacks still reign supreme;
Of how it would be to show at Perth,
For the "Guineas of the Queen".

It saw the hills of Aberdeen,
And a distant Scottish vale;
It beheld the highlands ruggedness,
And it heard the bagpipes wail.

It visioned its ancient ancestors,
Who roamed those hilly lands;
Of how the breed had been developed,
From those far off wild bands.

Of how they grew so valuable,
To be exported far and wide;
The growing of that Red brand beef,
Beneath that sleek, black hide.

But then it stopped and thought again,
This pride it could but scorn;
For sex had played a drastic trick,
The day that she was born.

But a lengthy list of herd names,
Passed quickly thru her view;
From east to west, they were the best,
Now why couldn't she be too.

The little calf woke with a start,
To gaze at the lowing herd;
It was a vision from the past,
That now appeared absurd.

Ah well! she thought with deep concern,
I cannot win them all;
I'll eat the best and pass the test,
To top the herd this fall.

I may not be the Queen of Perth,
Toronto or Chicago's fair;
But when it comes to herd improvement,
That's when I'll be there.

- January 1970 -

WHAT IS A GRANDMOTHER

A little old lady,
In an old rocking chair;
A smile on her face,
And snow white hair.

A lavender dress,
Trimmed with lace;
A stately lady,
Of a vanishing race.

A pillar of strength,
In time of need;
But needing her glasses,
In order to read.

With twinkling eyes,
That are full of fire;
And a loving heart,
That is full of desire.

Gentle hands,
That are wrinkled and fine;
A slender body,
And a supple spine.

A graceful lady,
Weaving a spell;
While she reads the tale,
Of "Little Nell".

Sitting and reading,
To children three;
While she rocks another,
Upon her knee.

Looking back,
To when she was young;
A hero yes,
But as yet unsung.

Growing older,
With truth and grace;
A contented smile,
On a contented face.

- December 1970 -

LIFE

Time is quickly passing,
While life slowly ebbs away;
So put not off until tomorrow,
What you can do today.

Can you look back with satisfaction,
On what has gone before;
Or does the past seem futile,
And make you rather sore.

Do you think you could be greater,
If you'd done if differently;
Or be happier if you'd listened,
To advice that was given free.

Experience costs a fortune,
But you all must learn somehow;
But many of the younger folks,
Put the horse behind the plow.

Now why is youth so wasted,
On the thoughtless and carefree;
When it could be more enjoyed,
By the sick and elderly.

Youth is as the springtime,
And no matter how you try;
You never miss the water,
Till the well runs dry.

Have you been as busy,
As the proverbial bee;
But find you've gotten no where,
But have naught to show you see.

You might have taken it easy,
Enjoyed life as you went;
No matter how you worked and saved,
Your savings are all spent.

Or can you see the mark you've left,
In a family that's full grown;
As now you are much older,
Your time of youth has flown.

Although you've scrimped and saved,
To raise them properly;
You can feel that you've accomplished much,
By extending the family tree.

Or if you've amassed a fortune,
To the grave it can't be taken;
For in neither Heaven or Hell,
Is there any place for spending.

So take advice that's freely given,
Enjoy life while you may;
You know not when your time will come,
Or how long the Lord will let you stay.

Youth for all is short and sweet,
But time speeds on I've said;
The years grow shorter as you age,
And you're a long time dead.

- December 1970 - January 1971 -

HERE AND HEREAFTER

Oh the farmer's life is a tough one,
This in the west we know;
For we must combat the elements,
As well as fight Trudeau.

He raises all our taxes,
Then drops the price of grain;
He forgets to raise our quota,
Till he drives us near insane.

The easy life on a western farm,
Is now a passing dream;
For credit now has disappeared,
The days are long and lean.

It's pay your debts or loose your shirt,
Its cash they do demand;
And interest rates have gone sky high,
In this democratic land.

The farmer's told what amount he sells,
And the price he will obtain;
Whether he be selling meat,
Or loads of golden grain.

And yet if he buys bread or milk,
The piper he must pay;
A group of serfs is all we are,
Working from day to day.

Try how you will you cannot make,
More than your daily bread;
No matter how you scrimp and save,
Your always in the red.

But the world must have its bread and meat,
Its fields of golden grain;
Supply you must what they demand,
Or you have lived in vain.

So struggle on ye farmer man,
Shirk not the toil or strife;
You may exist in Hell on Earth,
But it's a healthy life.

No doubt that heaven has a place,
Wherein us farmers dwell;
And up above the Aperture,
"You now may rest a spell".

- June 1969 -

29

WANDERLUST

I've rode the rods from East to West,
And then back East again;
I've worked a little everywhere,
In this our fair Domain.

I've fished the broad Pacific,
And been a smelter man in Trail;
As a miner in the North,
I certainly didn't fail.
I milked a cow in the Fraser,
In the Okanagan picked some fruit;
In the mountains I was a logger,
And big game I learned to shoot.

Then I moved on into Alberta,
And joined a cowboy band;
I rode the wildest horses,
Punched the best cows in the land.
I worked as an oil rigger,
Helped shovel grain and coal;
When industry and power came,
I was the first one up the pole.

I sashayed into Saskatchewan,
Where I worked out on a farm;
Growing wheat and oats and barley,
Feeding piglets in a barn.
I milked some cows, fed some steers,
And oil seeds I grew.
I took my turn at potash mining,
And of oil wells saw a few;
I learned to drive the big machines,
Self-propelled became my name;
As a fisherman and a hunter,
I walked the track to fame.

I marched on to Manitoba,
The gateway to the west;
Its vast amount of lakes and rivers,
Where fishing is the best.
Many minerals and terminals,
Attracted me while there;
On a mixed farm, I spent,
The best part of a year.

Then onward to Ontario,
Where industries take over;
With dairying and livestock,
Fruit, grass, corn and clover.
Salvaging the many feeders,
Which grew out in the west;
Minerals, cars and water power,
From the Great Lakes stand the test.

Then I crept eastward to Quebec,
Where tobacco and potatoes grow;
Pulpwood and pure maple syrup,
Helped to bring in my dough.
On small farms and at fishing,
I worked along the old St. Lawrence;
Making textiles, shoes and aluminum ware,
I used power from this source.

I sauntered on to Nova Scotia,
Where a ship builder I became;
A fisherman and big game hunter,
A sportsman was my name.
At lumbering, coal and woodworking,
I spent some time you see;
Grain, manufacturing, fruit and dairying,
My occupations came to be.

I rushed on into New Brunswick,
With the Bay of Fundy's tide;
Despite its winter weather,
I decided to reside.
As a sportsman and a lumberman,
I earned my bread and tea;
As a hydro man and fisherman,
I migrated towards the sea.

Then I sailed over to the Island,
Fur farming to explore;
But of wheat and fruit and cereals,
I found I could learn more.
I traveled a bit and fished a bit,
Then fed the fox and steers;
If I'd just had the time to spare,
I might have stayed for years.

But forward to Newfoundland,
To hunt and fish out there;
I extracted cod fish oil,
Tracked the otter to his lair.
At lumbering and mining,
I also tried my hand;
Newsprint I manufactured,
A product of this land.

I only had one section left,
In this our fair Domain;
So I mooched on in my mucklucks,
Across Eskimo terrain.
I saw the seal and polar bear,
Out in the ice and snow;
As a herdsman and prospector,
I was prepared to go.
For oil and uranium,
I traveled the barren waste;
But for modern development,
The natives have no taste.

I had worked my way from West to East,
And then back home again;
From coast to coast and South to North,
And across the intervening plain.
With all this work and wandering,
I've learnt a lot you know;
That one must take it as it is,
No matter where you go.
There's always work that you can find,
If willing you will be;
So be an independent man,
Rather than on charity.

- February 1971 -

DAYS GONE BY

There's a lonely little schoolhouse,
On a long and lonely road;
It stands alone in darkness,
'Tis now no ones abode.

'Twould shock the younger generation,
To know how great you were;
Even tho you're now abandoned,
They would wish they had been there.

If it could only tell you,
Of what had gone before;
Of all those exciting things,
That went on inside its doors.

Your building was a struggle,
For the early pioneer;
But you soon became the center,
Of things they held most dear.

For little barefoot children,
Made footprints to your door;
Seeking out the knowledge,
That they could not get before.

Some came to school with horses,
Others walked the weary miles;
The children's cheeks were rosy-red,
On their faces, healthy smiles.

There wasn't any snowploughs,
Nor buses small or great;
But you didn't skip a single day,
And stayed in, if you were late.

Out in the little school yard,
Surrounded by a hedge;
Stood a male and female toilet,
And a horse barn painted red.

Many games of prisoners base,
And of pom-pom-pull-away;
Were played around those buildings,
In the good old by gone days.

The dear old place was heated,
By a furnace or a stove;
On the cold days in winter,
We sat close to them, by jove.

There were two little cloakrooms,
To hang up your clothes and such;
As segregate the boys and girls,
Is a thing they thought they must.

The water came in five gallon cans,
With a dipper or a tin cup,
The floor was swept with a worn out broom,
And once a month mopped up.

The teacher's throne up at the front,
Was a desk of many drawers;
Which many pupils stood beside,
To recite their two times fours.

The top drawer was a place of mystery,
The home of register and strap;
When needed it was well applied,
I can vouch for that.

Attendance was from ten to fifty,
The teacher overworked I vow;
Having grades from one to ten,
Yet she taught them all some how.

Times were hard in those old days,
The teacher's wage was small;
From three hundred up to eight,
If she could collect at all.

On Sunday 'twas a meeting place,
For all the old and young;
To receive the sacred word of God,
And hear the old hymns sung.

But many of the evenings,
Were filled with joy and fun;
As to the pipe and fiddle,
Those sturdy rafters rung.

The noisy old piano,
Which was slightly out of tune;
Pounded out " Oh Promise Me",
As laughter filled the room.

Times have changed and you're alone,
Dark, deserted and forlorn;
The modern generation now,
All go by bus to town.

But are they any better off,
Then their parents were before;
Will they lead as straight a path,
To Heaven's golden shore.

- February 1971 -

SMOKE, SMOKE, SMOKE--

I'm driving a nail in my coffin,
As I take a cigarette from the pack;
But I've done it so very often,
There is now no turning back.

A slave I've become to the deadly weed,
No one can change me now;
I've tried and tried to kick it,
But I just cannot somehow.

And the price is getting higher,
So I cannot afford the stuff;
But I will starve to get it,
Although the starving's rough.

I crave the lift that it gives me,
The feeling of sweet repose;
I am deeply attracted to it,
Like a bee is to a rose.

When I awake in the morning early,
I bark like a baying hound;
And unless I quit the dirty weed,
No relief for it can be found.

I've become a blessed slave to it,
A moral and physical wreck;
And before it gets me mentally,
I'll ditch the habit by heck.

I'm tired of barking and coughing,
I'm tired of gasping for breath;
I'm tired of thinking of cancer,
That will surely mean my death.

I'm tired of getting thinner,
Of wasting away to a thread;
Yet I know some day because of it,
They are going to find me dead.

So all you young and haughty,
Take heed before it's too late;
Please don't ever start on it,
For it's an awful habit to break.

-Spring 1972 -

35

THE CHIEF

The Indian Chief lay dying,
Inside his teepee door;
Head raised upon some buffalo robes,
To view that distant shore.

His life was slowly ebbing,
As he made his last request;
For soon they would be burying,
The 'War Chief' of the West.

He had been born and raised,
On this rolling prairie wide;
And as a strong and growing boy,
Had learned to jump and ride.

And when young manhood came along,
He was a tall and robust lad,
Becoming the bravest warrior,
The band had ever had.

He showed them how to hunt and track,
When drought and blizzard raged;
He showed them how to trick the enemy,
When they were attacked and seized.

He signed the peace that brought about,
The end of war and strife;
He tried his best to get for them,
A better way of life.

He tried to unite together,
The tribes across the land;
But they remained aloof,
Like knolls of drifting sand.

He had hopes of a brave Red Nation,
In peace beside the White;
Living as neighbors together,
Ceasing to quarrel and fight.

Surrounded by his tribesmen,
Who kept his word with care;
He looked across the distant land,
Seeking his answer there.

For his last request was one of Love,
'Lord! make us brothers more';
And by the end of his request,
He'd reached the 'Heavenly Shore'.

- September 1972 -

A SAD FAREWELL

Farewell, farewell Saskatchewan,
I'm going to leave you now;
For sixty years I've lived here,
And I've survived somehow.

We pioneered together,
Near a century ago;
It was a rugged business,
I'd like to have you know.

The summers hot, the winters cold,
The flies were, Oh! dear me;
But there was the rolling grassland,
As far as one could see.

The hunting was delightful,
The fishing was supreme;
But when it came to breaking,
It was a different thing.

The stones were like the table top,
And the oxen mighty slow;
The insects drove us wild,
With no place else to go.

Other settlers came and went,
Yet some stuck on somehow;
It was a sort of challenge,
But I'm going to leave you now.

My usefulness if over,
In your rugged, robust clime;
I think I will retire,
To a climate more sublime.

But I'll look back with longing,
To the land I left behind;
The good years, the tough years,
Will linger in my mind.

For I can't forget a lifetime,
No matter where I go;
For my roots are in Saskatchewan,
I'd like to have you know.

- September 1972 -

HARMONY OF A HARVESTING HOUSEWIFE

Fall again has rolled around,
I'm afraid that harvest's here;
I heard hubby yell real loud,
"Will you come out here, Dear?"

"Your presence is required,
To make this small repair";
But half an hour later,
You're still standing there.

It's run and bring him this and that,
To save him time you see;
He doth require many tools,
And the servant must be me.

I've found out that a monkey wrench,
Has no family tree;
And that a rat-tail is a file,
For it has no legs you see.

And when he says, "just pass the hose",
It's not your socks he's seeking;
He must inflate an inner tube,
To see if it is leaking.

The wrenches come in fractions,
Which you may know by chance;
That burr is on a rivet put,
And not sticking to your pants.

Your knowledge is increasing,
In a different sort of way;
A crescent is a useful wrench,
Not a part of the moon they say.

Now hoses for hydraulics,
Are bisexual you see;
But whoever heard of little hoses,
That one could raise for free.

I've also learnt some new words,
Which a lawyer calls profane;
But in harvest time it also means,
Hubby's hit his thumb again.

Now next it's move the loader,
And I'm the one to push;
I'm glad I've got the poundage,
It goes back in a rush.

Now take the truck out to the field,
The combine he must fetch;
But be careful how you drive,
Or you'll end up in a ditch.

"Now wifey, Dear, you see that pipe,
The truck must go beneath";
But after you have bent it,
You hear him grit his teeth.

His steam starts in rising,
Like a kettle on the boil;
So I resolve to mend my ways,
Keeping out of sight awhile.

But soon his temper's cooling,
And he seeks my aid again;
This time it's "Will you shovel?"
In that bin of golden grain.

Now when you're fat and forty,
Or a little less or more;
You do not fit too easily,
Thru a granary's little door.

So you make a resolution,
That before another year;
You'll render off some poundage,
And learn to drive in a lower gear.

- November 1972 -

TO A TOM

With tail erect and ears alert,
The 'Old Warrior' trod the trail;
Sparks of fire from gray-green eyes,
Showed he'd never live to fail.

A harem he had of ladies four,
And he would not part with one;
The master of his universe,
But contested by his son.

The arched up back of black and white,
Meets that so black and fine;
While angry hair doth quickly rise,
Along those feline spines.

A flash of claw, a spurt of blood,
A loud low throated growl;
Find they must the superior one,
For these males on the prowl.

Oh! the wailing was terrific,
And it was a dreadful fight;
Both the victor and vanquished,
Emerged an awful sight.

The fur did fly and the growling sound,
Was as of a jungle beast;
It was a tremendous well fought fight,
To say the very least.

But the pride with which the winner left,
Was as of a warrior bold;
Battle scared by head held high,
A general to behold.

So young felines take this advice,
Before you think you've grown;
There's spunk in those 'Old Masters' yet,
Their manhood has not flown.

- June 1972 -

MODERN LIVING

It's hurry, hurry, hurry,
No matter where you go;
I wonder where its getting us,
That's what I'd like to know.

It's hurry when you're rising,
As you have slept too late;
'Twas really nice to snooze a bit,
You forgot you had a date.

It's hurry when you're working,
So you have time to rest;
So you can go a visiting,
Looking your very best.

It's hurry when you're traveling,
So you get there on time;
If you are late a little bit,
Your jobs not worth a dime.

It's hurry while you're eating,
So you can watch T.V.;
Thus you get indigestion,
And are really out of steam.

You're on life's Roller Coaster,
Slow down! and wait a spell;
Take time to live while you are here,
Why rush to Heaven or Hell.

- April 1972 -

MEMORIES

The elderly man sat rocking,
In an old broken down rocking chair;
Thinking back to the days of his childhood,
When he had neither worry nor care.

He thought of being a little lad,
In a suit of sailor blue;
He thought of the meadow where he had skipped,
And played with his sisters two.

A fleeting smile crossed his face,
As he thought of himself a lad;
Of his beautiful blue-eyed mother,
And his strong and stalwart dad.

He thought of the fun he used to have,
Down at the old swimming hole;
And of all the tricks he used to pull,
While just a boy in school.

Then he saw himself a lad,
In square top hat and gown;
Who took up the life of farming,
When to manhood he had grown.

He took himself a lovely bride,
Who bore him children three;
But the Heavenly Father claimed her too,
When they were still quite wee.

He thought of the sad, yet glorious times,
Of them loving one another;
Of father mothering all the three,
And of sisters mothering brother.

He thought of them as the years sped on,
When to adults they had grown;
Each going their own desired way,
Leaving him thus alone.

But he wouldn't change it a single bit,
As he loved and visited all three;
And grandchildren ten he'd watched grow up,
As he dangled them on his knee.

He thought of his wife Marie again,
And knew that he loved her still;
As darkness fell in the vale that night,
Of this earth he'd had his fill.

In the morning the family found him,
Still in his old rocking chair;
His face showed love and contentment,
With Marie in Heaven he's there.

- September 1970 -

A WEE GIRL

A - is for your angel face,
  That always wears a smile.

B - is for the babe you are,
  For girls are all the style.

C - is for the copyrights,
  We have reserved on you.

D - is for the dreams we have,
  Which now concern you too.

E - is for your eyes so bright,
  Are they grey or they blue.

F - is for the frown you wear,
  When you're deep in thought.

G - is for that girlish grin,
  The camera's often caught.

H - is for that happiness,
You've brought to mom and dad.

I - is for intelligence,
  Yours makes us very glad.

J - is for your joy in life,
  Long and happy may it be.

K - is for the kisses that,
  You share with dad and me.

L - is for the love you give,
  So free and tenderly.

M - is for your loving mother,
  When you sit upon her knee.

N - is for the naughtiness,
  You somehow cannot avoid.

O - is for the orneriness,
  You have a streak inside.

P - is for the pappa,
With whom you love to play.

Q - is for the questions,
  You ask us everyday.

R - is for the rising sun,
The time when you were born.

S - is for the smile you wear,
  You never seem forlorn.

T - is for the tiny teeth,
Sharp and white and clean.

U - is for the universe,
Of which you think you're Queen.

V - is for vitality,
With which you sometimes scream.

W - is for the work,
  We do for love of you.

X - is for excitement,
  Your arrival caused.

Y - is for your yellow hair,
Which crowns your little head.

Z - is for the zero hour,
  You must always be fed.

Just a little bit of heaven,
For those parents tried and true;
Their hopes and prayers were answered,
By a little mite like you.

- January 23, 1972 -

WHAT IS A BOY

What is a boy?
I'd like you to know;
He's a little wee man,
Just starting to grow.

Needing a bottle,
And change of pants;
Before showing off,
To uncles and aunts.

Starting to holler,
And then to talk;
Learning to creep.
And then to walk.

Cutting his teeth,
Taking a fall;
Suffering bruises,
And that isn't all.

Getting the ailments,
Of all childhood;
Being some bad,
But also some good.

Measles and mumps,
Cold and the pox;
Rundown shoes,
And holey socks.

A runny nose,
And ragged pants;
Big red spots,
From bees and ants.

Playing in mud,
All covered with dirt;
Running for kisses,
Whenever he's hurt.

With smudged face,
And dirty paws;
Caring nothing,
For grown up laws.

Climbing the fence,
Or riding a horse;
Taking a spanking,
As matter of course.

Starting to school,
All tidy and clean;
Enjoying the recesses,
That come in between.

Learning his lessons,
With effort no doubt;
And looking forward,
Until school is out.

Hunting for birds' eggs,
Early in spring;
Snaring a gopher,
On the end of a string.

Playing at hockey,
Tag, ball, fox and hare;
Teasing the girls,
And pulling their hair.

Now here he comes,
His hat all awry;
He's fighting again,
Just look at his eye.

But his laughter and chatter,
Show he's a boy;
His father's pride,
And his mother's joy.

Take advantage of his childhood,
Enjoy him while you can;
For in just a few short years,
He too will be a man.

- November 19, 1971 -

ON THE RUN

I wake in the morning early,
Just at the crack of dawn;
Jump into my blue jeans,
Pull my runners on.

Hop out to the kitchen,
Put water in the pot;
Soon the porridge is ready,
Come get it while it's hot.

Meanwhile I brew the coffee,
Black as black can be;
A pickup for the housewife,
Especially one like me.

Then it's rouse the children,
A great big job indeed;
They must catch a bus you know,
For their learning is in need.

Then scoot out to the stable,
To milk the mooley cow;
I wonder why I was so soft,
In ever learning how.

Pick the cackle berries,
Throw them a little feed;
Then rush the eggs into the fridge,
They must be fresh indeed,

Now rush out to the garden,
And plant a row of seeds;
Pick a mess of vegetables,
And pull a spot of weeds.

Then its time to grab the broom,
And sweep a little bit;
Don't forget to phone your neighbor,
Or she will have a fit.

Dust a bit, mop a bit,
Get dinner on the go;
The forenoon is nearly over,
I'd like to have you know.

Now with dinner over,
You sit and catch your breath;
And take a short siesta,
Before you're worked to death.

From the deepest slumber,
You wake up with a start;
You forgot to put the roast in,
Or bake the apple tart.

You do a bit of baking,
Clean up all the mess;
It's time to prepare the supper,
This I will confess.

Do up the dirty dishes,
Then it's chores again;
The weary day is ending,
Some of my plans in vain.

I snuggle down leg weary,
In my soft and cozy bed;
Praying that tomorrow,
I will somehow get ahead.

- January 1972 -

THE CHRISTMAS QUESTION

Now that Christmas is over,
I would like to know;
Where do all the stickers,
And wrapping paper go.

Where is all the laughter,
The blessing and good cheer;
Or have we with the tinsel,
Packed them for another year.

Where are all the ornaments,
The bells and stars held dear;
Packed away in boxes,
To be used again next year.

Where is that gorgeous evergreen,
With its spellbinding scent;
Its branches are all wilted,
And the aroma spent.

Where are all the candy canes,
Striped in red and white;
Where are all the cards from friends,
Colored gay and bright.

Gone is all the company,
The turmoil and the noise;
Gone is all the clamor,
Of many girls and boys.

Gone is the excitement,
The secrets and the thrills;
Gone is the momentous task,
Of getting stockings filled.

Yes, Christmas now has come and gone,
With the excitement and the thrills;
All that now is really left,
Is a host of unpaid bills.

Now! where are all of "Santa's Reindeer",
And Old Saint Nick himself;
Away back at the cold North Pole,
Looked after by a elf.

New Year's too will come and go,
As onward time doth roll;
Old Santa too will age a year,
Before restarting from the Pole.

- December 27, 1971 -

TO A HEN

There's a lot of lazy people,
In this old world today;
If they were more like the little hen,
When they sat, they at least could lay.

Even for that little hen,
They really are no match;
For when she only stands around,
For a living she can scratch.

She does not ask for welfare,
Get drunk or put in jail;
She does not smoke a cigarette,
Or on drugs go for a sail.

As a mother she's terrific,
She'll fight to the bitter end;
Against many enormous odds,
Her family she'll defend.

She'll never join the unemployed,
Nor her family will she neglect;
She won't starve to amass a fortune,
So give her, her due respect.

She does not need a baby-sitter,
Nor does she seek divorce;
As to a husband she's not choosy,
But lets nature take its course.

She rises very early,
Just as the sun is up;
She does not in her bed repose,
Or have coffee from a cup.

She'll do her daily dozen,
And each day an egg she'll lay;
Not like her human counterpart,
Who unemployed likes to stay.

She's a worker and a talker,
Like most good women are;
She does her own advertising,
And her products come up to par.

At packaging her foodstuff,
She isn't any cheater,
Nor at her crowing master,
Is she ever really bitter.

She never is a quitter,
And she's always on the run;
Now man could take some lessons,
The lazy son of a gun.

So look ye not on the little hen,
With sneers of disrespect,
If you'd follow in her footsteps,
You'd be a better man by heck.

- April 1972 -

WINTER OF 1964 - 65

Sunny old Saskatchewan,
Has got a fit of chills;
It's one of the coldest winters,
That's come to these old hills.

They talk about the Yukon,
When it's sixty-nine below;
But in sunny Saskatchewan,
It's blow, blow, blow.

The roads fill in with powder,
And then move on again;
The snow-plow keeps on coming,
But his efforts are in vain.

The glass crawls a little higher,
To afford us some relief'
But the wind makes up the difference,
And the colds beyond belief.

The thermometer hits the bottom,
And the wind starts in to blow;
The temperature keeps falling,
And it's snow! snow! snow!

Feed is getting shorter,
With no word of spring in sight;
The ground hog saw his shadow,
And I guess the guy is right.

Birds and beasts have perished,
In the storms that crossed our plains;
The wildlife is suffering,
And the livestock make no gains.

But the people of Saskatchewan,
Are a strong and hardy lot;
They're never very wealthy,
But hold on to what they've got.

But we'll have to live and tough it,
Or clasp our hands and pray;
But we never will desert it,
Only stay! stay! stay!

We'll survive this blinken winter,
To look back with memories bold;
To pass on to our descendants,
Its tales of snow and cold.

- February 1965 -

MODERN EDUCATION

Now modern education has all gone to hell;
If you will only listen, I'll show you how I tell.

It used to be you learned to write, read, subtract and add;
But now you just computerize, it has become the fad.

It used to be we wore our slacks, shorts were all forbid;
Now they wear the mini skirt, I wonder what they've hid.

The mini skirt it looks quite nice, if your figures hourglass;
But if you are the rotund type, you just amuse the class.

Now when the winter rolls around, some must catch a chill;
But now they wear the long fur coat to prevent the 'Winter Kill'.

Boys used to wear their hair cut short in pompadour or crew;
But now they let it grow so long, we wonder who is who.

The funniest thing I ever saw, it made me laugh by heck;
A man gone shiny up on top, but long curls down his neck.

We used to go to a country school, where one teacher taught the lot;
We had to sit and study hard or else the strap we got.

But now they go to town school with teachers quite a few;
This sending them out into the hall, I cannot yet see thru.

Detention is another thing, if enforced is quite O.K.;
But why give them detention then let them skip away.

The language and the stories that are invented in the place;
Many an old time barroom would consider a disgrace.

It makes one stop and wonder what this modern trend will do;
Will it benefit the many or more likely just a few.

And then there are the bright ones who to University are sent;
Amid the drugs and riots, their next few years are spent.

It makes us stop and wonder if the risk is worth the while;
To start our young teenagers out in this present style.

Will they have the guts and gumption, to withstand the evil trend;
Or will they fall in with the gang, and come to some bad end.

And when we weigh the pros and cons in our parental way;
Are we doing right by them, or does modern education pay?

- February 1970 -

THE RIDICULOUS AND THE SUBLIME

Did you ever live on a family farm,
Where January blasts are chill;
Where the summer sun is hot and dry,
Out in them thar hills.

The farmers are a cheerful lot,
Who always pay their bills;
For they believe in honesty,
Out in them thar hills.

The housewives are a happy lot,
With never many frills;
For they never know what they need do,
Out in them thar hills.

The corn has ears like elephants,
The pumpkins grow in hills;
The tatters are like coffee pots,
Out in them thar hills.

The cars they all need four wheel brakes,
As well as driver skills;
The roads go up as well as down,
Out in them thar hills.

The hunters they get lost or stuck,
Before they make their kills;
For 'East is West' and 'North is South'.
Out in them thar hills.

The cows they grow so sleek and fat,
They never get the chills;
For the grass is high as an ostrich eye,
Out in them thar hills.

The field mice all have curly tails,
The old folks run the stills;
The horses all have two short legs,
Out in them thar hills.

The children all grow big and strong,
With never many ills;
For they must be taught but to survive,
Out in them thar hills.

The hens they all lay soft boiled eggs,
Cause the roosters on the pill;
For they believe in saving work,
Out in them thar hills.

Now Trudeau is a mastermind,
But our wheat he cannot mill;
So please return the "Old Warhorse",
Back to them thar hills.

He takes our money to pay his taxes,
Till we can't afford a will;
So we are very loath to die,
Out in them thar hills.

- December 5 -10, 1969 -

INJUSTICE

The lonely coyote stood upon,
The crest of the distant hill;
He raised his nose to the evening air,
His cry was loud and shrill.

He called and called and called again,
But there was no answering cry;
For the mate he had chosen for his own,
Had just come home to die.

She lay in a hollow at the foot of the hill,
But no answer could she give;
She had been chased till her heart was broke,
So she had not long to live.

Three little mites of brown and grey,
Snuggled close to her stiffening form;
Seeking a bit of motherly love,
To protect them from all harm.

Now should man with his inventions,
Cause nature to suffer so;
Soon there'll be no wildlife left,
And then what will he do.

The pigeon and the dodo bird,
Have now become extinct;
And many more will follow soon,
If man does not stop to think.

So lets protect our wildlife,
With stricter regulations too;
And abolish all forms of hunting,
From the seat of a skidoo.

- February 1973 -

OBITUARY

Here's to Dear Old Dufferin,
They've taken you away;
Replaced you with a counterpart,
Which had not long to stay.

But yet your site will be held dear,
By many who passed thru;
As we look back on by gone days,
We cherish thoughts of you.

You saw us thru our primer,
Grades one, two, three and four;
You cheered us thru our entrance,
Some didn't ask for more.

And yet for those who wished it,
You passed us thru highschool;
To start us on 'Our Road of Life',
And to keep the 'Golden Rule'.

You didn't show distinction,
In religion, race or creed;
But gave us all the best you had,
And wished us all good speed.

Many Masters held they throne,
Too numerous to name;
Many souls that sat thy seats,
Pushed on to greater fame.

We were no little angels,
As anyone can guess;
But yet we learned our lessons,
And somehow passed the test.

Some who have passed thru your door,
Are scattered far and wide;
And yet a goodly number nearby still reside,
Some as yet are young and gay and some like you have passed away.

Now generations One, Two, Three,
Your four walls have attended;
Do not some of you feel sad,
To see its roots upended.

But do not sigh old school yard,
For the bell that rings no more;
Or the trample of the carefree feet,
That many times tread o'er.

But think yourself a sacred plot,
Remembered by many often;
And 'Here's to you, Old Dufferin',
You are gone by not forgotten.

- Spring 1960 -

NEW BORN

The moon itself was a shimmering orb,
As it sailed on its silvery sea;
The glistening glow of the glittering snow,
Was a sight for one to see.

The crackle and crunch my footsteps made,
Was as of a thundering herd;
Silence supreme for the moon was queen,
I was the only thing that stirred.

The dipping degrees that brought the freeze,
Under a clear blue sky;
My ears and nose I thought were froze,
But bravely on walked I.

Cool and crisp was the morning air,
As I checked the sleeping herd;
The coal-black backs were white with frost,
But never an animal stirred.

'Twas then I saw in a hollow of straw,
A tiny new born calf;
Jet black below top white as snow,
I had to stop and laugh.

Above her chin she seemed to grin,
And her eyes were shining bright;
She seemed to say in her own small way,
I've made it here alright.

Just give me a hand in this promised land,
And I'll pay you back some day;
So I carried her tenderly into the barn,
And placed her on some hay.

Returning then to my snug warm bed,
My heart was warm and light;
I'd saved the life of a newborn babe,
Which arrived on a cold, cold night.

- November - December 1972 -

61

TO A MOSQUITO

I was sleeping very soundly,
When there was a gentle hum;
The 'Dive Bomber' lit on target,
But I didn't hear him come.

He did not use his tail lights,
Nor drop his landing gear;
He nosed in on the airstrip,
Which was me I fear.

The pierce of his propeller,
Was the poking of a pin;
He was not very gentle,
As he eased his motor in.

The earth tremor was terrific,
As I let out a yell;
I bombed that poor mosquito,
And then I scratched like hell.

His fuselage was broken,
His fuel all spattered round;
It was a total write off,
So the agents found.

Now you dopey pilots,
I am posting up this sign;
Find another airport,
If you wish to wine and dine.

- July 1972 -

CANADIAN HISTORY

Our continent was first sighted by the Norsemen bold;
As Vineland it was known in the brave days of old.

Away up in our North land, lives the sturdy Eskimo;
He lives a life of hardship, amid the ice and snow.
Dressed in fur from head to foot, a noble hunter he;
To drive his dog, and kill his meat, is his security.

Oh Columbus found America, Cabot the great Cod Banks;
The English flag set on our soil, to him we give our thanks.

Cartier unto the Indians, was friendly as could be;
Secured their furs and took their chiefs back to gay Paree,
Sailed up the mighty river, a thousand miles or so,
As Canada's discoverer went down in history.

Then came Henry Hudson, who the North-West Passage sought,
Who lost his life in Hudson Bay, when by the ice floes caught.

He crossed the great Atlantic, twenty times and more;
And for the Eastern fur trade, opened up the door.
Port Royal, Quebec and Lake Champlain, are places he helped find;
The "Founder of New France", Champlain we have in mind.

Brebeuf the Jesuit Father, who to the Hurons came;
To teach and preach and baptize, and help the sick his game.
The Iroquois attacked them, wiping out the Huron tribe;
Torturing the missionaries, before they bravely died.

Montreal was founded by Mr. Maisonneuve,
A soldier and brave leader, who defied the Iroquois;
To protect himself and men, he shot their wily chief,
But for another twenty years, they found no true relief.

Adam Dollard was a soldier, who fought the Iroquois band;
On the mighty Long Sault Rapids was where he made his stand.
They lost their lives, but their plan had won;
The town was saved and their work well done.

Talon the great Intendant, who with a distant view;
Brought out wives for lonesome soldiers, tools and livestock, too.
He started work of many kinds, and thus the colony grew.

Frontenac the governor, who quelled the Iroquois,
Using pomp and glory, to keep them in their place;
For furs he brandy traded, which made the churchmen scoff,
Known as the fighting governor, he kept the English off.

Madeleine the maiden, the one who saved the fort,
We'll fight for "King and Country" was her brave retort.
Her men were few, her nerve immense;
She won the day, at the Iroquois expense.

La Salle the trader and the sailor, the farmer at Lachine,
Sailed the Mississippi from its source to mouth;
Set the flag of France on Louisiana soil;
Lost his life in ambush, while hunting in the south.

Radisson and Groseilliers a fur trading pair of boys,
Got a lot of furs, near Great Lakes and Hudson Bay;
But the greater part of these, the Governor took for free,
So they joined the English and formed the H.B.C.
With Prince Rupert for its governor, and a million miles of soil;
But they quarreled with the English, and with the French did toil.
And then again reversed themselves and with the English stood;
Where Groseilliers disappeared and Radisson stayed for good.

Henry Kelsey came from England. to work for the H.B.C.;
He crossed into Saskatchewan and made friends with the Cree.
The buffalo and the grizzly bear, the first white man to see;
Of Fort York became the Governor, after writing a dictionary.

La Verendrye was a dreamer, who sought the Western Sea;
And on his exploration, took three of his family.
They traveled with the Indians across the Western lea;
Built a Fort at Winnipeg and one at La Prairie.

Jean was killed soon after, in a Sioux attack;
Louis and Francois saw the Rockies before turning back.
Trouble started at Fort La Rain; where Pierre was stranded;
He never reached the mountains, but the fur trade they expanded.

Montcalm, the leader of the French, a brave and able man;
Lost his life in Old Quebec on the Plains of Abraham.
Vaudriel and Bigot, a pair of traitorous men,
Hampered every move he planned.
Refused him men and guns, and lost the cause of France;
Brought about its downfall in the year of fifty-nine.

Wolfe was the one victorious, who took the Plains that day;
A frail and sickly soldier, who led the English horde.
His brains made up for his lack of brawn;
But he died too while the cannons roared.

A monument stands for these heroes bold,
Uniting the enemies of the days of old.

A brave and cunning Chieftain, of the Ottawa tribe;
Friendly to the French but the English couldn't abide.
Nine English Forts destroyed, while attacking with his band;
Pontiac was killed by an Indian on his land.

Three times Hearne sought the river, known as the Coppermine;
And for the H.B.C. did extend the fur trade line.
After failing twice, he sailed it to the Arctic;
The first white man to reach it overland.
Led across the wasteland by Chief Matonabee,
He found Slave Lake and River and Fort Cumberland.

Joseph Brant the Mohawk Chief, a loyalist of great fame;
For aiding the British in the war, a "Six Nations" Chief became.
He traveled over to England, royalty for to see;
To interest them in Indian aid this side of the sea.
He opened the first Protestant Church in Old Ontario,
Named in his honor is Brantford, a city which we all know.

A general brave and statesman wise, is what we call Sir Guy,
He passed the "Act of Old Quebec" in the year of '74;
Which to a revolution, opened up the door.
He floated down the river to Quebec from Montreal;
And by his brave leadership saved it from a fall.

An immigrant from USA, a fur trader, Peter Pond;
Spent three winters in Manitoba and Saskatchewan.
Pushed on into Alberta to Athabasca Lake,
Traded furs, planted garden, and accurate maps did make.
Joined the North West Company, but a second trader killed;
Left his home and company, with the murder never billed.

Captain Cook the sailor, an English captain he;
His work was exploration on our Eastern Sea.
New Zealand and Australia were his discoveries,
He found the cure for scurvy upon the citrus tree.
He sailed the wide Pacific, on Canada's western sea;
The world he circled twice. and was killed in Hawaii.

Mackenzie sought the Arctic, on the river that bears his name;
A hundred days to the ocean and back to Chipewyan.
Many hardships they endured, to reach their destination;
To plant a cross on Whale Island, and return to civilization.

On the waters of the Peace in May of Ninety-three,
Began a dangerous journey, to seek the Western Sea.
Included in the group were eleven stalwart men,
To reach the vast Pacific, was their greatest yen.
The Great Divide was crossed on the twelfth of June,
After traveling on the Fraser, overland thru the bush,
Up the Bella Coola, they reached the ocean soon.
"In July of 1793, From Canada by Land,"
Was the inscription painted by Mackenzie's hand.

Next came George Vancouver, and Island his name bore;
His work to command at Nootka, and chart our western shore.
The winters in Hawaii, the summers on the sea;
He sought the North-East passage and said there wasn't one.
He made a map of our western coast, famed in accuracy.

Simon Fraser built some forts, in the center of B.C.;
Along the Parsnip River, the fur trade he extended,
He traveled the dangerous Fraser from its source to mouth,
Ended at Westminister, instead of farther south.

As a geographer and surveyor, Thompson was the best we know;
Thirteen years with the Hudson Bay and to the Norwesters did go.
Charted source of Mississippi and Lake Superior's shore;
Crossed the Rocky Mountains, a dozen times or more;
Raced the Great Columbia from its source to mouth;
Lost the race, but charted it, from the north to south.

Thomas Douglas was a generous Scot, who to Red River came;
He started there a colony under the 'Kildonan' name;
After many trials and hardships, and the Norwesters attack;
Selkirk came to aid his settlement and bring more settlers back.

Governor Semple and twenty others were killed at Seven Oaks;
Selkirk and one hundred Swiss, reprisals for this sought.
Capturing Fort William and several Norwesters caught;
But after a lengthy lawsuit, damages had to pay;
With health and money almost gone, in three years passed away.

He built Fort Victoria, named for the gracious Queen;
When the 49th parallel as our boundary was seen.
James Douglas was the Governor of Vancouver Isle,
Transferred onto the mainland in a little while;
When gold was found on the Fraser River, he built the Caribou Road,
Brought law into the mining camps, upholding the British Code.

Father Lacombe the missionary, of Blackfoot and of Cree;
His aim to unite the red and white, in peace and security;
He built a school in Edmonton, a bridge on the Sturgeon River;
He brought settlers to Manitoba, to live by the old Red River.
He gained the confidence of the fierce Blackfoot tribe;
As President of the C.P.R., for one hour did reside;
He taught the people to read and write, and tended to their ills;
And at last became a hermit in Alberta's sunny hills.

Colonel French, who formed the Mounties, to help control the West;
"Maintain the Right" their motto, at which they did their best.
The ones to move Chief Piapot, who blocked the railway track;
They stopped the whiskey smuggling, and brought law breakers back;
Put the Indians on reservation, and helped protect the white;
Kept law and order from East to West, and stood up for the right.

Van Horne was chosen to command a gang of railroad men,
Given nineteen hundred miles of the C.P.R. to build;
From Winnipeg to Vancouver, mountain pass and prairie trail;
The East and West uniting, his energy didn't fail.

So in November Seventy-five, the 'Golden Spike' was drive;
To make the longest railway in the world;
From Atlantic to Pacific, for union they had striven;
And the flag of our Domain was unfurled.

- 1958 -

LIFE OF SIR WINSTON CHURCHILL

Born in the year of 1874, among that century's great,
Of British royal line, and American motherhood;
He grew to be a forceful, stalwart boy,
The "Democratic Way of Life" was all he understood.

At Harrow and Sandhurst College he took his education,
Then into a military career, led by his determination;
From there to the African wars to fight with the cavalry,
Then to the Boer Expedition, a hero when he broke free.

In 1900, at twenty-six became a Conservative M.P.,
Then switched his support to the Liberals in the year of 1903;
In 1905 he joined the ranks in the Liberal political game,
Meanwhile he wrote several books of literary fame.

In 1908 he married a pretty British girl,
And from this happy union arrived a boy and three girls;
The death of daughter Mary, nearly broke his heart,
When she was only very young, he found they had to part.

In 1911 he had the foresight to see the Kaiser's Plan,
In fourteen had his navy ready, to protect the rights of man;
But due to defeat at Dardanelies resigned his navy post,
And joined the troops in Flanders Fields as an ordinary man.

But soon moved up, from experience and education,
And by the year of seventeen became Minister of Munitions;
And when the war was over, as a speaker gaining fame,
Became Britain's greatest Orator, in the "parliamentary game".

In Nineteen Twenty-two when the Liberal Party fell,
Sir Winston took up art and writing and rested for a spell;
In the intervening time wrote historic volumes four,
On the deeds and actions of the Empire, in the First World War.

In 1924 to the Conservative ranks returned,
And Chancellor of the Exchequer he became;
In Twenty-six there was a strike which he worked to end,
In 29, lost his office, and in the Thirties rested on his fame.

In the year of Thirty-eight, his foresight stood him well,
He warned the Chamberlain government not to trust the German horde;
To reject the Axis powers and be prepared for war,
Or the Nazis led by Hitler would blast the World to Hell.

The Second Great War became a fact on September third of '39,
He became the Admiralty's First Lord in a few hours time;
But nine months later on the eve of France's fall,
He formed a war time government and became responsible for us all.

He could promise nothing but "blood and toil and sweat and tears",
But yet they trusted him, forgetting all their fears;
"V for Victory" was his sign, that spurred the Allied on,
To bar the march of Nazi troops, outnumbering them four to one.

Bombs fell like rain from o'er head but never did he shirk,
And his determination beat the Germans at the "Landing of Dunkirk";
His "Little Boats of Britain" plied back across the foam,
To save the Allied troops and return them to their home.

And when the war was ended in Nineteen Forty-five,
Churchill led the opposition, very much alive;
Then in the year of Fifty-one, became Britain's Lord Supreme,
And in the year of Fifty-three, was knighted by the Queen.

On her "Grand Old Adviser" knighthood she bestowed,
The Order of the Garter was his to have and hold;
The highest and the oldest honor, a commoner ever got,
The "Nobel Prize" was also his in "Literary Art".

He was a man on many trades, soldier, statesman he,
Painter, writer, bricklayer were just another three;
As "Britain's Greatest Commoner" at this he did excel,
An honorable citizen of the U.S.A. as well.

At four score years resigned, as Minister Supreme,
But held his "Parliamentary Seat" in honor of his Queen;
And when eight years were added, retired from the strife,
Then spent two years enjoying a happy, private life.

On the twenty-second day in the year of Sixty-five,
One of our greatest "War Lords" passed away;
A heart attack which struck him, a few short days before,
Relieved him of his earthly toil, to reside on Heaven's shore.

A Royal funeral took place in January of Sixty-five,
When the "Old War Horse" went to his final rest;
Laid in his birthplace of Bienheim, Oxfordshire,
Respected by all the world, and for mankind to admire.

A "Great Old Warrior" has passed on, to his just reward,
The man who lived the longest as a parliamentary steward;
He lived and worked for freedom for us all,
And led the Democratic World with his flaming sword.

- 1965 -

SIGNS OF SPRING

The Old Goose told me spring is here,
So I know it's on its way;
The gander told her the facts of life,
So she started in to lay.

For the Old Grey Goose is a wise old bird,
Of this I will avow;
She knows if Spring is early or late,
For she can tell somehow.

Do you wonder what the Old Goose said?
One morning as she awoke;
Spring is here! Spring is here!
And it really is no joke.

I have a pain around my gizzard,
But it is settling down;
So she began to seek a place,
On which to build a mound.

She looked and honked for many an hour,
Until a place she saw;
Then the construction work began,
In the bright and golden straw.

Now Mr. Goose meanwhile stood by,
With a sexy look in his beady eye;
His major roll in this part of life,
Was to give advice to his bossy wife.

Then when she began to lay,
A large white egg, every other day;
He stood his guard like an eagle bold,
Of each invader taking hold.

And when a clutch of snow white eggs,
Lay tucked beneath her breast;
It was worth ones very life,
To venture near the nest.

But four short weeks have come and gone,
And tapping doth commence;
And soon the green and yellow mites,
Struggle through that marble fence.

The honking and the waddling,
Were comical to behold;
When Mr. and Mrs. Goose trekked off,
With nine little balls of gold.

The noise and the commotion,
On the Old Duck Pond that day;
Let everybody really know,
That summer's here to stay.

- August, 1970 -

THOUGHTS FROM ABROAD

Christmas time is drawing nigh,
Excitement's in the air;
Everyone is going home,
How I wish I could be there.

Where young and old alike will sing,
Those carols old and new;
Bringing back sweet memories of,
When friends were quite a few.

Santa time has rolled around,
For yet another year;
But many in this wide, wide world,
Will not celebrate we fear.

The season's one for you to give,
Love and health and cheer;
The time for all to lay aside,
Greed and hate and fear.

If Old Santa could but give,
A gift for Peace for all;
He'd have his sleigh packed to the top,
With trips home for one and all.

He'd transport the lonely wanderer,
The sailor on the sea;
The soldiers in the foreign lands,
For loved ones at home to see.

Now Christmas is a time of Joy,
And Peace of Earth to man;
But Santa cannot bring us Peace,
'Tis a thing, only the Good Lord can.

- December 20, 1971 -

INTO THE PAST

What has become of the stately chief,
Who roamed the plains of the west;
He's been replaced by the farmer man,
And the biggest farms, and the best.

What has become of the rolling prairie,
On which he lived and roamed;
It's been replaced by a reservation,
On which his spirit is entombed.

What has become of his native pride,
His honor and his respect;
It's been replaced by a crave to drink,
And to look for trouble by heck.

What has become of the Indian brave,
With his feathers and paint of war;
He has been replaced by a shiftless man,
With no will power or spunk anymore.

What has become of the buffalo,
That was his staple fare;
They've vanished from the prairie wide,
While the Indian gets welfare.

What has become of his pinto pony,
He rode like the wind so free;
It's been replaced by the motor car,
Which costs a lot you see.

What has become of his bow and arrow,
With which he killed his food;
It's been replaced by rifle fire,
But does he live as good?

What has become of the Pipe of Peace,
Smoked twixt the white and red;
The cigarette has taken its place,
Hence many of both are dead.

What has become of his beaded clothes,
Useful and pretty and soft;
They've been replaced by the mini skirt,
Which looks too much aloft.

What has become of the moccasin feet,
Leaving their tracks in the snow;
They've been replaced by the motor ski,
Which costs a lot of dough.

What has become of his tidy braids,
Hanging neatly down his back;
They've been replaced by the hippie cut,
Of which there is no lack.

What has become of the pemmican,
Made of berries and meat;
It's been replaced by store bought food,
Which is traded for booze on the street.

What has become of the water clear,
They drank wherever they roamed;
It's been replaced by barley beer,
On which they're often stoned.

Now why not abolish the reservation,
Assign him a piece of land;
Give him equal work, and equal rights,
And let him again, become a man.

- December 5, 1970 -

MY HEALTH RULES

I drink my milk and water,
But no tea or coffee please;
I eat fresh fruit and vegetables,
And also meat and cheese.

I wash my hands before I eat.
I bathe myself, once every week;
I brush my teeth three times a day,
And eat by meals in the nicest way.

On hankie clean my nose I blow,
And to my bed I early go;
Ten hours sleep is what I need,
And my health rules I try to heed.

Outside I play most every day,
In sunshine and fresh air;
With windows opened up, I sleep,
For my health rules I try to keep.

I brush my hair, keep my nails clean,
And from my mouth keep things unclean;
So I will grow to my full size,
And grow to be healthy, happy and wise.

- 1962 -

RAIN

It's raining, raining, raining,
The water's pouring out;
It seems as if the Heavens,
Have sprung a leak no doubt.

It's raining, raining, raining,
Every day or so;
If it doesn't stop it pretty soon,
Where can the water go.

It's flooding in the low spots,
It's washing on the hill;
The flats are getting waterlogged,
The farmer's had his fill.

The water's laying everywhere,
No matter where you look;
There's now a little river,
Where used to be a brook.

The last two weeks, it's rained and rained,
Before that it was dry;
The garden is all drowned out,
It's enough to make me cry.

The frogs have taken over,
Where cutworms used to dwell;
For Sunny Old Saskatchewan,
Has all gone to hell.

I guess we need a Noah's Ark,
Instead of house or flat;
For the cellars are all flooding,
Now how can one stop that?

The crops are growing taller,
And then they're falling flat;
You cannot work your fallow,
The weeds are like a mat.

But we are not complaining,
And I will tell you why;
For I'd rather see Saskatchewan,
Inclined to be wet than dry.

If in the thirties you had farmed,
When soil was on the move;
You'd know how much we hate the drought,
And why the rain we love.

Now farming is a job of chance,
You take the weather that you get;
You thank the Lord for what he gives,
And make the best of it.

So wear a smile, oh farmer man,
Do not swear or cry;
For in the year of Seventy-one,
Saskatchewan may be dry.

- July, 1970 -

DAVID HORNELL, V.C.

The midnight sun was shining in June of forty-four,
But the night was bright as noon, on Iceland's rocky shore.

As a crew of eight Canadians, for subs patrolled the seas;
Their work to protect our waters, from enemy artillery.

Their mission almost ended, across the tumbling foam;
A tiny speck was sighted, "A sub so near our home".

"Action Stations" was the call, as the aircraft thundered thru;
The gunners did not miss their target; and the U-boat answered too.

Sea and sky were rocked with fire; as the battle rose and fell;
Within were seven gallant Canadians, under Captain D. Hornell.

The U-boat badly damaged, sank slowly out of sight;
'Twas then the Captain realized, how serious was their plight.

"Prepare for landing" was the message; signaled out the very last;
In a cold North wind and twelve foot waves, it proved quite a task.

After bouncing badly, and losing a dingy, too;
Four in, four out, was the only way, to save the weary crew.

But their faith in their commander, was wondrous to behold;
Towards the safety of his fellow man, he had a heart of gold.

For twenty-one endless hours, with neither food nor drink;
These brave airmen floated, in the cold and briny drink.

Two crew members met their Maker, of exhaustion from the sea;
The Captain gave the brief, sad rites very reverently.

He stood the brunt of hardships, while cheering his comrades on;
Thinking not of his personal needs, but doing what had to be done.

The rubber dingy capsized once, but they righted it again;
Then a lifeboat was lost, while dropping from the rescue plane.

At last a rescue plane arrived, to rush them to the land;
But they could not wake the Captain, his Maker held his hand.

The Victoria Cross was his award, which he deserved full fair;
It was awarded posthumously, for the Captain wasn't there.

- October 23 - 25, 1968 -

MR. MOON

Now Mr. Moon has many uses,
To numerous to mention,
I will only list a few,
Which is my strict intention.

Many, many years ago,
You were worshiped far and wide,
As a guiding light at night,
For those who on earth reside.

Many saw your features,
As a god who watched at night;
To help the wayward traveler,
And aid him in his plight.

Others saw your heavenly body,
As the featured hunk of cheese;
But others were far wiser,
And did disapprove of these.

Many older living folk,
By you predict a weather change;
Windy, wet, warm, cold or dry,
They can cover every range.

We know that you affect the tides,
That brush our coastal shores;
You push and pull them back and forth,
Causing the Tidal Bore.

But I believe your greatest use,
As in the heavens you reside;
Is the part you play in plain old love,
While Mr. and Miss their joys confide.

But then your solitude was invaded,
By members of the human race;
When the U.S. Government decided,
To put astronauts on your face.

So please excuse us Mr. Moon,
I hope your not offended;
Please keep on shining for all humans,
Until time on earth has ended.

- November, 1970 -

AN ODE TO A BEARD

There are beards of many colors,
There are those of many hues;
They'll grow upon a Frenchman,
They'll grow upon a Jew;
And even on a Billy Goat,
Tho' I'm not meaning you.

Now there are many reasons,
Why they're grown so 'tis said;
Some say that they improve the looks,
And some protect the head;
But then I wouldn't know, I never had the grace;
To grow a bunch of whiskers, all scattered o'er my face.

Some are long, some are short,
But even at their best;
They'll only do to frighten kids.
Or make a mouse's nest;
Now don't let insult cash you in,
Take this with a grain of salt and only grin.

Some are soft and silky, others only stiff,
And stand out on a fellows face, like a porky in a pif;
But a poor fellow can't complain,
And always be a grousin';
For now what little mite would care,
Which one he built a house in.

But grow it long, and do it well,
Stand by the first set cause;
For this I'd say to all old men,
And when you've passed your three score-ten;
You might pass as Santa Claus,
(Enough insult to a poor beard - Amen.)

- December, 1943 -

THIS CANADA OF OURS

From Atlantic to Pacific, across our country wide,
Ten independent provinces, standing side by side;
The east coast and the west coast, joined by prairie land,
As a unified Dominion, may we forever stand.

We have B.C. with its fruit and fish, its lumber and its gold,
Its mild climate and scenic view, its beauty to behold;
The grandeur of its mountains, its power limits untold,
A rugged land to labor in, but a haven for the old.

Alberta with its rangeland, its herds and rolling hills,
Its oil to raise its income, and its stampede for the thrills;
Its cowboys and its Indians, its vegetables and so forth,
Its long Alaska Highway that reaches to the North.

Now Saskatchewan is the wheat land, its prairie reaching wide,
With cattle, grain, and lumber, growing side by side;
With minerals and oil to be extracted from the lands;
Where once the Indian roamed in large and extensive bands.

Manitoba's next in line, with her fisheries galore,
With the famous port of Churchill, on the Hudson Shore;
With grain, and fur and mining, where tatters grow the best,
With the grain Exchange and stockyards, is the gateway to the West.

Our Great Lakes are situated in Old Ontario,
From rugged north to balmy south, where the fruit orchards grow.
Dairying and feeders, and pigs of many breeds;
Minerals and vegetables, enough to fill their needs.
The homeland of our sportsmen and Toronto's Royal Fair;
The manufacturing center of our Dominion is there.

With Superior and Erie, Huron and Ontario,
St. Lawrence the greatest waterway, the world will ever know;
With Honeymoon Bridge and Niagara Falls, across the mighty river,
Four of the greatest fresh water lakes, may they last forever.

Quebec, the home of the Cor.-de-bois, where French and English meet;
From rugged north to balmy south, both cultures compete.
Where Old World flavor still exists, right beside the new;
While in the St. Lawrence River Valley, fruit and industry grew.
With pulp and paper from the North, fishing on lake and shore;
With scenic view and sugar sweet, how could one wish for more.

In the Bay of Fundy, with its Tidal Bore;
Another of our provinces with fisheries galore,
Ridges, lakes and rivers in a rolling countryside;
Lumber, pulp and paper, and fertile valleys wide.
Dairying and agriculture, coal, gas and oil, too;
Fishing, furs and game and hydro's quite a few.
Winters are severe, with snow and rainfall thick,
One of the Maritimes, known as New Brunswick.

A little bit of Scotland dwells inside Nova Scotia's shore;
And Nova Scotia's "Bluenose" is remembered evermore.
With the cod banks and the herring, inland fishing, too;
In lumbering and woodwork, there's always lots to do.
With lots of cheese and powdered milk, flowing from the land;
Apples from Annapolis Valley are really something grand.
Newfoundland's iron is turned to steel and shipped throughout the world;
While the naval base at Halifax, helps keep our flag unfurled.

A long and narrow island in the gulf of Old St. Lawrence;
The densest peopled province of our fair domain.
With many roads and railroads, airports and scenic view;
A pleasant place to live in, with its fox fur farming, too.
With many bays and inlets, where her fish are caught;
Of our many provinces, it's the smallest of the lot.
Farming is intensive here, livestock raising too;
Prince Edward Island is the province, I've described to you.

Newfoundland is the latest province, to join the prosperous ten;
With lumbering and minerals, and many stalwart men.
A plateau marked with many hills, a sheer and rocky shore;
And Gander's Airport Terminal, to Europe is the door.
Lobster, herring, cod and salmon on the Grand Banks are found;
In a cold and snowy climate, game hunting does abound.
The Transatlantic Cable at Trinity Bay begins;
The U.S. Naval Base at Argentea helped us the War to win.

Thru a million miles of wasteland, where man has seldom trod;
Underneath the Northern Lights, close to the ways of God,
Here lies miles and miles of barren land, covered by ice and snow;
Far from the city's noisy streets deserted where ever you go.
Here lives the sturdy Eskimo, an igloo for his home;
May he in this land he loves so well in freedom always roam.
There's Mackenzie and Keewatin, with Franklin in-between;
There's copper, gold and oil here, but furs remain supreme.

It is the home for the caribou, food for the native bands;
Including many islands in this barren arctic land.
But the Eskimo's life is changing in this cold and arctic land;
He's getting an education, this we're given to understand.
But will he still be happy after he has journeyed forth,
Will he be free to love his life in this backward rugged north.

Now all that's left is the Yukon, where mineral wealth is great;
Where man and beast died off like flies, in the rush of ninety-eight.
Where Robert Service lived and wrote, in a realistic way;
Where Sam McGee and Dan McGroo learned to cuss and pray.
Where summer is short, and winter is long, and daylight hours strange;
Crossed by many rapid rivers, and a rugged mountain range.
Where the strong are getting stronger, and the weak die one by one;
Where Mount Logan towers upward to reach the midnight sun.

So now you see our country is a vast and varied land;
May we unified and peaceful, walk on hand in hand.
Reaching out in distance, thru seven zones of time;
Extending from Port Peelee, to a Northern Arctic clime.
And may Democratic policy continue at our head;
And we as true Canadians be forever born and bred.

- December, 1967 - January, 1968 -

TEN BLACK CROWS

Ten black crows in the meadow sat,
Cawing over this and that;
One decided 'twas time to dine,
He flew away, then there were nine.

Nine large crows roosting on a limb,
Everyone as black as sin;
Discussing what would be their fate,
One flew down, then there were eight.

Eight big crows, sitting in a line,
Shaking their feathers, black and fine;
Talking of a place called Heaven,
One flew away, then there were seven.

Seven crows in an excited state,
Sitting on the old barn gate;
One said, it must gather sticks,
She flew away, then there were six.

Six saucy crows raising quite a fuss,
First they'd chatter, then they'd cuss;
One decided to take a dive,
He flew down, then there were five.

Five hungry crows, starting into caw,
Each one telling what he saw;
The bull let out an awful roar,
One got scared, so then there were four.

Four shiny crows, looking bright,
One got angry and decided to fight;
Fight she did; but had to flee,
Leaving just a group of three.

Three lonely crows feeling kinda sad,
Wondering why they had been so bad;
The wise old owl said, "WHO! WHO!"
One took fright, so then there were two.

Two silly crows sitting side by side,
Wondering if their friend had died;
They thought that they might have some fun,
But one fell asleep, leaving only one.

One old crow, left on the gate,
Thinking it was very late;
Started dreaming how his sins to atone,
Now the old meadow land is all alone.

- January, 1972 -

THE WESTERN FARMER

Here's to the western farmer,
A man of muscle and brawn;
Here's to the western farmer,
A Liberal Government pawn.

Here's to the sucker that he is,
Trying to fish for a buck;
Changing his plans so as to live,
With a little bit of luck.

They push you here and shove you there,
Until you're a mental wreck;
Trying to find a way to swim,
Instead of drown by heck.

The cattle prices are very good,
If you have whatever they need;
But if it is too small or large,
It just pays for the feed.

Taxes are up and pigs are down,
The grain you cannot sell;
I wonder why you don't sit down,
And say, "Please go to Hell".

But then we have the lovely weather,
And Saskatchewan's summer sun;
Which makes farming rather pleasant,
For the "poor old son of a gun".

But if it's rain he's needing,
The sky is mostly clear;
And when we need the sunshine most,
It will likely hail I fear.

Or else those rain clouds will pile up,
And gently turn to snow;
When the crop is looking good,
And the combine is ready to go.

But then the farmer is a patient man,
He holds his job most dear;
He'll never give in but still hold on,
So he'll try again next year.

- July, 1970 -

MY VIEWS OF THE BUSH

You can talk about your bush land,
Where little houses hide;
But give me the sunny prairie,
With grain land rolling wide.

I'll take the hills and valleys,
As long as they are tree bare;
But in that burnt off woodland,
You'll never find me there.

It makes you feel so lonely,
So desolate and small;
It makes you wish incessantly,
For the dear old prairie call.

There's firewood on every hand,
And burnt trees scattered o'er the land;
The spruces stand up like specters bold,
Like giant corpses grey and cold.

There may be wealth in the bushland,
Where life is hard but free;
But make the rolling prairie,
The year round home for me.

Now that my trip is over,
And back I wend my way;
To that far distant grain land,
It's where I want to stay.

- July 28, 1944 -

RECOLLECTIONS

The little old lady sat knitting,
As gently she racked too and fro;
Thinking thoughts of her childhood,
In the days of the long, long ago.

She thought of her fair skinned mother,
Who was a beauty to behold;
Tall and slim and graceful,
With hair of a russet gold.

She thought of her stalwart father,
As handsome as he could be;
And how she used to brush his hair,
While sitting upon his knee.

She thought of the day she started school,
The excitement and the fears;
And of how she worked to get high marks,
Throughout the coming years.

She thought of her sisters and brothers,
Who by now to Heaven had gone;
To join her mother and father,
Thus leaving her all alone.

She recalled her many playmates,
And all the fun she'd had;
Of how she helped her mother,
And pestered her dear old dad.

Of how she grew to womanhood,
With tresses long and red;
Of how she married her childhood beau,
Who like her parents, now was dead.

Of how she was broken hearted,
When the accident took place;
Wiping out three happy lives,
And erasing the smile from her face.

She dreamed of the day she left her home,
As higher learning she sought;
Of how she traveled to distant lands,
And by dark-skinned natives was caught.

Of her lonely life as a missionary,
In the hot and humid lands;
Of the hunger and hardship suffered there,
By the carefree native bands.

Of her return to her old home town,
Amid cheering and gay fanfare;
To move into the Old Folks Home,
And retire sedately there.

And although her time was running out,
She was contented with her lot;
She had her future paid for,
In the little family plot.

Another week has come and gone,
And another soul has departed;
The little "Old Rocker" is silent tonight,
And many friends are downhearted.

- October, 1970 -

MORNING ON THE FARM

Rise in the morning early,
That's when my day begins;
The sun is shining brightly,
No time to count my sins.

Rush to start the fire,
Get some water on;
When it starts to boil,
Start to sing this song.

It's time to get up, it's time to get up;
It's time to get up today;
It's time to get up, it's time to get up;
You must be on your way.

Mix the porridge pretty quick,
Make some coffee, too;
Hurry now or else you'll see,
Mother in a stew.

One must rush to get the cows,
Another feed the chicks;
From these very simple things,
We must get our kicks.

There's cows to milk and calves to feed,
Pigs and poultry, too;
In the morning on the farm,
There's always lots to do.

We eat our breakfast in a rush,
Hunt clothes and books up spry,
For if we fail to catch the bus,
We'll know the reason why.

There's lunch to make and faces wash,
Ma! "how's my neck and ears?"
Now brush your teeth and comb your hair,
And be good "My Little Dears".

Oh me, oh my, at last they're off,
Now I can catch my breath;
This new fangled education,
Is about to be my death.

- 1964 -

TIME

The silver circle slowly sailed,
Across the starlit sky;
As I stood on the earth below,
And watched the clouds roll by.

I felt so insignificant and small,
In all of nature's world;
While he looked from way up there,
To see every flag unfurled.

He knows whereof we earthlings come,
From monkeys, Mars or man;
But he does not disclose a hint,
Of how we fit God's plan.

He saw Anthony and Cleopatra,
A floating down the Nile;
He saw the building of the Pyramids,
In Egyptian slavery style.

He watched the Birth of Christ,
And Old Herod's power sway;
He saw the crucifixion deed,
And the Lord's return that day.

He helped Columbus find America,
And saw it become a nation;
He saw her as a democracy,
Helping to advance salvation.

He saw the British Commonwealth,
From Celts and Saxons grow;
Until it was an Empire,
"Which the sun never sets on", you know.

He's seen Ireland's little Leprechaun,
And Russia's gay Hussars;
Saw the advance in travel,
From ox to motor car.

He sailed over death and destruction,
In World Wars One and Two;
And other forms of chaos,
Numbering quite a few.

He saw the "Little Boats of Britain",
Ply back across the foam;
While Mr. Winston Churchill,
Protected Queen and home.

He observed the floods and famine,
In China and Japan;
Starvation and over-population,
In India and Siam.

The airplane and rocket ship,
May have disturbed his peace of mind;
But a million miles of moonlight,
Between him and earth you'll find.

Some astronauts alighted,
On his moon dust plain one day;
Took some samples of his surface,
And inspected Tranquillity Bay.

But all of us common people,
Who gaze at him at night;
Think of his peaceful features,
And his soft and silvery light.

So Mr. Moon, you wise Old Sage,
I hold you in respect;
May you continue to watch o'r us,
And many on your face reflect.

- November, 1970 -

"WHAT WOULD WE DO WITHOUT CHRISTMAS"

Oh, what would we do without Christmas?
The happiest time of the year;
A time of loving and giving,
A time for laughter and cheer.

Oh, what would we do without Christmas?
All the tinsel, the trinkets and toys;
All the candies, the nuts and the oranges,
For good little girls and boys.

Oh, what would we do without Christmas?
With all of its ribbons and bows;
Its noise of laughter and dancing,
And the traditional mistletoe.

Oh, what would we do without Christmas?
And the Spirit of good old St. Nick;
With boys and girls who gorge themselves,
But yet never seem to get sick.

Oh, what would we do without Christmas?
Santa, his reindeer and sleigh;
Visiting all around the world,
To give his gifts away.

Oh, what would we do without Christmas?
The merriest time of the year;
The time for presents and dancing,
The season for liquid cheer.

Oh, what would we do without Christmas?
The carols, the bells and the tree;
The thoughts of ones who are far away,
And hopes that they think of me.

Oh, what would we do without Christmas?
Old Santa and all his elves;
All the hymns and songs of gladness,
Sorry, we'd feel for ourselves.

Oh, what would we do without Christmas?
Its a sign of the end of the year;
We look forward with thoughts of the future,
And thoughts of the past, we revere.

Oh, what would we do without Christmas?
In memory of the babe born in flight;
So lets give thanks for a Merry Christmas,
And to all tired children, "Good Night".

- December 27, 1970 -

93

THE STORM

The breeze was blowing softly,
And I saw the flowers nod;
The sun was shining brightly,
Straight from the Throne of God.

The brook was flowing gently,
As I watched from a hill that day;
And in a nearby pasture field,
I saw an oak tree sway.

I sat in silent wonderment,
As not a sound I heard;
Not the babble of the running brook,
Nor the song of a happy bird.

Then I looked at the western sky,
And I found my answer there;
The movement of the darkening clouds,
Made me stand and stare.

A boiling cauldron of black and white,
Moved slowly in on me;
While brilliant flashes came and went,
A sight for all to see.

The distant sky was a raging maine,
But the white capped waves were clouds;
They looked to me like an angry mob,
In many shades of duds.

And then the thunder vent its power,
Like a lion's mighty roar;
It caused the very earth to shake,
As it had never shook before.

You could hear a mighty moaning,
As the clouds rolled over me;
There was a calm and silent moment,
When lightening struck that tree.

There was a smell of brimstone,
And the old oak tree split asunder;
A hundred years of patient growth,
Destroyed by nature's blunder.

The rain came down in torrents,
From the dark clouds overhead;
And I became a sodden mass,
As the hailstones fell like lead.

The tumbling clouds rolled to the east,
The sun came out behind;
I had viewed a sight of nature's strength,
That would never leave my mind.

It made me see how small I was,
How weak and insecure;
How nature's force was in control,
As God's in Heaven that's for sure.

- October, 1969 -

DAY DREAMING

Did you ever rise in the morning,
At five or a little before;
When the sun is shining brightly,
To do your morning chores.

The dew is sparkling on the grass,
As you circle the docile cows;
You gaze in wonder at nature's beauty,
As long as time allows.

You deeply breath the morning air,
Thinking how lucky you are;
Enjoying in full all nature's gifts,
Without a worry or care.

You see a field of the greenest grass,
A waving in the breeze;
You notice many a delicate flower,
As the fluff floats off the trees.

You hear the song of the native lark,
As it says to you, "Good Morn";
You hear the caw of the noisy crow,
As he helps himself to the corn.

The leaves are whispering in the breeze,
As the birds commence to sing;
The old crow gives a warning croak,
As the magpies take to wing.

You hear the cry of the hungry hawk,
As it starts out on the prowl;
You hear the scream of the noisy jay,
And the sleepy drawl of the owl.

You watch the sun send forth its rays,
As it mounts the orb of the day;
For morn has come and night has fled,
Making one feel young and gay.

The flowers hang their heavy heads,
And you see the long grass weaving;
The wind is slowly mounting up,
And the morning dew is rising.

You awake with a start from your revelry,
You cannot spend more time;
Work is calling and you must go,
As the cows march on in line.

- September, 1969 -

96

SUMMER IN SASKATCHEWAN

When It's summer in Saskatchewan,
That's where I long to be;
It then becomes a beauty spot,
Which everyone likes to see.

The sky is blue, and the clouds are high,
The days sunny and bright;
The stars come out to peep about,
While the moon doth cross the night.

The wind it is a gentle breeze,
As the flowers bow and nod;
Making one feel close to nature,
And so near the "Throne of God".

Now the rain, it rains, so gently,
Like dew drops on the run;
And then the skies clear quickly,
Bringing out the sun.

A rainbow appears so suddenly,
It's beauty we behold;
It makes one as excited,
As to have found the pot of gold.

One can smell the wild flowers,
The alfalfa and the clover;
There's no other perfume,
Half so sweet, the whole world over.

The livestock are so sleek and fat,
There are fields of golden grain;
It's heaven in Saskatchewan,
If we only get the rain.

But when the summer's over,
Then we should vacate the place;
And journey farther southward,
For an extended time of grace.

To return again in spring time,
As the early robins do;
To spend yet another summer,
As a native tried and true.

In the winter it's quite different.
But somehow stay we do;
For Sunny Old Saskatchewan,
Is the home of me and you.

- January, 1970 -

KING OF THE ROOST

The little banty rooster, is of a noble breed,
He grows so fat and saucy, but eats very little feed;
He has more spunk and energy, than anything I know,
A coat of many colours, and a very sexy crow.

With head erect, and a fighting look in his beady little eye,
Just like the many coloured peacock, he goes strutting by;
The other birds all step aside, and do not say a thing.
We look at him and think of a noble prince or king.

With a ring of gold around his neck, and across his back,
His head a brilliant apple red, his tail a shiny black;
Fleck of gold throughout his breast, with spots of blue or green,
I think that he's the prettiest bird that I have ever seen.

He'll fight his weight in wildcats, and not be scared at all,
He's inherited enough conceit, to have grown ten feet tall;
He'll collect himself a harem, numbering quite a few,
And orders that he issues them causes quite a stew.

And he is quite the family man, this you will allow,
For mother banty has a brood, that's hard to count, I vow;
Cream and tan with spots of brown, and also lightening fast,
As they take off like balls of fluff, hiding in the grass.

He really is a pompous male, much like the human form,
He likes to sputter, fume and cuss creating a regular storm;
And if he should meet up with another crusty male,
Watch the blood and feathers fly, from either head or tail.

Now one can't help admire, this fighting little cock,
With a body like a pigeon, and a nerve as hard as rock;
If there were just more humans with as much spunk and gall,
This world would not be half as bad, in fact, not bad at all.

- January, 1970 -

A BUSHMAN'S LAMENT

Ah, now that I have cut my beard,
How chilly I do feel,
I only got it partly reared,
When off it came, a-weel,
As the Scotty Boy would say,
I'll grow a better one someday.

I feel so lonesome now you see,
For 'twas the better part of me,
Oh now 'tis gone, I am so sad,
For 'twas the best I ever had,
Not because 'twas cute or handsome,
But because 'twas warm and winsome.

It was only a rat's nest you may guess,
To keep it pretty I did my best,
Its color was, I never said,
A mottled brown with spots of red,
Ah well 'tis gone, forever heed,
A razor did that sorrowful deed.

I wonder why I miss it so,
No one will really ever know,
How close a friend it came to be,
And how dear it was to me,
But one must sacrifice a lot,
When returning to a civilized spot.

But Mr. Burns he oft did say,
Best laid plans of mice and men, "gang aft Aglee",
Alas I have removed my beard,
To which you mites were so endeared,
But this I'll say to every friend,
Of a great beard it is the End.

- February, 1944 -

CALM, COLD, AND CLEAR

We listen to the forecast,
With shreds of hope and fear;
But all they'll ever tell us,
It that it's calm, cold and clear.

It's in the morning early,
At noon and night we hear;
In Sunny Old Saskatchewan,
It's calm, cold and clear.

The barometer is rising,
But the degrees are stuck I fear;
For in Sunny Old Saskatchewan,
It's calm, cold and clear.

It's clear, calm and cold,
Three short words they say;
But it describes Saskatchewan,
In a superior sort of way,

At night it drops to fifty,
At noon it makes a high;
It's just twenty-five and cold,
Beneath a calm, clear sky.

The wind will rise a bit,
And the snow go sifting by;
So we shiver in Saskatchewan,
Beneath a cold, clear sky.

When the wind it reaches twenty,
And the degrees are yet below;
The sun is shining brightly,
But it still is clear and cold.

The moon itself has a golden ring,
The sun dogs stand out bold;
But we cannot seem to get a change,
It still says, clear and cold.

And then the snow starts falling,
And the sky is overcast;
The thermometer is rising,
A break in sight at last.

But by the time the sun has risen,
Our hopes have passed away;
For on the calm and sunny prairie,
It's a cold, clear day.

For forty days we've suffered,
Without a break in sight;
The sun shines in the daytime,
And the stars shine bright at night.

It's the winters in Saskatchewan,
So many hope and fear;
So they vacate this province,
Because it's so cold, calm and clear.

When you are young and robust,
You enjoy this rugged mold;
But as old age creeps up on you,
You hate the cold, cold, cold.

So from sunny old Saskatchewan,
I would like to move away;
When they keep predicting,
It's a clear, cold, calm day.

- January 31, - February 2, 1969 -

REMEMBRANCE DAY

Let us look back to the time of wars,
When our soldiers fought on foreign shores;
With fire and shot and cannon roar,
Through the night destruction tore.

On land and sea and in the air,
They fought with a courage rare;
They fought for what was right and fair,
Those who know, are the ones who were there.

Where bombs and shrapnel and bullets fell,
The trenches were a living hell;
Machine and man rushed on pel mel,
How any survived, only God can tell.

Ypres and Passchendaele, Anzir and Dunkirk,
The Canadians were marching where the danger lurked;
Through both wars with the Allies they worked,
Did their very best and from their duty never shirked.

Then came the peace that they all sought,
That for each other they had fought;
They paid the price so dearly bought,
We pray that it was not for nought.

November 11th dawns cold and clear,
It rolls around to us every year;
Two minutes silence we hold dear,
May it protect us from all fear.

'Tis the day we think of those who died,
Resting in Flanders, side by side;
Where poppies blow our dead abide,
While we live on but our feelings hide.

Let us work hard for what they won,
To keep the peace from sun to sun;
To stop chaos before it begun,
That all may rest when day is done.

- October 20 - 22, 1968 -

ODE TO A CAR

She's a rattling little Chevie,
For she travels right along;
Over hills and valleys,
As her driver sings a song.

"Oh, these new cars may be fine,
But give me that Chev of mine;
Roll along little Chevie, roll along."

Some say bright lights are best,
But for me on her request;
It's roll along little Chevie, roll along.

Oh a brother's mighty handy,
You all know that is true;
But when it comes to getting gas,
I'm telling this to you.

It's nice to have a brother,
Whose gas is right at hand;
Who doesn't own a dog that bites,
But one who understands.

Without gas it will not run,
But for me it's lots of fun;
Roll along little Chevie, roll along.

A car requires water,
A horse needs but a drink;
So we'll not need to stop halfway,
When the driver doesn't think.

Many tires may go flat,
But thank-gosh mine don't do that;
Roll along little Chevie, roll along.

Many engines will run right,
Many doors may shut up tight;
But to me it seems alright,
Although it's not a pretty sight.

Just a little piece of string,
And a firecracker bright;
Just a jolly bunch together,
And then things go just right.

Many bronco's may be wild,
Of that he's mighty sure;
But when it comes to roping cars,
He jumps right out the door.

Oh your bronco's may be fine,
But give me that car of mine;
Roll along little Chevie, roll along.

Now these may be its bad points,
On them we should not dwell;
For as long as it keeps rolling,
We all think it is swell.

Oh these new cars may be fine,
But give me that car of mine;
Keep on rolling little Chevie, rolling on.

- 1941 -

A MONARCH

The noble elk stood broadside,
As the hunter drew a bead;
A spurt of flame, a dull impact,
A lucky shot indeed.

For slowly sank the Monarch,
To the pine strewn forest floor;
His life blood flowed like water,
The Monarch was no more.

Large and limp the warrior lay,
His last great battle lost;
He'd strove to be Prince of his realm,
A King at any cost.

He'd kept his herd together,
This Monarch of his clan;
Defeating all his enemies,
Till along came murderous man.

He'd been a proper father,
Fed all his children well;
Watched over all with loving care,
And like a warrior fell.

Now man has no such principles,
He'll hunt or kill for fun;
Why not make him the hunted,
And give the elk the gun.

- December, 1971 -

GARDENING ON THE PRAIRIE

Did you ever grow a garden,
On the prairie in the west;
Where the moisture is inadequate,
And the soil not the best.

Where the wind blows like a hurricane,
And stones are thick and big;
Where the bugs move in by thousands,
Till you could almost dance a jig.

You start out in the springtime,
And you work your soil well;
You fertilize and bug dust,
And then you pray like hell.

You dig your rows and drop your seeds,
Cover them and pack;
Cross your fingers that they'll grow,
"Oh Dear" my aching back.

You mark your rows so carefully,
With little sticks or stones;
And by the time it's planted,
It's "Oh, my weary bones".

Now's the time to watch and wait,
So you observe it every day;
To see if it will germinate,
And keep the pests away.

With anxious eye you watch the sky,
For any sign of rain;
But the sun is hot and the wind is dry,
It near drives you insane.

But at last a little shower,
Moves up and across the sky;
You hope and pray 'twill come your way,
But nary a drop falls nigh.

So you set up your water works,
Sprinkler, motor, pipe and all;
And with a smile of satisfaction,
You watch the water fall.

Boy! are you ever happy,
For in another day or so;
All your little seedlings,
Will have started into grow.

The weeds it seems,
They also like the sun and moisture too;
For they grow even faster,
So what are you to do?

You must pick and pull and cultivate,
And work from morn till night;
The weeds they seem to keep ahead,
Now isn't it a fright.

At last you've reached the other end,
And your corners all are clean;
You think you'll take a breather now,
But look! It makes you scream.

The little peas so nicely up,
Have started into fall;
The onions have a withered look,
Lettuce, there's none left at all.

It's bugs and worms and maggots,
Beetles, thrips and aphids, too;
If it wasn't for the insect dust,
What would we really do?

We run right quick to get the can,
Before all our work is lost;
"Dear me!" upon the radio,
They have predicted frost.

So you dust and scratch to cover up,
All the tender little plants;
In hopes that "Jack" won't get them,
Or you'd like to kick his pants.

Now a month has come and gone,
With sunshine and moisture too;
You've begun to think you've got it made,
But nature isn't through.

The hail it struck one afternoon,
When the clock said half past four;
So the garden had a punctured look,
It did not have before.

But then the sun came out again;
And we could not weep for long;
For the heart of a prairie gardener,
Needs to be sturdy and strong.

And like a wilted pansy,
With the coming of the rain;
In a few short days and nights,
It has revived again.

Now the bee is mighty handy,
This I have to admit;
And in these modern times,
They have invented seedless set.

But to give you plenty pumpkin,
Cucs, citron, marrow too;
Being nature's little helper,
Is the job allotted you.
Then the hens and geese thought they would like,
Some peas and carrots too;
Just as he had decided,
It was time to have a stew.

Fall at last has rolled around,
And we must reap our spoil;
So it's dig or pick or can or freeze,
With never ceasing toil.

So rush you must from dawn to dark,
To beat the frost and snow;
Thinking not of what you'd rather do,
Or where you'd like to go.

Now despite the bugs and rust and drought,
We loved our garden plot;
Even though it was a worry,
And we had to work a lot.

But when the season's over,
And our winter fare is stored;
We look with admiration,
Then thank the blessed Lord.

And may we when another year,
Has quickly rolled around;
Have health and wealth and spirit,
To plant the same old ground.

- November, 1969 -

BABY BOY ALPHABET

A - is for the ailments,
That all children get.

B - is for the baby boy,
Who cries when he is wet.

C - is for the colic,
He is sure to get.

D - is for the diapers,
That must be washed.

E - is for his energy,
He has lots, by gosh.

F - is for his friendly face,
So do not let him cry.

G - is for his baby grin,
When he waves good-bye.

H - is for the happiness,
He brings to you and I.

I - is for the intelligence,
We hope he'll have some day.

J - is for his joy in living,
Bless him, will you Lord, we pray?

K - is for the kisses,
He has lots to spare.

L - is for the love you give,
Make sure its always there.

M - is for the anxious mother,
To whom he turns for care.

N - is for the night times,
He wakens for a bottle.

O - is for his open mouth,
Issuing noise, you'd like to throttle.

P - is for his pappa,
Who keeps him from all harm.

Q - is for his quaintest acts,
   That he doth perform.

R - is for his rubber pants,
   Which suffer in a storm.

S - is for that sleepy smile,
   That flits across his face.

T - is for the toys he has,
   Scattered every place.

U - is for the understanding,
   You must give him every day.

V - is for the voice he has,
   If mother's far away.

W - is for the way he walks,
   While just a little tad.

X - is for (e)xonerate,
   For he's never really bad.

Y - is for the yelling,
   Before he learns to talk.

Z - is for the zeal he has,
   While giving out a squawk.

All in all he's quite a boy,
Which he's bound to be;
Just a little mite to love,
   Right from A to Z(ee).

- January 15, 1972 -

DREAM WANDERING

Last night as I lay on my pillow,
In my soft and cozy bed;
I saw visions of countries before me,
And this is what they said.

I saw Eskimos up in Alaska,
Mushing on sleigh dog terrain;
I saw farmers picking purple grapes,
Out in sunny Spain.

I saw fruit orchards in Niagara,
And mountaineers in old Tibet;
I saw fishing boats on the blue Pacific,
And all of their nets were set.

I saw paddy workers in old Japan,
And factory men in London town;
The elephant hunter on the African veldt,
Was a native brawn and brown.

I went with a Peon in Mexico,
To a long-horned cattle station;
Then scouted the outback of Australia,
And its wonders of creation.

I rode a camel on Egyptian sands,
And helped excavate a tomb;
Watched a Civil War from Irish shores,
And in Scotland worked a loom.

I joined a penguin colony,
On Antarctica's frozen shore;
I woke with a start for my feet were cold,
And I can't go back anymore.

- November, 1971 -

BUS RIDING IN SASKATCHEWAN

Education in Saskatchewan is supposed to be the best;
They tell us it's the highest, from the east unto the west.
But when one tries to get it, it's really mighty grim;
For "Sunny Old Saskatchewan" may get a weather whim.

Now education and centralization, go hand in hand you see;
But these far reaching bus routes, were never meant for me.
Your rising very early, to catch it at the door;
For many of us have to travel, twenty miles or more.

When the sun is shining bright, and there isn't any rain;
When the birds are singing sweetly, and the road is just maintained,
To cover all that mileage, in a worn out bus is fine;
But in any other weather, it really cramps your spine.

When the rain comes down in torrents, and mud is everywhere;
You duck and dive for either ditch, and wish you were not there.
You slip and slide, and shiver and shake, to reach your destination;
All for that so called government whim "Centralized Education".

And in the spring, or in the fall with roads an icy glare;
You twist and turn round curves and grades, you wish were never there.
The frozen ruts grow deeper, the roads are really rough;
And of that so called gravel, there's never quite enough.

Now there are minor mishaps, which no one can foretell;
Like a motor conking out, or some gears have gone to hell.
A flat tire needs a spare, which the driver cannot carry;
Or just a little mud hole, that one is forced to ferry.

But the winter time is worst of all, this I can truly state;
For you start out mighty early, and get home very late.
It's dark when they leave in the morning, and also dark at night;
Thus the time of labor is very long, for many a little mite.

The January blasts are blowing, across the prairie wide;
While the roads fill in with snow fingers, lying side by side.
We listen and we wonder, as morning rolls around;
If any new snow has fallen, and hope the wind goes down.

We wonder if the bus will complete its scheduled route;
Or if the so-called bus driver, has already chickened out.
You get the children ready, thinking it will surely come;
You watch, you wait, you wonder and then start cussing some.

You call each successive neighbor, to see how far he got;
You wonder if its worth the worry, and your mind is full of doubts.
Then you start in sympathizing with the poor bus driver's lot;
Where risk is high and wages small, and a bunch of frisky sprouts.

But learning is the needed thing, for the coming generation;
So struggle we must to get them off, to get their education.
Battle the elements indeed, we must regardless of our likes,
It's sure a lot more complicated, than when parents were the tykes.

We often wish they'd spend our taxes, on improving transportation;
Then on so many new fangled methods of modern education.
But modernize and specialize, is the thing that's on the go;
It matters not if our pockets broke, or our nerves are plum shot, too.

- 1969 -

THE FARMER

Here's to the man he might have been,
If his livelihood was secure;
They cannot really starve him out,
But they always keep him poor.

The cattle prices are very good,
If you have what the buyer wants;
But if it is not top grade stuff,
They'll rob you of your pants.

And when he's built a dairy herd,
The price will fall I fear;
Why not milk to drink for the politician,
Instead of wine or beer.

We could flavor it with chocolate,
Gin, rum or even spice;
Then they'd consume the surplus,
Now wouldn't that be nice.

But we love the sunny weather,
On Saskatchewan's rolling plains;
It would be like heaven here,
If we got the needed rains.

But if it's rain he's needing most,
The sky will be sure to clear;
Or else the dark clouds will pile up,
And bring the hail I fear.

Or when it's time to combine,
And the grain is nice and dry;
The snowflakes will gently fall from,
A dark and cloudy sky.

But he got himself a crop of rape,
Wheat, oats and barley too;
But finds he cannot sell too much,
So his creditors start to stew.

But you cannot reap if you do not sow,
At least so the Good Book said;
So maybe he would be better off,
If only he'd stayed in bed.

But the farmer is an ornery cuss,
Somehow he won't give in;
He'll sweat and swear with words to spare,
Overwork is his greatest sin.

Yet he does not like a handout,
And he's never without work;
He's the most independent buggar,
Yet, you never see him shirk.

So we wish you well, oh farmer man,
May your accounts not be in the red;
And may all who know respect you,
For you're the "Salt of the Earth" 'tis said.

- November 19, 1971 -

THE FOG

The fog was thick and hazy,
Across the vale that night;
It made one stop and wonder,
And feel the pangs of fright.

I stood very still and listened,
To a far off motor's drone;
I knew that someone else was there,
But yet I felt alone.

Bright lights were dim orange beacons,
But then they faded too;
The grey-white shroud was closing in,
There was nothing one could do.

I felt crushed and smothered,
Within an airless tomb;
I felt lonely and downhearted,
Filled with a sense of doom.

The motor's drone grew louder,
It seemed to implore from below;
I stood and waited petrified,
I knew not which way to go.

And then the world exploded,
Not far from where I stood;
The whole hill seemed to tremble,
And flames spread to the woods.

The grey-orange glow extended,
To cover quite a space;
There lay the plane upended,
Of people not a trace.

I felt very insignificant,
Small and insecure;
As the fog again closed in,
My thought I must endure.

I seemed as in a dream-world,
The scene--a bad nightmare;
I quickly closed my eyes up tight,
In hopes it wasn't there.

But then I opened quick again,
When I heard a siren wail;
An ambulance and patrol car,
Were seeking out the trail.

But the fog enclosed the victims,
So I ran with all my might;
So I could reach the thoroughfare,
And direct the searchers' light.

I stumbled through the whiteness,
And dampness filled my throat;
I felt encased in feathers,
Or as if floating in a boat.

I reached the graveled highway,
And stood as in a daze;
Waiting for their headlights,
To come protruding through the haze.

In coherent language,
I tried desperately to explain;
But they knew before they reached them,
Their efforts were in vain.

- January, 1972 -

117

DECEMBER 16, 1972

The other day "Old Santa" came,
To our little town;
In suit of red and whiskers white,
He drove himself around.

He could have had an airplane,
A 'copter or a bus;
But he came by horse and cutter,
And created quite a fuss.

He drove along the main street,
Right up to the big tree;
With his bells a ringing,
For all the kids to see.

The following was terrific,
Of kids racing along behind;
While many of the elders watched,
With their childhood in mind.

The old mare stepped out sprightly,
As if she remembered when;
Old Santa was a by word,
On plain, hillside and glen.

The old and young were joined together,
Their hearts and minds were one;
The elderly were remembering,
While the young joined in the fun.

Now may Old Santa join us,
Again another year;
And in his good old fashioned way,
Bring faith and hope and cheer.

- December 19, 1972 -

118

THE GREAT DEPRESSION

The Great Depression struck us,
In the year of twenty-nine;
For ten long years it lasted,
With no change or help Devine.

The sky was dark with drifting soil,
The grass was dry and brown;
The farmer hadn't a dollar to spend,
If he should go to town.

It took every cent that he could make,
To supply his clothes and food;
And when he had a bit to sell,
The prices were not good.

Seven dollars for a muley cow,
If she was big and fat;
Otherwise you paid the freight,
Now what do you think of that.

Eggs were sold by the dozen then,
From three to five cents, that's all;
You traded them in at the local store,
If they would take them at all.

A can of cream was worth two bucks,
Usually less, but never more;
And we worked like hell to get it,
So it sometimes made us sore.

Wheat was sold by the bushel,
For as low as twenty-one cents;
No wonder the western farmer,
Wore patch upon patch on his pants.

You grew a garden, if you could,
But water you must fetch;
If by chance you had a well,
A slough, dugout or ditch.

The hoppers were a menace,
And poison them we must;
For they filled the hot and cloudless sky,
Like a cloud of moving dust.

The roadsides were in hopper motion,
And they never seemed to stop;
As you ambled through the dry brown grass,
It was Zing, snap, crackle, pop.

You cut your crop with the binder,
With a "Poverty Box" attached;
You could not waste a single straw,
So hard for a living you'd scratched.

The wind was steady, hot and dry,
Taking moisture as it went;
Leaving everything parched and brown,
And man's hard work all spent.

The soil was piled, fence-to-fence,
In banks of drifting sand;
The lights of cars on a windy day,
Were a glow across the land.

So many a prairie farmer,
Was like a man bereft;
He just up and packed his bag,
As he had no spirit left.

Now the easterners took pity,
On their poor prairie kin;
Emptying out their attics,
They shipped food and clothing in.

Now some if it was useless,
But most was heaven sent;
For the people on the prairie,
Were both broke and badly bent.

Then there were the Cod fish,
For which the Maritimes we thank;
We baked it long, in an oven hot,
And then we ate the plank.

Now many were the hobo's,
Across this fair domain;
They rode the rods from east to west,
Then back home again.

There was no work for them to do,
As money was too tight;
They were a carefree happy lot,
But for survival, they must fight.

Like a band of wandering gypsies,
The hobo rode the rail;
Coming from nowhere and going nowhere,
Like a boat without a sail.

A dollar a day was the going wage,
If one could find some work;
It was survival of the fittest,
So one tried hard not to shirk.

The government paid out half his wage,
If you would hire a man;
But then you had to feed him,
Under this employment plan.

Then there was that monthly check,
Ten dollars that many did resent;
Relief it was from dire need,
And so very carefully spent.

Now in those long and hungry years,
You could not travel very far;
So you made a Bennet Buggy,
From your poor old gasless car.

A pole in front and a tired team,
Ambled down the dusty trail;
You knew you had transportation,
If your tires didn't fail.

We ground our grain to make our bread,
As flour we could not well afford;
Now gopher pie they said was good,
When hunger was a burning sword.

Our shoes and socks we wore in holes,
But the latter you could jump;
It made them wear just twice as long,
Although the insteps had some humps.

Now father had his homemade snuff,
Packed carefully in a tin;
From tobacco, salt and coffee grounds,
When those hard times moved in.

You bought your pipe tobacco,
But the hank or by the twist;
Just ten cents for half a pound,
And then crush it in your fist.

To get sufficient coffee,
You had to improvise a lot;
You browned your wheat and ground it,
And mixed it with coffee in the pot.

We made our soap from tallow,
With a dash of lye and scent;
It sure chased out the dirt,
With little money spent.

Now pigweed greens were very good,
And mushrooms were a treat;
They were full of many vitamins,
So we hunted them to eat.

You canned your beef, and salted pork,
Picked wild fruit if you could;
You only bought what you must have,
It was plain but wholesome food.

We went out to the bush to cut,
Our wood, both dry and green;
We had to use the proverbial axe,
As chain saws we'd never seen.

You saved the thread, if you ripped a seam,
And yarn from homeknit socks;
All was carefully wound and saved,
In a mouse proof little box.

We had our supply of pots and pans,
Which grew old and sprung a leak;
But we never threw a one away,
As the "mendit card" we'd seek.

Our tinware had the measles,
If you turned them upside down;
The tiny bolts upon the bottom,
Would make an angel frown.

Now as liquor you could not afford,
So moonshine you must cook;
Now wheat, sugar and water,
And know-how was all it took.

We made our own entertainment,
Which in those days was a boon;
We'd dance all night to the school piano,
Which was always out of tune.

Or else a card game we would have,
A lunch and cup of tea;
Discuss our problems with a friend,
It made them much less you see.

We listened to the radio,
The hockey games and songs;
"Twas in the Dirty Thirties,
That Wilf Cater came along.

And we listened in on Foster Hewitt,
With a loud "He Shoots, He Scores";
It helped relieve the tension,
On those depression "Mental Sores".

Now mother was the family barber,
And she had to curl all the hair;
With tongs or wavers, heated in a lamp,
If she found the time to spare.

You washed your clothes on the washboard,
And dried them out in the sun;
It was tiresome work indeed,
And never very much fun.

You made yourself a patchwork quilt,
Then had a quilting bee;
Invited all your neighbours in,
And served them lunch and tea.

There were many barefoot little children,
Who walked those dusty roads to school;
They could not neglect their learning,
As education was the rule.

With supper over we gathered round,
The table close and soon;
For work and study must be done,
With one coal oil lamp to light the room.

One who has survived the thirties,
Is as saving as can be;
They won't throw out a single thing,
Its inbred in them you see.

But somehow we managed to survive,
The Depression in the West;
The Dirty Thirties came and went,
And most Westerners stood the test.

It was followed soon by World War II,
Which was harder to endure;
But the Westerner is a hardy one,
By now you know I'm sure.

- January 1 - 5, 1974 -

JUST A HOUSEWIFE

The Census man to our house came,
Just the other day;
He gave us forms to fill June 1st,
On how we work and play.

Now we the hard-worked housewife,
Don't count you must admit;
Although we labour all day long,
It does not count one bit.

Now a gardener's wage is rather good,
And they are often sought;
Although we grow a great big one,
Yet it is counted nought.

As dairy maid we are supreme,
Yet wages we don't get;
It counts not on the census form,
That you can really bet.

The poultry man makes quite a lot,
With fryers, eggs and chicks;
Although we supply ourselves the same,
We are only country hicks.

Although a secretary, vet and driver,
Teacher, nurse and cook;
We are entered as "Just a Housewife",
In Canada's counting book.

If we could draw the wages,
For all the jobs we do;
We could live the life of Riley,
But we'd be bored clean though.

But the thing that really makes me sore,
In this land of mechanization;
Is why they count the housewife, nought,
When she's "the backbone of the nation".

They can computerize the census,
Your taxes or your wages;
But they still need mothers in this world,
As they have down through the ages.

I wonder what they'd surely get,
If two computers they would mate;
The housewife then could stop awhile,
For a rest at any rate.

So if we made a drastic change,
Taking up a single job in life;
We'd at least be a dot on the census sheet;
Not just a blank spot housewife.

- June, 1971 -

THE HUNT

Well fall has rolled around again,
And hunting season's here;
The hunter's wife is now the boss,
While father's gone for deer.

He'll prepare himself for days ahead,
He'll work himself to death;
To earn himself a hunting spree,
And then walk till out of breath.

He'll buy a gun and lots of shells,
A license and a suit;
And then the little whitetail,
He must go out and shoot.

He'll rise in early morning,
Before the light of day;
Gulp down a hurried breakfast,
And then he's on his way.

He'll drive out many miles,
Then walk as many more;
Through bush, o'er hill and valley,
Until his feet are sore.

If we'd suggest he work as hard,
When he was still at home;
He'd ask if we were just plum nuts,
Or cracked up in the dome.

He had walked many a weary mile,
And never fired a shell;
The time is nearly dusk,
And he's as tired as hell.

As over a nearby tree lined rise,
Came a five-point in full stride;
The hunter slowly raised his gun,
The chest on sight he spied.

He carefully pulled the trigger back,
So not to spoil his aim;
But the buck kept right on coming,
He thought he'd fired in vain.

But its stride it quickly shortened,
And its manly chest showed red;
Another charging stride or two,
And at his feet fell dead.

Now his search was over,
He had acquired his kill;
The let down was terrific,
But the meat would fill the bill.

Now work he must to dress his kill,
He cannot rest as yet;
The excitement over for this time,
But he'll be back next year, you bet.

- November 18, 1971 -

THE GOPHER

Sitting straight and tall,
On a pock marked knoll;
Whistling through his whiskers,
Beside his personal hole.

With never blinking beady eyes,
So very bright and quick;
His front paws held up daintily,
While giving his tail a flick.

He whistles out a challenge,
Of catch me if you can;
But if you make a sudden move,
Why down his hole he's ran.

But if you'll just have patience,
He will all danger spurn;
And with his saucy chatter,
Will announce the spring's return.

He is a perfect nuisance,
This I'll have to say;
But we like his cheerful whistle,
Saying "Spring is on the way".

- March, 1973 -

BALER TWINE

Twin strings around a bale of hay,
Are as useful as can be;
But they're not half as useful,
As they later are to me.

I can use a pair of them,
To tie a little calf,
The way he pulls to break them,
Doth make a person laugh.

They even work on roosters,
In butchering time you know;
It is a little wifely hint,
To hold him head and toe.

Now there's a fence needs fixing,
But a hammer is hard to find;
So wifey dear just never fear,
Grab one of those baler twines.

And then there are the garden rows,
Which straight they need must be;
Now baler twine is just the thing,
For wifey dear to see.

Next there is that old milk cow,
With long sharp horns you see;
But snare them with a baler twine,
And she's as timid as can be.

There also is the one that kicks,
So high she'd lift your hat;
But double twine in figure eight,
Will very soon fix that.

Now if your pants are slipping,
Across that mucky yard;
Your bound to catch your toe in one,
Landing flat and mighty hard.
Of course you get up swearing,
And rather quite a mess;
You forgot the many uses,
For that twine I will confess.

- May, 1973 -

130

ON LOOKING BACK

I drove slowly down the highway,
As the prairie sun sank low;
Thinking of the difference,
From a hundred years ago.

A black ribbon stretched beneath me,
Where once a prairie trail;
Wound slowly up the hillside,
And down into the vale.

On either side the grain land,
Reaching far and wide;
Where once the massive buffalo,
Wandered side by side.

I saw the large machinery,
Go roaring back and forth;
Where once the wild Indians,
Roamed from South to North.

Then I beheld a farmstead,
With a shelter belt out back;
It has replaced my vision of,
A Run-down settler's shack.

We see a modern car or truck,
Quickly by us pass;
Where once the noble horse,
Was rode by every lad and lass.

We see the towns and cities,
With their turmoil and their noise;
Where once the level prairie rang,
With war hoops of redskin boys.

We see oil wells and antenna,
All along our route;
Where once the lonely coyote,
Let his voice ring out.

And then there is the jet plane,
Which zooms across the sky;
Where once the pretty song bird,
Did gaily sing and fly.

Now progress is the symbol,
For which one highly pays;
But are we any happier,
Than in those bygone days.

- December, 1971 -

131

MY VIEWS OF THE TELEPHONE

The most amazing thing we have,
Is that phone upon the wall;
You must run to answer it,
To find out who has called.

It's usually a near by friend,
Calling up to have a chat;
To discuss the present weather,
Or with tales of this or that.

But it may be your neighbor,
Who is in need of help;
Or perhaps a salesman,
You would really like to scalp.

We never see our neighbors now,
Since we've joined the old "rat race";
But we love to hear their cheery voice,
If we cannot see their face.

Now it may be long distance,
From a friend or family;
Or just some goofy kid near by,
Acting smart you see.

It often rings at the worst time,
Sometimes early, sometimes late;
It's sure to catch you in the bath,
Or some other dreadful state.

Then there is the fun of listening,
To hear what is going on;
It may be sickness, death or birth,
Or the neighbor's friends are down.

Perhaps an old friend has passed on,
Or a neighbor has had twins;
Then perhaps 'twas an accident,
Some of your friends were in.

The neighbor's cow was ill you know,
But doing just fine now;
Your daughter's cat had a dozen kits,
By phone they told you how.

Your cousin's banty has the roop.
But the pony's doing fine;
All these things you hear about,
When you're on the party line.

Now if some one would like the line,
When you are only chatting;
Why don't they politely ask,
Instead of "rat-tat-tatting".

Now tongues were made long, long ago,
Before we had the telephone;
So if you'd like it when its busy,
Why not ask or leave alone.

There's times when it is out of whack,
It makes one cuss you know;
For you must wait for the repair man,
And can't even let him know.

But all in all we think it's great,
And most of us know it's fine;
For wouldn't life be dull at times,
Without the party line.

- March, 1973 -

PROBLEMS

I sat beneath the muley cow,
Upon an old tin pail;
She took one cross-eyed look at me,
And hit me with her tail.

Thinking me a great big fly,
One swat was not enough;
So beside the other ear,
I received a well aimed cuff.

I place my head against her flank,
Her two front teats I took;
So very carefully she stepped back,
And landed on my foot.

Now with Scotch determination,
And plans that couldn't fail;
I gently grabbed the two back teats,
This time she kicked the pail.

That will teach you not to pinch me,
Or I'll be bound to retaliate;
So she walked off and left me,
Sitting at the barnyard gate.

But that Irish fortitude,
Would not let me be beat;
So I got a set of kickers,
And secured both her hind feet.

I tied her down both fore and aft,
But she still could wiggle free;
My patience now had ended,
So I tried profanity.

It is surprising the effect,
Those harsh words had on her;
She must have been a preacher's cow,
For it almost made her purr.

Then she turned around to look at me,
With nerve you'll seldom find;
I thought that she would lick me,
Right on my big behind.

But don't you be mistaken,
And don't you be misled;
When she turned to lick me,
She kicked at me instead.

But I survived the ordeal,
I really can't see how;
But with a few more problems,
I broke that consarned cow.

- June, 1973 -

OLD FRIENDS

Ye, I was walking down the street,
When an old friend I chanced to meet.

I scarcely recognized his face,
But yet I knew it from some place.

I greeted him with hand outstretched,
As my memories I searched.

He smiled at me with a knowing look,
As his trembling hand I shook.

His dark brown hair had turned to grey,
His dimples too had gone away.

A shiny spot stood out on top,
His figure too had gone to pot.

But yet the voice was kind and clear,
And speech brought back those memories dear.

We talked and chatted for a while,
Rehashing things quite out of style.

Of old times that had come and gone,
We chatted on and on and on.

Of old friends that had come and went,
Of deeds well done and time well spent.

We laughed and joked and reminisced,
And as parting friends we kissed.

Although the premonition brought me pain,
I knew I'd never see him again.

For time as always passes on,
And old friends, too soon, are dead and gone.

- July, 1973 -

TO A BUTTERCUP

On a grassy knoll,
On the side of a hill;
Nestled in grass,
So thick and still.

Bunches of buttercups,
Yellow as gold;
Nodding and beckoning,
So sweet to behold.

Little short stems,
Bright and green;
Supporting gold nuggets,
That many have seen.

Struggling to live,
Where animals trod;
A speck of beauty,
Created by God.

- March, 1973 -

CONFEDERATION

Oh Canada, our homeland has reached it's hundredth year,
And it will make another of that I have no fear;
From a tiny Fort at Old Quebec, it grew at a rapid pace;
Until it now consists of almost every race;
From Atlantic to Pacific, stretching far and wide;
With every creed and custom tucked away inside.

Let us think back to long ago, when all the world was new,
Columbus found America in Fourteen Ninety-two;
And in five years Cabot discovered Newfoundland's Great Cod Banks;
But to Amerigo Vespucci for a name we give our thanks.

Let us look back with due respect on our discoverers of old,
Cartier, Frobisher and Hudson are classed among the bold;
Thompson, Radisson and Fraser may be added, too;
Maissonneuve and Dollard to mention just a few;
And don't leave out the missionaries or Madeliene De Vercheres;
They all helped weld together this fair domain of ours.

Champlain, the "Father of New France" started to build our nation,
Then the Empire Loyalists came to improve the situation;
Prosecuted in the south, they fled to a friendly land,
But suffered many other hardships; they couldn't understand.

The Indian tribes were numerous in this undiscovered land,
Believed to have reached this continent from a foreign strand;
The fur traders too, were brave and bold, while traveling in a band,
But Mackenzie reached the farthest, "Crossing Canada by Land".

Nova Scotia and New Brunswick, Quebec and Old Ontario,Were the first to be
united a hundred years ago;
The Confederation Fathers who numbered thirty-three,
Worked long and hard to build this land, for folks like you and me.

The courage, hope and wisdom of the seven leading men,
Brought about expansion in this our fair Domain;
The plan of Confederation by Mr. Galt was born;
Cartier, Tilly, Tupper, McGee, MacDonald and Brown;
Spurred the movement forward to Union and Renown.

The Indian tribes were many, across this wide domain,
The Huron, Cree and Iroquois, lived on the eastern plain;
The Assiniboine, Algonquin, Blackfoot and the Cree;
Lived in the prairie provinces and were hostile as could be;
The Haida, Tlingit and Bell Coola lived on the B.C. coast;
Totem carving and salmon fishing occupied them the most.

The homesteader lived in his little shack, away out on the plain,
A lonely life, a brave little wife and a sod roof to keep out the rain;
He broke with an ox and a walking plough, sowing his seed by hand,
He was the backbone of our nation that opened up this land.

The men of the "Royal Mounted", who rode three hundred strong,
To keep the law and order, and punished those in the wrong;
To help the weak and needy in this vast unpeopled land;
And to keep the hostile Indian restricted to his band;
The days were long, the nights were hard, they rode thru snow and rain,
Their hearts were brave, their coats were red, "The Riders of the Plains".
The colony of Red river was attacked by Louis Riel;
He took control for six months thus the colony fell;
The way the Canadian settlers were treated was a sin;
So in the summer of seventy, the Dominion troops marched in;
They put the insurrection down and Riel fled to U.S.A.;
Manitoba thus was formed for protection so they say.

Then Canada's eyes turned westward to meet another storm,
The most extensive project by their government ever borne;
Two thousand miles of railroad constructed by Van Horne;
In the town of Craigellachie, the golden spike was drive;
The bands of steel were joined in the year of Eighty-five;
And the Confederation policy became very much alive.

Now B.C. wanted union and connection with the rest,
Which privilege she did trade for the line of railway track;
To be completed in ten years joining the east and west;
Five days for the journey out and five for coming back.

In 1873 Prince Edward Island province, the smallest of the lot,
Entered into Confederation and this is what she got;
A steamship line to the mainland her railway debts were paid;
And a telegraphic cable from mainland to island laid.

The vast unpeopled territory of our great north west,
The last home of the Indian, and the mighty buffalo beast;
Controlled by governor and council until the year of seventy-three;
Then the Royal mounted men moved in to keep it free.

Next the Metis from Manitoba, started a mass migration,
The unsettled land of Saskatchewan was their destination;
They confiscated land after selling out their right,
Demanded titles in Saskatchewan calling Riel to lead the fight.

He drew up an army of a thousand metis men,
Added on some Indians and then the war began;
He set up headquarters at Batoche, many Indians refused to join;
But he got assistance from Big Bear by using a heavenly sign;
In the spring of Eighty-five twelve mounted men were slain;
Then the Frog Lake Massacre took place, when the metis struck again.

Then on to Fort Pitt to attack the Hudson Bay Fort,
But the defenders escaped to Battleford thou the area was lost;
With the aid of eastern troops they defeated the rebel band.
Louis Riel was captured while escaping from the land.

He was tried and hung at Regina for treason so they say,
Poundmaker surrendered at Battleford and lived to a ripe old age;
It was the last uprising in this our democratic nation,
Now the Indian lives in luxury on his reservation.

Five years after the rebellions end; the settlers boom began,
It was the time to test the grit of every woman and her man;
For fifteen years the populace grew at a rapid rate,
And then they carved Sask. - Alta. from the territorial state.

Now Confederation was nine provinces wide,
With the North West Territories standing close beside;
But in the year of Forty-nine another joined the clan,
With the rugged island of Newfoundland filling out the span.
Thus our unified Dominion has passed its hundredth year,
May all this talk of Separatists gradually disappear;
Do not you think those worthy men, who organized this plan,
Would think it rather childish to let it all disband.

- February - March 1968 -

TO A MOUSE

I was working in the garden,
Plodding slowly down the row;
The tiller set in deeply,
The task was hard and slow.

When from out a strawy spot,
Appeared a streak of grey;
I stopped and looked in wonderment,
As he quickly dashed away.

And when he'd reached some twenty feet,
He turned in great surprise;
He looked at me with utter scorn,
In those dark and beady eyes.

He raised himself on two hind feet,
His front feet held aloft;
Twitched his nose and gnashed his teeth,
Looked at me and scoffed.

"You know you nearly killed me,
I think you are a louse;
Why should you disturb me,
And wreck my little house."

"I only had six inches square,
Of scrubby garden soil;
On which I spent a lot of time,
Of love and work and toil".

And so I stopped the tiller,
And watched him with a sigh;
As that little field mouse,
Turned again to fly.

I did not try to stop him.
Give chase or interfere;
I wished him well upon his way,
And better luck next year.

- May, 1973 -

141

THE MAN IN THE MOON

Oh the man in the moon is an astronaut,
From the good old U. S. of A.;
They packed their ship to take a trip,
Not knowing how long they'd stay.

They knew not if they'd make it,
Nor what up there they'd find;
But they blasted off into outer space,
With a brave and open mind.

A million miles they traveled,
Out in the universe;
Landing right on target,
And for the journey were no worse.

They found a barren wasteland,
Which they explored somewhat;
But rocks and sand and soil,
Was about all that they got.

For they found it uninhabited,
And not of cheese, as we've heard them say;
But the man in the moon is an astronaut,
From the good old U. S. of A.

The features of that mighty orb,
Are valleys deep and wide;
No doubt the mouth is a dried up lake,
Where no man doth reside.

They found no life upon its face,
And they didn't have long to stay;
But some day it may be a stepping stone,
To the rest of the "Milky Way".

- June, 1973 -

142

MY ANIMAL ALPHABET

A - is for the Antelope,
   Tan and small and fleet.

B - is for the big Bear,
   Who loves his honey sweet.

C - is for the pussy Cat,
   Who falls upon his feet.

D - is for the collie Dog,
   Everyone's best friend.

E - is for the Elephant,
   With a trunk, upon one end.

F - is for the tiny Fawn,
   Who carries nature's blend.

G - is for the tall Giraffe,
   Whose neck doth never end.

H - is for the Hippopotamus,
   Who is large and gray.

I - is for the Ibex,
   Who in Asia doth stay.

J - is for the Jaguar,
Who is yellow trimmed with black.

K - is for the Kangaroo,
   With long legs at the back.

L - is for the little Lamb,
Who is woolly, white and soft.

M - is for the Monkey,
   By his tail he swings aloft.

N - is for the Narwhal,
     Who lives out in the deep.

O - is for the wise old owl,
     Who sees us while we sleep.

P - is for the little Pig,
     Who eats with great delight.

Q - is for the timid Quail,
     Who runs off in a fright.

R - is for the tiny Rabbit,
     Who sits on his hind feet.

S - is for the saucy Squirrel,
     Who loves some nuts to eat.

T - is for the Turkey tom,
     Which you like as meat.

U - is for the Unicorn,
     Which is now extinct.

V - is for the Vulture brave,
     Who is black as ink.

W - is for the Water Buffalo,
     Who wades into drink.

X - is for the Xerus brown,
     Of fur a good source.

Y - is for the shaggy Yak,
     Who is long haired, of course.

Z - is for the two-toned Zebra,
Known as the candy striped horse.

- September, 1973 -

MY MOTHER

Who thought me pretty, tho I was plain,
Who bore me on a bed of pain;
Yet loved me enough, to do again,
My Mother!

Who rose from her warm bed at night,
To feed me, or console my fright;
To hold me very close and tight,
My Mother!

Who warmed my bottle at the stove,
While for me she thanked the Lord above;
I'm sure it was an act of love,
My Mother!

Who bathed her grouchy little bear,
Who powdered me with loving care;
Who washed and combed my tousled hair,
My Mother!

Who changed my pants when I was wet,
Who rocked and sang so I didn't fret;
Who had to stand for a lot you bet,
My Mother!

Who took me from my little cot,
When I was just a little tot;
And set me on my cold, cold pot,
My Mother!

Who made my clothes and tied my shoes,
Who tucked me in for a little snooze;
Yet my sex she couldn't choose,
My Mother!

Who neglected all her other cares,
But took no time to shed some tears;
Who watched o'er me for several years,
My Mother!

Who watched me as I quickly grew,
Walked at one, talked at two;
Kissed my bruises quite a few,
My Mother!

Who picked me up if I should fall,
Kept me within her beck and call;
Played with me at tag or ball,
My Mother!

Who showed me how to work and play,
Told me the words I shouldn't say;
Sent me to bed at close of day,
My Mother!

Who saw me off to public school,
Shed tears enough to fill a pool;
As education was the rule,
My Mother!

Who guided me as I older grew,
Advising me what not to do;
Applying spankings quite a few,
My Mother!

But now that I have older grown,
Raising a family of my own;
I appreciate the care she'd shown,
My Mother!

Altho to heaven you have gone,
I dedicate to you this song;
As I look back on days long gone,
Thank-you Mother!

- September, 1974 -

TO A DAUGHTER

What is a daughter?
I really don't know;
She was once a wee girl,
Just starting to grow.

A tiny wee tot,
With a smile or tear;
But always so happy,
When someone was near.

With diapers and dresses,
And blankets to wash;
A whole lot of work,
But worth it by gosh!

Getting some teeth,
And growing more hair;
As good as gold,
When company was there.

With freckles and pigtails,
And dirt on her face;
Getting under ones feet,
And all over the place.

Learning to talk,
And play Peek-A-Boo;
Putting on her clothes,
And tying her own shoe.

Playing with dolls,
And the rest of her toys;
But as yet showing no interest,
In sex or the boys.

Helping you bake,
And trying to sew;
Then she's off to school,
The first thing you know.

Learning her lessons,
To read and to write;
Losing her plumpness,
And just double in height.

But she grew tall and straight,
With poise and with grace;
She learned how to dress,
And fix up her face.

Curling her hair,
And learning to dance;
Going on dates,
When she got the chance.

Doing her homework,
Or reading a book;
Balancing her budget,
By hook or by crook.

Finishing school,
Off to college and all;
Got her diploma,
Only this fall.

Now she's a lady,
I'll have you to know;
With long curly hair,
And having a beau.

Soon she'll be married,
And leaving the nest;
I'm sure that you'll miss her,
But wish her the best.

The generation's advancing,
And rightfully so;
For "We are all growing older",
It's a fact we all know.

- May - June, 1974 -

NATURE

Did you ever lie on a grassy knoll,
In the springtime of the year;
And listen very carefully,
To hear what you could hear.

Now there is Mister Robin,
With his puffed out rosy breast;
Telling of his true love,
As he struts his very best.

And Mister Earthworm cussing,
In his elongated sort of way;
Because that domineering robin,
Has moved in here to stay.

Then there is that big ant hill,
Right over by the fence;
The noise and the commotion,
You'd think would be intense.

But not a single sound emits,
From that pyramid in motion;
So we just watch and wonder,
At that organized commotion.

And there sits Mister Chipmunk,
As saucy as can be;
Daring all his counter parts,
To take his family tree.

Now over there beneath some leaves,
I hear a squeaking sound;
It is the nest of Mrs. Mouse,
I'm sure that I have found.

She's telling them to settle down,
In that nest so warm and soft;
And warning them that danger is near,
From that old bird aloft.

For over there upon a tree,
His eyes as bright as fire;
Sits a black and noisy bird,
Venting out his ire.

The buzzing of a bumble bee,
As he flits from flower to flower;
Gives you the deep impression that,
He is a man of power.

Then you hear a cheerful whistle,
From a little mound near by;
It's Mrs. Gopher watching you,
With twitching nose and beady eye.

And there just down beneath me,
Is a rustling, slithering sound;
Mr. Snake has gone out hunting,
For his breakfast, I am bound.

So I decided its time to move,
And terminate my reverie;
But I've learnt that nature's little ones,
Are as busy as can be.

- March, 1974 -

GONE BUT NOT FORGOTTEN

Last night as I lay on my pillow,
Last night as I lay in my bed;
The dreams of the past and future,
Floated slowly thru my head.

I saw myself as an infant,
On the snow drifted track to the barn;
Following the footsteps of father,
Who watched me from all harm.

I saw an old coal oil lantern,
Making long shadows on the snow;
The smoke curling around the elongated glass,
As it gently swung to and fro.

We entered the sweet smelling stable,
Where the cows lay in a long row;
The horses munched from their mangers,
While the lantern cast an eerie glow.

The mother cat mewed a welcome,
As she knew she was to be fed;
And four little spotted kittens,
Curled up in her new made bed.

I helped lug in the oat sheaves,
And portion them out with care;
Everything was so warm and cozy,
It was a childhood thrill to be there.

I watched with fascination,
As father milked the spotted cow;
It was a wonder of nature,
To a small child somehow.

Now everything has changed you see,
For automation is so fast;
The path is cleared by power,
And the lantern, a thing of the past.

The yard light beams across corrals,
Where the livestock lay asleep;
The farmer feeds them quickly,
With no time for children to peep.

The coming generation,
Are losing nature's touch;
All that matters is mechanization,
Love don't count for much.

But mechanization is expensive,
So the young folks haven't a chance;
They move to the cities' bright lights,
For in farming there's left no romance.

- November, 1972 -

TO A COW

They talk about the dairy cow,
That don't milk on holidays;
But she don't understand yet,
That unemployment pays.

Now if we had a five day cow,
It couldn't last for long;
For they'd soon form a union,
Every lady strong.

I'll admit it would be nice,
To take a holiday;
But I think I have a better plan,
So this I'd like to say.

If that female bovine,
Would only fill the pail;
With lots of cream along with milk,
When we pumped her tail.

But I suppose the young folk,
Would think up a promotion;
To install a motor,
To keep the tail in motion.

But many of the 'young folk',
Refuse to milk a cow;
It is beneath their dignity,
It's not that they know not how.

So they rush off to the city,
And are soon in the red;
Or work like hell to eat and drink,
From that same old quadruped.

Now many things they help make,
But somehow they're way behind;
That lowly cow's away up front,
If you only look you'll find.

She can provide the following,
With skill and ease and grace;
She is a built in factory,
For all the human race.

There's milk and cream and butter,
Glue, leather, hair and meat;
Fertilizer, soap and bonemeal,
And also the cheese we eat.

So why not uphold the dairy cow,
With praise and care and feed;
Don't keep on complaining,
She's a wondrous thing indeed.

- December, 1972 -

HOLIDAY TRAFFIC

I was speeding down the highway,
On a dark December day;
Heading for my home town,
In a province far away.

The blacktop was a ribbon,
Of icy glare and snow;
But I had to keep on going,
For it was the only way to go.

T'was then the snowstorm struck us,
Like a sheet of blinding rain;
My thoughts were very hectic,
And my language quite profane.

The highway was a tunnel,
Of white and blowing snow;
The Pass was soon impassable,
So we had no where to go.

We waited for the snowplow,
And when the pass was cleared;
There'd been a dreadful accident,
Just as we all had feared.

We were very thankful, and
That night when prayers were said;
We thanked the Lord profusely,
We were not among the dead.

Next morn when we continued,
We vowed in sad refrain;
Regardless of the hurry,
We would never speed again.

For how many dead and dying,
Crippled, injured and in pain;
Are found on every highway,
Because so many drive insane.

As a little bit of alcohol,
Or an extra tired mind;
A little bit of carelessness,
And recklessness combined.

Add these to extra traffic,
And poor road conditions found;
It is not safe to travel,
When a holiday rolls around.

- January 13, 1973 -

MODERN TRENDS

Oh the younger generation,
Are different you'll allow;
Sometimes I like them very much,
And at times I don't somehow.

But when you see a mini skirt,
Come marching down the street;
It makes one stop and wonder,
What next your going to meet?

For most animals have feathers,
Fur or even quills;
To cover up what ever they should,
And keep out many chills.

But the human is an animal,
The queerest that I've seen;
It likes to show off both its ends,
And most that's in between.

Now! How many have the figure?
To do justice to the mini;
Knock-knees or bow legs protrude,
Or else they're too fat or skinny.

The maxi coat's another thing,
I don't know what it's for;
Unless to keep out the breeze,
Twixt the mini and the floor.

On top some wear a feather duster,
A bristle broom or mop;
I wonder when the modern trend,
Will ever change or stop.

Some don't wear shoes upon their feet,
When out in public places;
It makes one think they want to run,
From the law or in the races.

Then there is the way they live,
The modern clannish fad;
How will the little children know,
Whom to call mom or dad?

But I suppose the time will come,
When they have older grown;
They'll settle down, as people should,
When their 'Wild Oats' they've sown.

But may it not have ill effects,
On generations three;
The one to come, the one that's here,
And mainly, on you and me.

- January, 1973 -

IRISH FRUIT

I was digging little tatters,
In the old potato patch;
The soil was very hard and wet,
So I must get down and scratch.

Me hands got rather dirty,
And my knees were partly green;
For the crop of wild tomatoes,
Was the best I'd ever seen.

The blue burrs were terrific,
And they stuck to me like glue;
So you can just imagine why,
The air above was blue.

I bent my poor old creaking back,
And pulled the vines with care;
In hopes that many tubers,
Would emerge into the air.

But I was disappointed,
For not a one came forth;
So I must kneel right down to dig,
For all that I was worth.

My first chop struck a large potato,
Severing it near in half;
I vowed that I would dig more gentle,
As that irked my Scottish half.

I scraped a bit with my little hoe,
But all I got was skin;
So I knelt again on bended knee,
And dug my fingers in.

I vowed I'd get the Irish fruit,
And my efforts weren't in vain;
But my knees they suffered bruises,
Till I thought I'd need a cane.

But I kept right on digging,
Despite the mud and stones;
For I value those potatoes,
More than my aching bones.

Then when winter rolled around,
I enjoyed my Irish fare;
Thinking back unto September,
As those tatters I did pare.

- March, 1974 -

THE DECK OF CARDS

Let us take that lowly deck of cards,
And place it on the table;
I know not who invented it,
But I'll explain what I am able.

You see now before you,
The Ace which is counted high;
It represents our God above,
And the sun up in the sky.

There is only one of each;,
The Sun and God above;
The sun controls our life on earth,
And God we trust and love.

The little Deuce is only two,
But he really has some might,
For he divides a twenty-four hour span,
Into two parts, day and night.

He also divides the Bible,
This small but mighty two;
Thus we have before us,
The Old Testament and the New.

The little Trey shows us a lot,
On how we should divide our day;
Time for rest, time for work,
And also time for play.

Our Bible has three holy spirits,
To guide our soul we boast;
So enjoy a life of deep fulfillment,
With the Father, Son and Holy Ghost.

We have four seasons in a year,
Which you may all recall;
They fill up the total calendar,
Namely, summer, winter, spring and fall.

There were four biblical evangelists,
Whom are now dead and gone;
But they are well known to us all,
As Matthew, Mark, Luke and John.

Now in the book of Holy Scripture,
There were virgins ten;
Five were wise and five were foolish,
And so can be most men.

The six stands for the days we work,
At honest labor and love;
To make the world a better place,
In which to live and move.

The seven stands for the day of rest,
Which the Good Lord really needed;
He thus created a day of worship,
Which man has always heeded.

Now when its reached the seventh day,
Our week has been completed;
One quarter of a calendar month,
And then the week's repeated.

The eight stands for the righteous ones,
Who survived the mighty flood;
Noah, his wife, the son's wives,
And three sons of his blood.

The nine stands for the ailing Lepers,
That while healing sick he cured;
It shows the advantage of having faith,
In all works of the Lord,

Nine also stands for the months it takes,
To create a new made life;
May you be blessed with all of this,
When you are man or wife,

The ten is for the ten commandments,
Which Moses carried down the mount;
Which if we follow carefully,
We can make our whole life count.

Now the King represents our Lord on High,
Who resides in Heaven as our Father;
Whom we should worship above all else,
As we do our own father and mother.

The Queen stands for the blessed Virgin,
Mother of Christ, who died on the Cross;
Giving his life to right all wrong,
But to the world its greatest loss.

The four Queens stand for the times of life,
In the female part of the race;
A baby, a girl, a little mother,
And an elderly lady with grace.

Now the Jack represents the Knave or devil,
To which man doth often turn;
But would we not be better men,
If for this evil we did not yearn.

Now thirteen cards there are in each suit,
And four suits make the deck;
Four seasons there are in every year,
And thirteen weeks in each by heck.

Twelve faces we have in every deck,
Which make up quite a horde;
Twelve months there are in every year,
And twelve apostles had the Lord.
Three hundred and sixty-five days has our calendar year,
And so our deck has spots;
The Joker stands for the extra one,
When leap year is what we've got.

So you see I have before me,
A threesome needed much by man;
A calendar, bible and deck of cards,
Now beat that trio, if you can.

February, 1974

TO THE POOL
FARM LIFE 1924 - 1974

As we drive down the dusty highway,
Thru fields of golden grain;
We see spread out before us,
That expanse of Western plain.

And in every little Western town,
Is a structure, large and tall;
With four red letters in a golden square,
Near the top of a silver wall.

But these many superstructures,
Have not been here too long;
For it is but fifty years ago,
To the day, that you were born.

Now let's look back to those good old days,
When both of us were young;
I was just a child then,
And your laurels were yet unsung.

Now our generation,
Has topped life's peak or crest;
And you've become the largest company,
In this growing west.

Now farming in Saskatchewan,
Has changed a lot you know;
For we're a lot more mechanized,
Than fifty years ago.

We used to be small farmers,
With neighbors close at hand;
But now we live unto ourselves,
With acres and acres of land.

We used to call upon our friends,
To pass the time of day;
But now as far as neighbors go,
We're a hundred miles away.

We used to farm with horses,
Four, six, or eight a span;
But now we're mechanized and dieselized,
Almost to a man.

Your future power a little colt,
Playing happily you'd find;
But did you ever see a tractor,
With a tractorette behind.

We rode the plow despite the stones,
Or walked slowly on behind;
Now we have a disker,
And the largest tractor we can find.

The stones we picked with team and boat,
A tiresome job indeed;
Now we use the picker,
To do this back breaking deed.

We used to plant our seed grain,
With four horses on a drill;
Now a dicker does it,
Even some have auto-fill.

We pickled grain, and shoveled it,
And filled our drill by hand;
Now they spray with chemicals,
But our feed value is not as grand.

We used to fertilize our land,
With good old cow manure;
Now we buy it by the bag,
At a price that's high for sure.

We used to use a binder,
To tie our crop in sheaves;
Now a power combine,
Gets the grain but not the leaves.

We used to thrash our crop,
With an engine run by steam;
But the combine now is self-propelled,
More modern it would seem.

We had a crew of twenty men,
Stook wagons hauled by teams;
We worked from daylight until dark,
A full day it would seem.

Now it's just a combine,
And a truck to move the grain away;
We do not start till ten o'clock,
So must turn night to day.

We hauled our grain down a prairie trail,
To a nearby little town;
The horses plodded their weary way,
As we watched nature all around.

Our expenses were not very great,
Our income, it was small;
But we took great pride,
In paying up our bills in the fall.

But now we hire a big truck,
So our quota we can fill;
And when year's end has rolled around,
We're left with unpaid bills.

Bur farming in Saskatchewan,
Has changed a lot you see;
Or have you really stopped and thought,
How it used to be.

It used to be our taxes,
Got paid up in the fall;
Now they've got so very high,
We can't pay them at all.

We used to get our milk and cream,
From a bovine with four feet;
But now it comes in a box or can,
Marked dried, condensed or sweet.

It used to be we had a garden,
Some chickens and a sow;
We had time for work, time for rest,
And time for play, somehow.

The farmer owned his small farm then,
And he worked from morn till night;
He did not owe a single soul,
Was the most contented man in sight.

But now he worries all the time,
It's the Jones's he must beat;
He's rushing here, and rushing there,
As with his neighbor he must compete.

But expenses keep on rising,
And our income has gone flat;
But no matter what we do,
We cannot alter that.

So now its work and worry,
From morning until night;
If we're to prolong existence,
We must put up a fight.

But both the ends are fighting,
To reach a central goal;
And the farmer's in the middle,
Away down in the hole.

But somehow your superstructure,
Represents the farmers' worth;
Large and tall and steadfast,
It's his symbol of rebirth.

And if he is persistent,
He'll somehow make it pay;
To live his life on the land he loves,
If your behind him all the way.

March - April, 1974

THE FLU BUG

Somehow or other, just the other day,
The flu bug bit me,
Cause he couldn't stay away.

He bit so hard, I fell into my bed,
With an ache in my stomach,
And a pain in my head.

I shivered and I shook, I cussed and I swore,
Cause I couldn't stand up,
On that "gall darned" floor.

My knees did quiver, my head did spin,
For when you get the flu,
You're sure done in.

I had hallucinations, my mind was weak,
My throat was dry,
And I could hardly speak.

I just laid around, all wrapped up,
And near froze to death,
With the heater turned up.

I had me a bark and a sniffle nose,
My head was hot,
And my feet were froze.

I'd sit awhile, then sleep a spell,
Sure done nothing,
And felt like hell.

I sure couldn't think, and didn't want to eat,
Lost a few pounds,
But sure could sleep.

Had to lay around, a few more days,
Had to rest up,
And my head was in a haze.

But the flu bug died, and I survived,
Guess I should be thankful,
That I'm still alive.

February, 1974

MOTHER'S INFLUENCE

A mother's troubles never end,
This I'd like to state;
Experience I've had, not just with one,
But numbering up to eight.

There's the worry and frustration,
The diet and the bills;
For you must see those little tots,
Arrive without any ills.

There's the doctor and the nurses,
The needles and the pills;
The "cutty sark", that you must wear,
Which hasn't any frills.

There's the case room, and the ether,
And the thoughts that you might die;
But its really, truly worth it,
When you hear that lusty cry.

There's the formulas, and wet diapers,
And night feeding time you know;
There's hiccups, burps and bellyaches,
For those wee mites must grow.

There's baths to give, and hair to brush,
And their nails that must be cut;
There's toys to pick, and clothes to wash,
Dear me that pin must be shut.

There's vaccinations and inoculations,
And teeth they have to get;
And you must feed them when they're hungry,
And change them when they're wet.

Now there's measles, mumps and whooping cough,
The chicken pox and itch;
There's cuts and bruises, scrapes and wounds,
That sometimes need a stitch.

And then there are those tantrums,
All children get somehow;
You never know, if you should spank,
Or sympathize, I vow.

If you let them get their way,
You're soft, and spoil them bad;
But if you spank them, well, you know
You're crabby, mean and mad.

There are the years they go to school,
The lunch pails and the books;
The rising early to catch a bus,
We must by hook or crook.

There's clothes to hunt, shoes to tie,
And pants that need a patch;
Then there are those elusive socks,
That never seem to match.

Then there is the homework,
That somehow must get done;
You push a bit, and help a bit,
Even tho it's far from fun.

But somehow the years, they soon pass by,
And teenagers they've become;
They're racing here and running there,
Adulthood, they think is fun.

There's wedding bells to help them ring,
And fond advice to give;
There's knowing when not to interfere,
And let them, their own life live.

But somehow, they keep on growing,
And soon they're off from home;
It makes one feel much older,
To find that they are gone.

But sometimes I wonder, if its worth,
All the worry and the tension;
I believe that mothers surely need,
A big frustration pension.

August, 1974

SPEEDING

Away up in the mountain,
In a cabin old and worn;
Lives a lonely little mountaineer,
Who is sad eyed and forlorn.

His back is bent, his hair is gray,
But his will is yet so strong;
He feels if he can save some lives,
In return for his act so wrong.

For years he has resided there,
Living close to nature's way;
Many people ask the question,
Why does he ever stay.

No one can really answer,
Why he lives so close to God;
Unless to pay, for his erring ways,
When the trails of youth he trod.

For it was on this self same mountain,
Nigh fifty years ago;
That four of his dearest ones,
Passed away you know.

The car was traveling swiftly,
The bridge was getting old;
There was a dreadful crashing,
For the brakes had failed to hold.

His pretty wife and children three,
Sank beneath the raging foam;
So near the place, that marks their grave,
He since has made his home.

He alone did reach the shore,
That sad and fateful day;
And since has deemed it necessary,
Near that bridge to stay.

To act as an assistant,
Should others miss their way;
And need themselves a helping hand,
In this old world to stay.

So all you young fool hardy,
Take heed before too late;
Do not overdrive your vehicle,
Or the same, may be your fate.

August, 1974

DARK HORSE

Nine horses went to the post that day;
And one was the favorite "Fly Away".

Number seven was the one he had;
Perhaps 'twas good, perhaps 'twas bad.

'Twas a grueling course they had to run;
It was for the money, and not for fun.

The track was long and the jumps were high;
Either man or horse, might deem to die.

A careless step, or a broken stride;
Would mean the end, on this strenuous ride.

Nine horses pranced into the gate;
They broke together, and run out straight.

The first four jumps were cleared on time;
By all the horses, but number nine.

He missed his step, and the rider fell;
He rose again, and raced on, pel mel.

Across the lea, and up the slope;
Number five went down, his leg was broke.

Over the crest, and on to the wall;
Where one and four both took a fall.

Five horses left, and one was the bay;
Still leading the field, was "Fly Away".

On they raced, with slowing stride;
There was one more hurdle, in this grueling ride.

On this last jump, two failed the test;
Although they'd tried their very best.

Three horses raced along the track;
The pace was telling and one fell back.

Two were left, a black and a bay;
Number three and "Fly Away".

'Twas a black nose first, across the line;
A true "Dark Horse" came in on time.

A garland of roses, on a sleek black back;
For a freckled faced kid had led the track.

June, 1973

PRAYER OF THANKS

Thank you Lord -
For health and wealth,
Although it isn't great;
Thank you Lord -
For happiness,
Tho of mind, it's just a state.

Thank you Lord -
For all my senses,
Numbering one to five;
Thank you Lord -
For seeing that,
I got to this world alive.

Thank you Lord -
That I can see,
The flowers and the sky;
Thank you Lord -
That I can hear,
The songs of birds that fly.

Thank you Lord -
For all my limbs,
That are both strong and straight;
Thank you Lord -
For a clear mind;
Free from fear and hate.

Thank you Lord -
For my daily bread,
Although for it I work;
Thank you Lord -
For making me,
One who will not shirk.

Thank you Lord -
For life on earth,
Although at times 'twas hell;
Thank you Lord -
Keep a Heavenly seat,
So I can rest a spell.

Summer, 1973

175

NO TIME FOR TEARS

Down on the farm where I have lived,
For close to fifty years;
There's only time to do the work,
And never time for tears.

The old cow had a big bull calf,
Which died when it was born;
Now momma's feeling lonely,
Ate off all my corn.

The old sow had a dozen pigs,
She laid on six I fear;
You curse a bit, you swear a bit,
But take no time for tears.

The chickens scratched the garden,
The turkeys got the roup;
Mother's getting angry,
About to fly the coup.

The cat had kittens the other day,
Which she hasn't done in years;
On my plushy front room rug,
But I had no time for tears.

The crop it looked a bumper,
But the worms left only spears;
So the farmer tightened up his belt,
For he' got no time for tears.

The summer fallow's gone to weeds,
At least so it appears;
Shirk not from work, oh farmer man,
You have no time for tears.

The truck it wouldn't start today,
The tractor striped its gears;
We hope and pray somehow to pay,
If we take no time for tears.

The puppy had an accident,
In the bed of daughter dear;
She done a lot of swearing,
But took no time for tears.

January 5, 1972

THE FARMING INDUSTRY

Now farming is an industry,
In this good old prairie west;
For here is old Saskatchewan,
It's one of the very best.

It's healthy and it's beautiful,
In spaces open wide;
But somehow the many farmers,
No longer here reside.

The profits are diminishing,
The hours growing long;
To stick it out, your needs must be
Rich and tough and strong.

Now Trudeau says to subsidize,
A calf a seventy-five;
But do you really think that,
It will keep the industry alive.

A few years back they told us,
Increase your herds you know;
For by the year of eighty,
Famine will be "touch and go".

Then we listened meekly,
And now we're in a bind;
For a market for the extra,
Our government cannot find.

And more years back they told us,
Sow grain to feed the nation;
Then they forced on us a quota,
Without any explanation.

Then there was the summer fallow,
Which they bonused, as you know;
It was a political sideline,
So too much grain we wouldn't grow.

They also paid a bonus,
For sowing land to grass;
To feed those cows they said to grow,
To feed the starving mass.

We switched to cows and grass you know,
So the price has gone to hell;
The price of grain is up again,
For we haven't much to sell.

We can't afford to fatten,
Those steers they said to grow;
Nor can we afford those new machines,
That high priced grain to ow.

Because, before we could pay for them,
The price would be sure to drop;
And somehow the payments,
Or the interest never stop.

And then there is the problem,
Of machines you can't get hold;
And if you buy a new repair,
It is worth its weight in gold.

They say we're a thriving industry,
We are if the pay is work;
But as far as money goes,
We're about to loose our shirt.

Now to subsidize this industry,
Don't seem to meet the need;
For subsidization can't keep up,
With the organized strikers greed.

But we cannot strike like the other guy,
For the cows and pigs must eat;
Somehow they do not feed themselves,
While we sit upon our seat.

In the farming industry,
Overtime don't count for much;
You work like hell, long hours most days,
But with nature you keep in touch.

If somehow we could manage it,
To deal with the consumer direct;
Perhaps we'd all get our just dues,
Or they could starve by heck.

Now why not set up a commission,
To balance income and expense;
Of over a period, say fifteen years,
Would make a bit of sense.

Then draw a line of decent living,
With points above and below;
And aid the farmer to level off,
When he gets too far below.

When he is above a decent living,
Pay income tax he must;
So why not return some of this tax,
When his income bites the dust.

Let his price for produce sold,
Vary with the living cost;
For the way things are going now,
This industry is all but lost.

Now we produce a lot of things,
That everyone must eat;
There's cereal, flour, butter and eggs,
There's bread and milk and meat.

There's only cream we get enough,
To cover the expense;
And then at it, you work so hard,
It don't make any sense.

Of course, you could mechanize,
To save your time and work;
But there's that big expense again,
And away goes your little shirt.

Many workers make a wage,
With only his two bare hands;
While a farmer has a lot tied up,
In machinery and acres of land.

He cannot make the net wage,
Of his barehanded counterpart;
Although he's slaved his life away,
And in debt, been from the start.

So why not put on the prairies,
More "finished product" plants;
Set up a prairie trade commission,
And ship products to other lands.

If an average living wage,
To the farmer you could guarantee;
We'd work like hell the year around,
To improve this industry.

He'd risk the elements of nature,
With the "Good Lord" take a chance;
He'd do his best, regardless of
Your political can's and cant's.

He'd produce the basic needs of life,
Have land, fresh air and sun;
With a little stabilization,
This farming could be fun.

November, 1974

WASTE NOT, WANT NOT

Why not wake in the morning early,
And climb right out of bed;
What is the sense of wasting life,
For you're a long time dead.

You laid around for nine long months,
Before the day that you were born;
And when you reached this Universe,
Of your life it was the morn.

Now God gave you the instinct,
To wake for food and drink;
He also gave to you a brain,
With which to plan and think.

He planned that if he got you here,
Provided with a goal;
That you could work to earn your keep,
And take care of your soul.

Now some people lie in bed,
Just to think and plan;
But why not get up and at it,
To prove that you're a man.

There are the days when you are young,
With ambition, guts and gas;
It makes no difference who you are,
Or whether you be lad or lass.

181

But then as you do older grow,
These qualities seem to fade;
So use them well, while you are young,
For you're a long time dead.

It is when you older grow,
Ambition fades away;
Replaced by laziness and lassitude,
Or so the Old Folks say.

And then time takes its toll,
And even that is gone;
Until we to the earth return,
As we rightfully belong.

So all you young and healthy,
Do not waste your time;
When early, morning rolls around,
Why don't you rise and shine.

Show the Lord, he done a job,
That proves, "Your Salt", your worth;
And did not waste the time or place,
When he put you on this earth.

December, 1974

THE LITTLE OLD LOG HOUSE

As you drive along the highway,
In your big black Cadillac;
You pass a little old log house,
That brings fond memories back.

It takes you back a hundred years,
When your grandparents first were wed;
Times were really different then,
And those old folks now are dead.

The paved road you are traveling on,
Was a rolling prairie trail;
Full of stones and badger holes,
But those oxen never failed,

The logs were carefully cut and peeled,
Straight and strong and true;
That's why that little old log shack,
Remains for you to view.

As we lovingly look back,
On those old tales that we've heard;
It is not for us to doubt them,
Or to despise their solemn word.

For we see the old black cook stove,
With its oven large and hot;
Its shiny silver scroll work,
And big black cooking pot.

But the aroma of the new made bread,
The stew and pork and beans;
No wonder that old time housewife,
Was worshiped as a queen.

Her work was hard and tedious,
But her heart was strong and free;
So lets admit she was a woman,
Better far then you or me.

Those old folks now are resting,
And the prairie sod is gone;
The old house is still standing,
But deserted and alone.

The windows are all broken,
The chinking too is gone;
The stove pipe also missing,
But fond memories linger on.

So destroy it not, you modern man,
For a few feet more of grain;
As it gives us back our heritage,
And shows their struggle was not in vain.

As their hearts and their determination,
Were much like those self same trees;
If they had not been of the best wood,
There wouldn't be no you or me.

July, 1973

"PALS"

Down the busy byway,
Walked a lonely little lad;
Beside him was his closest friend,
And I do not mean his dad.

The big Newfoundland canine,
All spotted brown and white;
Was his closest companion,
Whether it be day or night.

He cared not if his face was clean,
Or his hair was all awry;
If he had wore his ragged pants,
Or had one big discolored eye.

For the love that passed between the two,
Was very beautiful to see;
It was the joining of two hearts,
Both of them trusting and carefree.

He slept upon a colored mat,
At the foot of his little friend's bed;
If a stranger were to enter,
They would surely find him dead.

If his little master stirred,
Or cried out in the night;
He'd gently lick his little hand,
To tell him "all was right".

With eyes alert, and ears upraised,
He'd watch while his master ate;
With the patience of the noble breed,
Waiting, for scraps from his plate.

And if the little boy left home,
His friend was close beside;
Matching the little boy's footsteps,
With his manly canine stride.

"Twas thus the two of them took off,
Along that busy road;
But fate played a trick on them that day,
They never reached their goal.

The big van came swerving down the hill,
The controls had given way;
The driver had not a single chance,
He could only sit and pray.

The little lad knew only fear,
He could not jump or move;
He could only stand like a statue,
His life with the Lord above.

But just before it reached him,
His cry of fear burst forth;
'Twas then his canine friend took part,
In his last great deed on earth.

For they had counted not, with that dog,
As he too heard the cry of fear;
So a living streak of brown and white,
Shot by as the truck drew near.

The little lad lay in the ditch,
He had escaped disaster;
But his dearest pal, he lay close by,
He'd given his life for his master.

July, 1973

ODE TO THE NORTH

It's a rich land, a poor land,
A lonely land, and cold;
It's a tough land, a rough land,
But beautiful to behold.

It's a hard land, a cruel land,
A land of ice and snow;
It's a bleak land, a bitter land,
No matter where you go.

It's a silent land, a still land,
A land that's white and clear;
A wild land, a thrilling land,
At all times of the year.

It's a vibrant land, a pretty land,
A land of moss and deer;
It's a green land, a lovely land,
In the springtime of the year.

It's a hunter's land, a traveler's land,
A wild land and free;
It's a great land, for the young man,
But not for folks like me.

November, 1973

THAT OLD LAMP

Sitting there on the shelf,
All covered with dust;
Is a thing from the past,
A pioneers must.

The chimney is dirty,
Still covered with smoke;
A nostalgic reminder,
For some older folk.

The bowl is empty,
But needs only a fill;
Then a flick of a match,
And we'd have a light still.

But many a modern,
In snug self-repose;
Laugh at that lamp,
And look down their nose.

The burner they say,
Don't give any light;
And the wicks hard to turn,
Because it's too tight.

But lets give it credit,
Where credit is due;
With a nod of respect,
To the old, from the new.

For most of our parents,
With it seemed to live;
A beacon of friendship,
They were willing to give.

A guide to the lost,
In those pioneer days;
A sigh of some life,
For which they often prayed.

They sewed and they knit,
Read the Bible and news;
By your orange colored light,
Discussed different views.

Much more was the work,
Much less was the waste;
Done by that old lamp,
Than with power and haste.

It has not been so long,
Since power took it's place;
But no doubt it's a boon,
To the human race.

But oft, yet it's needed,
When the power fails;
So faithfully, we keep it,
As time onward sails.

November, 1974

AGE OF WISDOM

Now I'm growing older,
And my hair is turning gray;
Time is swiftly passing,
And my youth has flown away.

My step is getting slower,
And my figure's stoutening out;
My breath is getting shorter,
And no doubt I'll get the gout.

But my brain is getting larger,
Since the days of carefree youth;
When everyone is rather dumb,
Even silly and uncouth.

But just try and tell those youngsters,
How to improve their ways;
They only laugh and scoff at you,
And do not think it pays.

If they would only listen,
How much cost and pain they'd save;
But if you try and tell them much,
They say you only rave.

They think that you're a fogey,
And your tales of youth untrue;
They never seem to understand,
That you grew up and older too.

December, 1974

LONELY

Last night as I lay on the prairie,
I gazed at the stars in the sky;
I wondered if ever my sweetheart,
Would reach that Sweet Bye and Bye.

She left me for love of another,
A roaming sort of a guy;
I would have murdered to save her,
But for thoughts of that Sweet Bye and Bye.

She left me with little misgiving,
With never a tear in her eye;
She smiled and said she was sorry,
She'd see me in the Sweet Bye and Bye.

If I could but forgive and forget her,
But a tear I still get in my eyes;
As I feel that I'll be without her,
When I get to that Sweet Bye and Bye.

But a hope still lingers within me,
To be true to our love I will try;
Perhaps God willing I'll meet her,
And we'll dwell in that Sweet Bye and Bye.

Summer, 1973

THE DIRTY THIRTIES

The bright years, the golden years,
The years when I was young;
The hard years, the lean years,
When we of Depression sung.

The blowing years, the drifting years,
As the sand dunes built up high;
The sunny years, the cloudless years,
When no rain fell from the sky.

The scarce years, the low years,
When prices hit the dirt;
But close years, and neighborly years,
When you even shared your shirt.

They were loving years and caring years,
When we all helped one another;
They were sad years, yet glad years,
When we all worked for each other.

They were dry years and windy years,
The years that are long gone by;
Yet happy years, and good years,
As we think back with a sigh.

They were friendly years and family years,
The years when we were spry;
They were tough years, and rough years,
But somehow we got by.

December, 1973

WINTER TRAVEL

I was riding down the highway,
In a Greyhound bus one day;
The winter month of January,
Had all but passed away.

The wind became terrific,
Across the southern land;
The blacktop lay before us,
Like a dark grey velvet band.

A fence of white, just four feet high,
Was drifting all around;
With a little break in wind drift,
One could sometimes see the ground.

The lights of oncoming vehicles,
Were a glow of orange thru white;
The afternoon was terrible,
And the evening proved a fright.

It made one feel insignificant,
In a smothered sort of way;
Lonely, lost and awful small,
Is all I've got to say.

But the bus was warm and comfy,
And no one spoke of fear;
We put our faith in the driver,
And his ability to steer.

The blacktop was getting narrower,
And in places filling in;
If the wind got up much higher,
Traveling surely would be grim.

The driver sat there stoic,
His expression showed no fear;
His eyes were ever watchful,
Lest trouble should appear.

Our speed was slowly falling,
As the snow was falling fast;
We knew not if we would make it,
But town lights showed up at last.

Then when we had rested,
With a coffee break you know;
The wind had started falling,
And no more we saw the snow.

Our spirits started rising,
And we took to the road again;
Thankful that our driver,
Was full of grit and trained.

January, 1975

THE FARMER

I'm a poor, poor farmer,
As broke as I can tell;
But then it is no wonder,
Since livestock prices went to hell.

Now Blakney said 'produce more food',
For those in other nations;
And then he drops our price of beef,
Without any explanation.

Oh the bill collector's at the door,
He holds my I.O.U.;
Near every day I get a dunner,
When ever the mail gets thru.

The banker looks as if he'd like
To shake me by the hand;
But then that's understandable,
He holds the mortgage on my land.

My car it uses gas and oil,
It seems to cost a lot;
It seems I cannot pay for it,
With money I don't got.

There's seed to buy and spray to get,
There's fertilizer, too;
But my bank account is empty,
Now what am I to do.

There's grub to buy and food to get,
To keep the winter chills away;
And I'm just a poor old farmer,
Getting poorer every day.

There's clothes to buy to keep us warm,
For we can't change like the rabbit;
But then among the farming class,
Streaking could become a habit.

Now I could write an N.S.F. cheque,
To pay up what I have spent;
Then they'd put me in jail,
And I'd get free grub and rent.

Now wouldn't it be better,
If they'd kept the prices high;
I'd still be working yet for them,
Instead of them supporting I.

For when other prices kept on rising,
A poorer farmer I become;
I raised the beef they wanted,
But I'm broke, I am by gum.

But if I had failed to listen,
And worked things out my way;
I'd be a damn sight better off,
As my debts I then could pay.

December, 1974

196

DEDICATION TO A SCHOOL BUS DRIVER

Here's to the bus driver that you are,
Who ever you may be;
I'm glad i'ts you that's doing it,
For it sure as hell won't be me.

You must transport a group of little monsters,
Down that long, long trail to school;
Some have respect and listen,
Others like to act the fool.

The biggest mischiefs' of the bunch,
Collect down at the back;
Where all the dirty stories fly,
Or someone sets out a tack.

A punch will fly or a book will fall,
Accidentally of course;
Then you're looked on as a grouch,
If discipline you enforce.

Then there's the bus that you must drive,
Sometimes it's shinny, big and new;
But most school busses age a lot,
Due to what they must go thru.

Sometimes the roads are very good,
But then more oft they're not;
And as sure as the wind comes up,
In a snow drift you are caught.

The side road are a terror,
The main roads bad enough;
But still and all you have to try it,
Or some family's in a huff.

Then there's that probability,
That you will perchance get stuck;
So that before you try it,
Your fingers you cross for luck.

Now summer's more delightful,
For the rain's not quite as bad;
Although there are several times,
That the road looks mighty sad.

But walking in the summer rain,
Is nicer than the snow;
But no matter what the weather,
That school bus has to go.

And regardless of the circumstance,
That school bus must go forth;
And due to many little monsters,
"Tis the most thankless job on earth.

But then there are the good days;
The good roads and sunshine;
To balance out the problems,
And bring life back in line.

But if parents only stopped and thought,
How many life miles he rules;
While taking thirty little children,
Back and forth to school.

They'd tell those little children,
To behave themselves each day;
Or they'd spank their little bottoms,
In the good old-fashioned way.

January, 1975

POOR MOTHER

I'm bending over picking berries,
In that old strawberry patch;
And the skitter bugs are biting,
So it needs that I must scratch.

Now one must always bend down low,
To reach those berries red;
So you must kneel on your prayer bones,
Or stand on feet and head.

Those horse flies too, like your position,
As they go droning past;
But then the pappa of them all,
Alights upon your ass.

I jump a bit and swear a bit,
Look where I've put my feet;
I cry a bit and sigh a bit,
For they're on berries red and sweet.

But then I move my great big feet,
And start on down the row;
I look at all those nice green leaves,
And wonder how they grow.

Now water them you surely must,
To make those berries red;
They are the king of all the fruits,
Or so I've heard it said.

But my back is getting tired,
And my knees are getting sore;
But I cannot stop my picking,
As long as there is more.

So you struggle forward to the end,
Of that long row of red and green;
Then to the entire household,
You are the generous queen.

It's - Say Mom, I want a berry,
Oh give me quite a few;
I like those berries very much,
And Mom, I love you too."

Now if all that Irish blarney,
Could be used in picking fruit;
Mother's work would sure be easier,
And she might get more fruit to boot.

Although I sometimes wonder,
How many berries disappear;
When mother gets her little helpers,
It's quite a few, I fear.

February, 1975

FARMER'S WIFE

The farmer's wife has a varied life,
This I will admit;
She's a working fool from morn till night,
So let's consider it.

In the morning very early,
She's the rooster of the clan;
She starts to crow to rise them all,
Even her old man.

Next it is a chef she is,
With breakfast on the make;
But before the forenoon's over,
She's a baker of a cake.

With the breakfast over,
She becomes the milkmaid of the farm;
This is the hour of the day,
She retires to the barn.

A cleaning lady she becomes,
On completion of the chores;
For who but Mrs. Housewife,
Is going to sweep the floors.

Then there is the gardener,
Whose duties she must do;
For who'll provide the peas and carrots,
For in that Irish stew.

Now there are the dishes,
That somehow must get done;
Mother is elected,
Although she's on the run.

The sewing is another chore,
That somehow do she must;
The new things she does not mind,
But patching is the worst.

Next there is the washing,
She hates to start at all;
But she is the manager of,
Her private Laundromat.

Don't forget the children,
That by nature's law she bears;
She hopes they come in singles,
As work piles up in pairs.

So you see another job,
Is added to the list;
A nursemaid is her title now,
And the wee ones do insist.

And then when there is illness,
A doctor is her degree;
For who gives out the pills and salve,
And holds the patient on her knee.

And hubby too must have his turn,
With aspirin or vicks;
A back rub too is often needed,
So a masseur she is for kicks.

There also are the little chores,
Around the house you know;
Like building just a little shelf,
Or fixing a chair or hoe.

Then it is a carpenter,
Call her next I trust;
For if she did not do it,
Then it's a fact you must.

An accountant she becomes,
Once a year for fact;
When it's time to help fill out,
That blooming income tax.

And then there are the part time jobs,
That she must help you with;
Like being vet to an ailing cow,
Or helping pull a calf.

And yet when your loving husband,
Needs help to mend and repair;
Who is the other party,
Who always must be there.

Now she's a package policy,
With a score of jobs I'm sure;
But when she gets her wages,
It still leaves her mighty poor.

Now there is twenty-four hours in every day,
That she must be on call;
If she got wages for each job,
Their sum would you appall.

Now just twelve hours a day we'll plan for,
At two-twenty-five minimum wage;
Makes over four hundred dollars a day,
If a housewife you'd engage.

Over a hundred and sixty thousand,
Plus five hundred and thirty-five more;
So you see what love is worth,
From the financial score.

So when your filling out the census,
Do not sign a great big lie;
By saying, "She's Just a Housewife",
As the census sheet implies.

January, 1975

HEAVENLY TRAILS

The 'Trail of Life' is winding,
Slowly down the hidden vale;
We know not what lies before us,
Nor how smooth, will be that trail,
There's a lot of obscure potholes,
As we cross the grassy plain,
Many are the knolls of iniquity,
Ere the trail is smooth again.

There are rough roads and cross roads,
On which to loose our way;
There are good roads and bad roads,
Along which we might stray;
But we must choose the right road,
The smooth it always ain't;
For if life was always easy,
Everyone could be a saint.
It's those rough trails and bad trails,
That make us what we are;
But somehow we must stand the test,
To reach that Heavenly shore;
It's the good times, the bad times,
That makes our life worthwhile;
It's the happy times, the sad times,
We see in every mile.

It's a short life or a long life,
It depends on how we care;
But we have to make the best of it,
For there is none to spare;
Thus we must follow slowly,
Life's way to the Heavenly Vale;
Up many a rugged hillside,
Down many a sunny dale.

Across the wavy sea of Life,
Not knowing what's in store;
Until we reach our Father's Mansion,
On Heaven's golden shore.

December, 1974

WINTER OF 1974 - 75

What has happened to Saskatchewan,
In the year of seventy-four;
December now has rolled around,
And time is passing o'er.

There is no snow around as yet,
And we hope it stays away;
For Saskatchewan could be heaven,
If it didn't come to stay.

They say the geese are still around,
And some ducks are here we know;
Why even just the other day,
I really saw a crow.

The rabbits look peculiar,
Their white against the black;
Mother nature changed the weather,
But somehow forgot the Jack.

The willow trees are furring out,
The poplar's are in bud;
But when next spring has rolled around,
Will this be very good.

What has happened in Saskatchewan,
We hardly know the place;
For Mother Nature's left her,
With a desired dirty face.

October usually brings the snow,
And the cold and stormy days;
Which somehow never leave us,
Until April comes and stays.

November then gets colder,
And the snow it moves around;
The days get short and shorter,
And there's drifts upon the ground.

But this year is something different,
And I'm sure we're very glad;
For everybody greets you with,
It's the best one, I think we've had.

If only we can make it,
Past Christmas time and then;
The days start getting longer,
And we can look for Spring again.

December, 1974

FOND MEMORIES

Last night as I strolled across the farmyard,
I gazed at the stars in the sky;
I thought back to the days of my childhood,
Somehow the stars weren't as high.

For I used to look at the "Milky Way",
And imagine some folks lived there;
Dreaming about those far off lands,
At times I would just stand and stare.

I used to watch the northern lights,
As they danced away up high;
And I wondered where they always went,
When they reached the edge of the sky.

Now the distant hills don't seem so high,
Nor so tall is yonder tree;
But it isn't the change in nature's way,
So it must be the change in me.

Most things have changed since my childhood,
But the stars keep twinkling on;
There have been many joys and sorrows,
Many loved ones come and gone.

I'd like to return to my childhood,
When all our thoughts ran free;
Back to those days of carefree ways,
But we know that can never be.

So I live again those bygone days,
In memories fond and clear;
I return again to those happy times,
Away back in those yester-years.

January, 1975

207

TO A COTTONTAIL

I drove down the busy highway,
Cut off on an old side trail;
There is the glare of headlights,
Sat a great big cottontail.

His ears erect, his head held high,
His front paws held in prayer;
He sat and stared as the headlights glared,
He knew not I was there.

Yet he spotted danger quickly,
Taking off for fields afar;
He dodged a bit and raced a bit,
As I slowed the speeding car.

The lights they seemed to fascinate,
The mate that was more shy;
If she didn't watch her staggering steps,
She'd be condemned to die.

But I switched on the dimmer,
In hopes that she'd escape,
But I was not fast enough,
Alas it was too late.

Her snow white body lay beneath,
The wheel of my speeding car;
Bleeding and broken beyond repair,
As her lonely mate sped on afar.

She was just a wild animal,
That lay in a broken state;
But just as easy she could be human,
That suffered such a fate.

January, 1975

208

OUR LITTLE TOWN

There's the little town of Cut Knife,
In Saskatchewan's great Northwest;
Surrounded by some farmland,
Which is considered to be the best.

It was in the year of nineteen twelve,
This little town sprung up;
With the coming of the railway,
When the CP. was a pup.

It has grew and grew to quite a size,
Where near six hundred now reside;
A neat and tidy little town,
Where many old folks do abide.

Now main street lays straight North and South,
Where most of the stores are set;
Quite an array, you must allow,
They sell most anything you bet.

At the southern end of main,
There lies the railway track;
It's where the farmers haul their grain,
And buy Esso goods from Jack.

For here three elevators stand,
The Federal, Searle and Pool;
Fertilizer, oil and gas are sold,
Grease, antifreeze and twine, too.

Now Gallivan's garage is set up,
At the south end of main;
Located next is Margot's store,
A good clothing store 'tis plain.

Next we have a small building,
Used by cubs and scouts;
Then the Crown Mart lumber yard,
This half block does finish out.

You must step across the alley,
To our post office new and fine;
Then onto the grocery store,
Run by Mr. Dion.

Then comes the John Deere dealership,
Which don't carry too much anymore;
And then we have to cross the street,
To Florence's little grocery store.

Then we stroll a little further,
For Sandburg's Billiards is not far;
There is also lunch and coffee there,
Magazines, cigarettes and bars.

Then if one needs a prescription,
Vet supplies or spray for bugs;
They just walk a little farther,
Into the Rexall Drugs.

Now farther yet there is a building,
Used by the teenage group;
It's known as the Play Shoppe,
In summer when they work.

Next we have the library,
Where our mind can be improved;
It used to be the bake shop,
Where we bought the bread we loved.

The last business place on the block,
Is the large Oddfellows hall;
Where many groups collect or serve,
A well used building, all in all.

On the West side of the street,
On the South corner we all know;
Is a new type of building,
That improved our town and so.

There's a Doctor's office, barber shop,
Ice cream store and café;
You can get your coffee there,
At most any time of day.

Next there is the old Post Office,
Where the elderly go for free;
There's games and work and visiting,
And a social cup of tea.

Now Gordie's Second Hand Shop,
Is the next one on the street;
It's here you find some bargains,
That really can't be beat.

Next in line is Wettlaufer's,
The Ford garage as you know;
Gas, oil and grease and some repairs,
Keep several on the go.

Then there is a large store,
Which changed hands several times;
As Ranchland it is known,
Tops in the meat and grocery line.

Next we stroll into the Bank,
Where we hope we have some funds;
Managed by Mr. Leggott,
And his other trusty ones.

Now we reach the cross street,
Which they have not yet paved;
So at times you cross with care,
Or from the mud hole must be saved.

The other corner boasts the Co-op,
A modern store indeed;
From which you can get most anything,
When you are much in need.

They also have a storehouse next,
For livestock and poultry feed;
The Credit Union's next in line,
Where you can borrow if in need.

Then we walk up the street a bit,
To the Hotel Lucerne;
With meals and rooms and beer to sell,
For which many take their turn.

Then to the movie theater,
Which runs twice every week;
Thursday might and Saturday night,
If you entertainment seek.

Next let us look at the East side,
Where there are schools galore;
Where many town and country kids,
Get education, more and more.

Several Police it has acquired,
To keep peace twixt red and white;
To collect all the inebriated,
And tuck the town in for the night.

A Civic Center this town built,
With dance floor, ice surface, waiting room and lunch;
It's really quite a place you know,
If for sports you have a hunch.

Then there is the curling rink,
Which sets right beside the other;
There's many a mean rock thrown here,
By brother, sister, father and mother.

The largest place of business,
Located in the town;
Is owned by Mr. Finley,
Of province wide renown.

There is a garage, shop and hardware,
Grease, oil, gas and such;
Cars and machines of every size,
And small stuff not costing much.

Then just across the corner, is the liquor store,
It's where you also go if insurance you seek;
Where you pay your light and power,
And get the local paper once a week.

There is an apartment house,
At the West side of the town;
The headquarters of power and Sask-Tel,
And a municipal office of credit and renown.

Cut Knife also boasts a construction company,
That works the country around;
And at the East side of town,
Is where Mr. Novak's place is found.

There also is a gravel man,
Who does trucking night or day;
He is known as Mr. Breault,
And Cut Knife is where he stays.

In this little town there are three lodges,
And their female counterparts;
There's the Oddfellow, Elks and Masons,
Who on all jobs work with a heart.

And in this quiet little town,
There are churches four;
With a ladies group to help each out,
With its financial chore.

Now if you look farther,
Away out at the East side;
There is a well kept cemetery,
Where many old friends reside.

But the town is extending Westward,
Where the hospital was set;
It is the Nicest little place,
If ever ill you get.

Out that way too, is the museum,
To bring back memories old;
It may not look too modern,
But it's worth it's weight in gold.

Then there is a tiny campground,
Which is tidy, neat and clean;
It is not very large you know,
But it's as cute as I have seen.

And of course there is that Tomahawk,
That stands so very high;
I cannot see much use for it,
Except to dominate the sky.

All in all it's a tidy town,
Set out on the square;
If we can only keep it such,
And not let it fall in disrepair.

If we can keep it honest,
Upright, fair and clean;
It's one of the nicest towns,
That I have ever seen.

1974 - 1975

MY INCOME TAX

April too has come and gone,
And signs of Spring are here;
At last I've done my Income Tax,
For yet another year.

I've added up my income,
Subtracted my expense;
As for making anything,
I'm sitting on the fence.

The expenses have gone higher,
And my income has gone flat;
I can't stay here much longer,
Just sitting where I've sat.

My pants are getting thinner,
My temper's in a huff;
Its damn poor sitting up here,
But still I can't get off.

My hair is getting grayer,
And I'm getting bald on top;
My wrinkles are increasing,
And my figure's gone to pot.

Yet one must keep on trying,
Somehow to make ends meet;
To see if you can beat the game,
Or by the game, get beat.

Machinery prices have gone up,
Repairs you cannot find;
But you must borrow on your soul,
Tt's a new machine, you have in mind.'

214

Depreciation, you are allowed,
But somehow, it don't help much;
For if the payments you cannot meet,
You're in the lender's clutch.

So you patch, and mend, and cuss a bit,
And a struggle always on;
The "good old days" of pleasure farming,
Are indeed, forever gone.

So you borrow more, to pay for less,
And your interest claims it all;
So you end up owing everyone,
When the works done in the fall.

But then you've had the exercise,
And the right to work like hell;
You prove you are a healthy cuss,
But you'd like to rest a spell.

So that's why in the winter,
Mother Nature takes command;
By bringing us cold weather,
And freezing up the land.

Another year has come and gone,
And my pocket book is flat;
I'm still just that poor farmer man,
Sitting where I've sat.

Then you must hire someone,
To figure out what you've lost;
Or by our demanding government,
In the clink you might be tossed.

September, 1975

LISTENING AND WATCHING

Did you ever lie on a sunny slope,
In the spring time of the year;
And listen for "Old Mother Nature",
And what she'd let you hear.

There's little bugs a creeping,
Among the grass roots there;
Seeking out a feeding place,
Just where, they do not care.

There are butterflies a flitting,
From flower to grassy stem;
They seem so bright and happy,
I wish that I were them.

And then there are the fuzzy worms,
Brown and orange and black;
They'd start out in a straight line,
By wrinkling up their back.

The bees do hum, and flies do buzz,
From flower onto flower;
Collecting all the food they could,
In case of a springtime shower.

And then if one looks upward,
Into a cloudless sky;
You can hear the call of ducks and geese,
As they go winging by.

And there, upon that distant tree,
Sits a Crow in black attire;
Calling out across the vale,
To the mate of his desire.

And away beyond the fence line,
Lies a spotted, new-born calf;
The fuss and the commotion there,
Would really make you laugh.

A silent sweep from way up high,
And a scuttle thru the brush;
An ear splitting scream, that fills the air,
And then an awful hush.

But the stately robin, walks the lawn,
With little heed or care;
He carefully watches with two bright eyes,
For any earthworms there.

But sneaking very close behind,
On noiseless, padded feet;
Little knows, does Mr. Tom,
He'll soon be in fast retreat!

For watching from the nearby porch,
Is Rover large and quick;
He does not like this feline male,
And makes his motto stick.

But then across the old farm yard,
Walks a pussy with no fear;
The long white line all down his back,
Is a brand that belongs not here.

When Mr. Rooster sees him,
The commotion was supreme;
Rover too joined in the fun,
Of which "Odor" was the theme.

I then took off for distant parts,
As the smell I could not stand;
There was now no peace or quiet,
In "Mother Nature's" land.

October, 1975

WISHING

Are we ever satisfied,
With the time of year;
When it is coldest winter,
We wish that spring was here.

And then when Spring has rolled around,
And work is at full speed;
We wish the winter back again,
So we could rest indeed.

Now when July has rolled around,
And it is too hot you say;
You'd like a little touch of fall,
To drive the flies away.

But then when fall comes creeping up,
And there is harvesting to do;
Of those lazy days, despite the flies,
You wouldn't mind a few.

Now when the fall is over,
And Winter is here again;
We do not like the wind and snow,
But we like to rest, it's plain.

So why not quit complaining,
And enjoy the seasons, when you can;
There's time for work and time for play,
If you fit in with God's plan.

So organize and synchronize,
Yourself with seasons four;
And quit your darn complaining,
Or you really are a bore.

October, 1975

218

SASKATCHEWAN '74

What's happening in Saskatchewan,
In the Spring of seventy-four;
It rains, and rains, and rains and rains,
And then it rains some more.

It started very early,
Before the snow was gone;
It flooded out the garden,
The barnyard and the lawn.

We could not work our tatter patch,
It had become a slough;
So we put our garden on the high spots,
What else was there to do?

You started in to work your land,
In a jig-saw sort of way;
Many a tractor and large machine,
In a low spot had to stay.

Meantime you sloshed around the yard,
Which was ankle deep in mud;
The grass was slow in turning green,
And the trees forgot to bud.

The earthworms got scared of drowning,
So to the top they came;
Now for crows and ducks and magpies,
Eating them is the game.

So now I scare those varmints,
With a little pellet gun;
For berries, corn and lettuce,
Make earthworm eating fun.

Then hail it came one Sunday,
At the tea-time hour of four;
It striped the leaves and mowed the grass,
Thank God! there wasn't more.

It rained or froze near every day,
Somehow we couldn't win;
Lots of fields were swimming pools,
And some crops were mudded in.

Then on into the summer,
When July was here;
It got very dry in spots,
And crops suffered lots I fear.

And then it rained in showers small,
To rise our hopes again;
But frost crept in quite early,
As August days did wane.

Eventually we got the crop,
But it wasn't great I fear;
But then one can look forward,
To better things next year.

Spring, 1975

SPENDING

There's money to spend,
And money to lend,
And money to put in the bank.

There's money for girls,
And money for pearls,
And money for those we thanked.

There's money for pills,
And money for ills,
And money to keep us from harm.

There's money for dues,
And money for shoes,
And money to keep us warm.

There's money for food,
And other things good,
And money for even the frills.

There's money for taxes,
And money for rent,
And money to pay on the bills.

There's money for cars,
And some for cigars,
And money to spend on drink.

But budget it all,
For fear of a fall,
Into the financial drink.

October 1975

SPIRIT OF CHRISTMAS

Last night as I lay on my pillow,
In my cosy warm little bed;
I saw visions of Christmas before me,
Of Santa and Reindeer and sled.

Loaded and looking for chimneys,
As he drifted across the sky;
A smile spreading across his face,
And a twinkling in each little eye.

His whiskers and moustache a glistening,
And his hair as white as the snow;
His bells a shining and jingling,
As his reindeer danced to and fro.

"Tis a season of remembrance and writing,
"Tis a season of wishing and cheer;
"Tis a season of loving and giving,
"Tis a happy time of the year.

So imagine the spirit of Christmas,
Each one in their own private way;
And extend the season of giving,
To each and every day.

November 1975

"PRICES"

The farmer's like the old "Tom Cat",
Nine lives he has you know;
To take the blows beneath the belt,
Under the government of Trudeau.

They told us first to grow the grain,
To feed the nations' poor;
But then they dropped the price you know,
So our livelihood was insecure.

But they subsidized up just a bit,
To build up our low moral;
But told us our acreage to reduce,
Or no subsidy at all.

As the price of beef, it had gone up,
So we could make some gain;
Then we changed to livestock,
To consume this surplus of grain.

And we sowed our broke land down to grass,
For roughage for those cows;
Thinking now we had it made,
According to Trudeau's vows.

The price of pork then started up,
And the price of beef went low;
So subsidized the calf man,
Was the next step for Trudeau.

So then grain prices kept on rising,
And grain farmers grew some more;
But the low priced beef producer,
Got kicked right out the door.

So calves were kept that should have gone,
To market in the fall;
And we owed a loan we couldn't pay,
With no rise in price at all.

So another blow beneath the belt,
We took as a matter of course;
So try we must to get our income,
From yet another source.

So milk those cows and feed them,
That high priced good feed grain;
And then we took another blow,
Beneath the belt again.

They subsidized the dairyman,
Enticing him to raise production;
Then they cut his poundage,
Which caused him great destruction.

For to hold a shipping quota,
Eighty percent of it you had to fill;
But now they pay on seventy,
So how can you meet your bills.

The price of pigs is falling,
And the price of beef is flat;
It makes no difference to the consumer,
Now what do you think of that?

Now who gets this spread in price?
When the farmer's broke as hell;
If things don't change, I'm telling you
He'll need welfare for a spell.

For machines wear out that cost a lot,
And cannot be replaced;
And things break down that need repairs,
So with enormous debts we're faced.

He cannot reap if he does not sow,
And he cannot afford to sow;
So no matter which way he turns.
There is no way to go.

Now the farmer is the backbone,
Of this "Canadian Nation";
But he has almost reached a point,
Of political frustration.

So push him not dear Sir,
Or he may just rebel;
He's taken enough, political guff,
That he should say, "Go to Hell".

February 1976

MORNING CALL

Down on the farm,
About half-past four;
You're going to hear,
An awful roar.

It's time to rise,
For it's the time of the year;
To go to work,
For Spring is here.

It don't seem long,
Since winter came;
And you could play,
At the 'sleep-in' game.

But Spring is here,
And you must rise,
To play the game,
Of energize.

There's work to do,
For old and young;
For don't you know,
That 'Spring has Sprung'.

May 1, 1975

TO A BABY BOY

What is a baby?
I really don't know,
Just a wee speck of life,
Starting to grow.

An egg and a sperm,
United as one;
To create a new life,
In the nine months to come.

On a date set by nature,
No one can say when;
This tiny wee babe,
Makes his debut and then.

A pat on the bottom,
And then a big yell;
Gives him his own right,
To start to raise hell.

A red little face,
All wrinkled and sad;
But a sturdy wee mite,
To please mom and dad.

Nurtured and cared for,
A true mother's role;
A tiny wee tot,
With a heart and a soul.

There's formulas, schedules,
Late nights and all;
Each one of us answer,
To his beck and call.

A prince or a king,
He has become upon sight;
And rule us as such,
Doth this little mite.

It's fed and it's tended,
With love and with care;
And of total attention,
He demands his fair share.

He's rocked and he's burped,
He's spoiled rotten and all;
Little dreaming it might end,
When he gets just so tall.

He soon learns to smile,
And then to laugh;
Becomes the star figure,
Of each photograph.

Then comes those wee teeth,
And with most there's a squall;
Sharp as wee daggers,
There's twenty in all.

Then comes the first step,
After many a fall;
A few bumps and bruises,
And that isn't all.

A cut here and there,
And an odd bloody nose;
But soon he's running,
Whoops! there he goes.

He is grasping at life,
In his ardent young way;
He's learning real fast,
To work and to play.

Now give him, 'his day',
Yes, surely you can;
For this tiny wee fellow,
Will soon be a man.

October 1975

THE OLD AND NEW

The country's quickly changing,
This I'll have you know;
Where once the trees and sloughs were,
Now oats and barley grow.

Where once the prairie wool grew,
Ankle deep and green;
Now its mechanized machinery,
Is all that's ever seen.

There used to be the prairie trails,
Which across the prairie wound;
But now the graveled grid roads,
Everywhere are found.

It used to be the buffalo,
Wandered here and there;
But now inside a barb wire fence,
The cattle stand and stare.

You used to watch the lone rider,
Coming from afar;
Now on every byway,
Is the speedy motor car.

It used to be a team and wagon,
Hauled slowly down the road;
Now it is a big truck,
With five times the speed and load.

The trains day too is passing,
For the farmer man;
He'll have to haul his produce farther,
With a larger truck or van.

Now there are red-balls along the roadside,
To guide in planes from afar;
Where it used to be a novelty,
To own an old Ford car.

And the saddle horse or buggy,
Was a mode of travel grand;
Now its skidoo or motor bike,
That scoots across our land.

It used to be the walking plow,
Turned the virgin prairie soil;
Now with big machinery,
We spend our life in toil.

For tho we do a lot more work,
A lot more too we pay;
We really are no better off,
Then in those by-gone days.

November 1975

PIONEER HOUSEWIFE

"Twas in the year when the West was young,
And the pioneers came to stay;
Their food was not the fancy kind,
But was wholesome, I would say.

They made their meals on an old cookstove,
As black, as black as sin;
But the aroma from the burning wood,
Coaxed everybody in.
Now this busy housewife,
Baked and cooked for love;
The delicious food that she turned out,
With the help of that old stove.

The bread was brown and crusty,
The taste it was supreme;
It hit the spot and stayed there,
Making meals a dream.

The cakes and pies were also good,
With the filling from the wild;
There was no ready-mix made then,
Or an oven that could be dialed.

The work was mighty healthy,
And the taste was mighty good;
But now we turn a button,
Instead of cutting wood.

They picked their fruit out in the fields,
Or grew it in a garden plot;
Now we rush down to the store,
To see what they have got.

They used to cook their home made porridge,
From rolled oats or home cracked wheat;
Now the cereal boxes on the shelves,
Are numerous, bight and neat.

They churned their cream in a barrel churn,
Or shook it to and fro;
They worked and washed and salted it,
And the taste was great you know.

Now we buy our butter,
Down at the local store;
It costs about a buck a pound,
Or maybe even more.

The beef was canned or corned you see,
The pork was salted, dry or brine;
Jack Frost was their winter keeper,
But their meat always tasted fine.

Now we have our freezers,
Our cured meat needs we must buy;
But we somehow do it,
Although the bacteria count is high.

The pioneer had a garden,
It was her sacred plot;
She grew a lot of food there,
For in that old black cooking pot.

Now we buy them in a can,
The additives are great;
Many people never see them,
In their natural state.

They used to get their milk,
From a bovine with four feet;
Now we buy it boxed or canned,
Marked skimmed, condensed or sweet.

The hens they let them run at large,
No anemic eggs they laid;
They had more iron and vitamins,
Regardless of the grade.

But now the hens are captives,
So Grade A eggs they lay;
But the food value isn't there,
As in those good old days.

Now we have our water,
Running hot and cold;
They used to carry it, and heat it,
In those pioneer days of old.

The scrub board it was right in style,
In those by-gone days you know;
Lye soap was their detergent,
And sunshine made them glow.

They could not push a button,
To wash or dry their clothes;
There was no bleach or downy then,
They had not invented those.

But somehow these rustic pioneers,
Lived a very healthy life;
But he never could have made it,
Without his ever-loving wife.

She baked and cooked and cleaned for him,
And raised a family;
If they had not been a sturdy lot,
I wonder where we'd be.

January 1976

THE STRAP

Now years ago there was a strap,
Tucked in the old top drawer;
It let the teacher rule the roast,
So could she ask for more?

They respected her, and worked for her,
To learn a lot you know;
For obedience was the order,
In the long, long ago.

They say education has improved,
But I doubt it very much;
For they've taken away the teacher's strap,
And left her in the lurch.

Now many children go to school,
To waste their time away;
And laziness and rowdiness,
Is the order of the day.

For how can one poor teacher,
Supervise a bunch of kids;
Teach them whatever they should know,
The "do nots" and the "dids".

How can she keep the noisy quiet,
Make them all do what you expect;
Keep the lazy prodded on,
And make those "little terror's" show respect.

Make the wool gatherers pay attention,
And the rowdy settle down;
When even the faithful strap,
Is looked on with a frown.

What is education coming to?
When a teacher must spend her time;
Talking the lazy into working,
And making the bad ones mind.

Why is the teacher that we trust,
To improve our children's' minds;
Somehow can't be trusted,
When to paddle their behinds.

So put the strap on the teacher's desk,
Saying use it as you will;
And give that teacher half a chance,
To make use of her teaching skills.

For would you rather not your child,
Got that much needed strap;
Than coming home next June,
To say that he'd been zapped.

February 1976

ST. PATRICK'S GREETINGS

I wish you the luck of the Irish,
On this St. Patrick's Day;
As one Irishman to another,
This I'd like to say.

May joy and happiness follow you,
As sure as night comes after day;
And may St. Patrick's Leprechaun,
Steal your heart away.

May your March the 17th,
Be sunny bright and gay;
For many years to follow,
I wish in my Irish way.

March 14, 1976

DECEMBER 25TH - 10 P.M.

The children are all tired,
Their tummies filled up tight;
For its Christmas night on the prairie,
And the stars are shining bright.

The lights are hanging all awry,
Old Santa's taken flight;
For its Christmas night on the prairie,
And the stars are shining bright.

The Christmas tree looks barren,
And the floor's an awful sight;
For its Christmas night on the prairie,
And the stars are shining bright.

Mother is all tired out,
And father's still half tight;
For its Christmas night on the prairie,
And the stars are shining bright.

Your pockets are all empty,
And your credit's tied up tight;
For its Christmas night on the prairie,
And the stars are shining bright.

But then somehow we will survive,
Without too much trouble or fright,
For Christmas time will come again,
If we keep next year in sight.

December 1975 - January 1976

BYE-GONE EDUCATION

Across our widespread prairie,
Were built many one room schools;
Where we learned our A B C's,
And were taught the golden rule.

We were not pets or pampered,
Like children are today;
We did not have a heated bus,
To take us all the way.

We drove or rode or walked,
Many a weary mile;
We could not listen to the radio,
By simply turning on a dial.

And regardless of the weather,
Be it sleet or rain or snow;
We did not like to miss a day,
Somehow we had to go.

We did not have the grid roads,
The children have today;
We'd plod along a dusty trail,
Leaving footprints all the way.

Yet we were not bored with our daily trek,
As slowly on we trod;
We were very close to Nature's ways,
And near the wonders made by God.

We heard the gopher's spring like chirp,
As he stood upon a knoll;
We wondered how he knew his way,
To his own little private hole.

We'd watch the happy meadowlark,
On top of an old fence post;
As he'd give forth a burst of song,
From his bright yellow throat.

We saw moths and bees and butterflies,
As they went flitting past;
And many were the questions,
That we of the teacher asked.

We oft saw the harmless garter snake,
Asleep on the sunny road;
And watched him slither thru the grass,
To his more dark and safe abode.

We turned over stones to watch the ants,
As they carried their young away;
Wondering why they always worked,
And never stopped to play.

We saw many wild flowers,
Which are not around today;
And if we had some extra time,
We stopped to have a play.

But it you drove a horse or team,
There are times we'd have a race;Or else we picked up the strollers,
Adding a smile to their face.

Then, there were the times we rode,
Racing down that winding trail;
Six abreast it often was,
Each trying not to fail.

In winter as we rode along,
With some skiers on behind;
The curves and corners at high speed,
Was a thrill, you can't now find.

And there were the winter storms,
The breakups in the spring;
When you drove with care and courage,
As safety was the thing.

They saw that children now a days,
Have advantages you see;
But then in those olden days,
In fact, likewise had we.

January 1976

AGING

Now when our hair gets grayer,
And there are wrinkles in our skin;
We've lost our girlish figure,
And we are either fat or thin.

But time it seems has moved along,
And somehow we've changed too;
Our steps grow slower as we age,
No matter what we do.

Our hair fades more or thins a bit,
And our figure stoutens out;
Our legs get weak, but our head gets strong,
And we may have got the gout.

But our mind as yet is active,
And of our memories, we are fond;
We like to visit and discuss,
Those happy times long gone.

As long as we have got our health,
Of wealth, it matters not;
We should consider ourselves as privileged,
And make the best of what we've got.

Relive those memories, so long gone,
And in activity take part;
For tho we are aged in body,
We can still be young in heart.

We sometime stop and think a bit,
And wonder what we should do;
And wonder if we'll have accomplished much,
When our life on earth is thru.

Will we have left for the younger folk,
Something for which they'll care;
Or will we just be a passing thought,
Over which no one seems to care.

February 1976

THE BEST THINGS IN LIFE ARE FREE

Don't let anyone tell you different,
And no matter what you see;
There are many things that cost a lot,
But the best things in life are free.

There is the light that comes at break of day,
There are the green leaves on the tree;
There is the song of the yellow bird,
All these too are free.

There's the sun that shines from a cloudless sky,
There's the fresh air we cannot see;
There's the green grass growing on yonder hill,
Yes, the best things in life are free.

There's the love you share with dear ones,
And the smell of a bright sweet pea;
There's the ripple of the westerly wind,
All these too are free.

There's the twinkle in a pair of laughing eyes,
There's the beauty in nature we see;
There's the smile upon a happy face,
And these things too are free.

There's the sleep we get when we're tired,
As tired, as tired can be;
There's the joy in waking from this sleep,
And these things too are free.

There's the love of God from heaven above,
Which some are too blind to see;
There's the joy in living we all should have,
When the best things in life are free.

So stop and think as you go along,
Take time these things to see;
Complain you can of what costs a lot,
But the best things in life are free.

February 1976

DESTRUCTION

The golden sun was a glowing orb,
As it crossed the smoke filled sky;
The blowing blast was a holocaust,
In which many things would die.

I stood and watched as the fire spread,
Flames spreading far and fast;
There was naught to do, but stand and pray,
And I stood; my mind aghast.

The only thing that could save the day,
Was rain from a cloudless sky;
As wildlife kept rushing,
To the river banks nearby.

The smoke was slowly spreading,
Across the rolling prairie soil;
The sky was thick and hazy,
And the men, no more could toil.

But the air stayed hot and humid,
And the rain it failed to fall;
There was no hope of stopping it,
Not a single chance, at all.

I walked down to the river,
Praying fervently as I went;
That relief from the raging fire,
Would be surely Heaven sent.

It was then the fire fighters,
Came swooping down by plane;
The ejection of the chemical,
Performed the work of rain.

The fire started dying,
But smoke filled our lungs with pain;
We looked hopefully skyward,
And prayed for rain again.

And just as day was ending,
The clouds began to form;
We knew our prayers were answered,
In the presence of a storm.

Then the rain was gently falling,
Cleaning out the smoke filled air;
Blotted up by the grassless soil,
That was so black and bare.

The wildlife emerged,
From the river banks nearby;
Then all that was left to do,
Was count what had to die.

Now why should man be careless,
To destroy wildlife that way;
When the Good Lord put them on this earth,
And gave them the right to stay.

February 1976

TO A SASKATOON

Here's to a small sweet berry,
Found on the plains of the West;
For flavor and food value,
It is the very best.

It' been here since time beginning,
At least so the Indians say;
For they put it in their pemmican,
In those far off, by gone, days.

It's a native to Saskatchewan,
Although elsewhere it will sometimes grow;
But you do not see it cultivated,
It's a native fruit you know.

It seen us thru the thirties,
When depression reigned supreme;
It can't be bought in any store,
But of all the fruits, it's Queen.

This small dew-drop of purple,
Hanging from branches high;
Its taste is truly terrific,
It makes one really sigh.

It does not grow prolific,
Every year you know;
But when it's at its very best,
It's out to pick we go.

We drive down to the valley,
Where the soil contains some sand;
The sun seems rather hot there,
On a southern slope of land.

You climb a fence and follow,
A well-beaten crooked trail,
Then you take a cow path,
Up the hill and down the dale.

Over on that little hummock,
There they hang in clusters great;
Surrounded by some thorn bushes,
To protect them from their fate.

But we pick many berries,
And eat a lot I fear;
Leaving with our face and fingers purple,
And in hopes of more next year.

August 1976

243

TRANSPORTATION IN CANADA

Water -
It's a large land, a free land,
A land of spaces wide;
It's a traveled land, a changed land,
Where we all doth reside.

There used to be the Indian trails,
Before the white man came;
They followed thru the forests,
Pathways made by game.

They traveled down the rivers,
In a light birchbark canoe;
In water swift, they handled well,
And of pounds, carried quite a few.

Quickly made by the stranded traveler,
And easy to portage;
Of the Indian and fur trader,
Considered as a badge.

Then there developed the bateau,
A large flat bottomed boat;
Four oarsmen and a pilot,
To keep this ship afloat.

With a small mast and sail,
And six long setting poles;
To pilot thru the rapids,
Four tons to its goal.

Next came the sturdy Durham boat,
With long poles, oars and sail;
Twice the length, at eighty feet,
With ten times the load, it didn't fail.

Then they turned to steamships,
Of which "Accommodation" was the first;
Traveled from Montreal to Quebec,
With passengers and berths.

Next came the "Royal William",
Built in the year of thirty-one;
One hundred and sixty feet in length,
And a cargo of one hundred seventy tons.

244

Sold to the Spanish Government,
In the year of eighteen thirty-three;
Turned into a warship,
The first steam one, you see.

The next first for Canada,
Was the "Beaver" as you know;
Up and down the west coast forts,
It carried supplies both to and fro.

For fifty years it carried furs,
This steamer with a paddle wheel;
Until 'twas wrecked in Vancouver harbor,
By rocks which were well concealed.

But for larger boats they needed canals,
Which Canada must make;
But the U.S. switched to railways,
As the coverage was more great.

Now Canada, she built canals,
Numbering quite a few;
Lachine, Erie and Welland,
Cornwall and Rideau too.

In the year of Eighteen fifty-nine,
The steamboat to Red River came;
And then to the Saskatchewan,
Furs and supplies their game.

Railway -
So in the year of thirty-six,
Canada's first rail line was on;
Four horses were the power,
From La Prairie to St. John.

Then in the year of thirty-seven,
A steam engine they obtained;
And the beginning of the railway,
In Canada was ordained.

But with the spread of settlers,
Transportation must improve;
So the C.P.R. was started,
To help these settlers move.

Also too our fair Domain,
Depended on this rail;
For with the joining of East and West,
The Union couldn't fail.

So 'twas in November of Seventy-five,
The Golden Spike was driven;
The settlers got their supply line,
And the government- its Domain.

The train improved, as did the rails,
Across this fair Domain;
Far ahead of the first wood burner,
In the modern diesel train.

Roads -
Now these early pathways,
Down which the Indians ran;
Changed into a bridle path,
Used by ox, and horse, and man.

Then came the post-chaise,
A small two wheeled cart;
One horse and one passenger,
Down the trail he'd dart.

But the roads must need by widened,
Larger vehicles to accommodate;
In a caleche or cariole,
One rode right in state.

Two passengers and a driver,
Down these corduroy roads did go;
But travel was quite precarious,
And I'm sure was mighty slow.

Next came the stage coach,
With four or six horses in a span;
Eight or ten passengers there were,
Driven by an experienced man.

The baggage too was heavy,
And the roads were very poor;
There were many streams to cross,
With water up to the door.

But now lets journey westward,
In a Red River Cart, we could;
Box and wheels and axles,
All made of solid wood.

If one ox was our power,
Nine hundred pounds the load;
Twenty-five mile of creaking noise,
Each day down a winding road.

Now one might drive a pony,
So you cut your load to five;
But forty or fifty mile you went,
Without that creaking noise.

The Indians here used travois,
To move their goods and family;
Two sloping poles with a hide attached,
Pulled by an Indian pony.

Then came the prairie schooner,
To transport new settlers west;
A covered wagon pulled by oxen,
Must be strong to stand the test.

There were many single buggies,
And two horse democrats;
That covered many weary miles,
On hillsides or on flats.

Then the farmer had his wagon,
To haul his stock or grain;
Eighty bushel to a load,
Behind a spanking team.

Then too they surveyed the land,
And built roads on the square;
For things had to change you know,
With the coming of the car.

The first cars were the Model T.,
Built to cover roadways rough;
Side curtains filled with isinglass;
They were high, and black and tough.

Then next along came the Model A.,
With much more speed by far;
And each new kind improved,
Until we reached our modern car.

So many makes and models of cars,
Joined in the sale parade;
And trucks of every size and make,
You could get on cash or trade.

With the building of the highways,
The blacktopping and the grid;
The advancement of the transport truck,
Was the next great thing they did.

Air -
From the year of 1900 and into 1903,
Wright Brothers started travel in the air;
First with gliders, then with planes,
They made people stand and stare.

But in the last three quarters century,
Planes have changed a lot;
Monoplane, biplane, triplane and blimp,
Are only four, of what we've got.

Pontoon plane, seaplane and amphibian,
Fighter plane, cargo plane and jet;
Passenger planes and training planes,
And there is more to come as yet.

Helicopters and spray planes,
Of many kinds both great and small;
Canada has improved her air travel,
About which we can't complain at all.

There are also many private planes,
Across this widespread land;
There are many farmers with runways,
And a license from air command.

In the north land there's the dog team,
Thru the winter's wind and snow;
Then the helicopter took over,
Where other things couldn't go.

But some of the northern natives,
Still use the caribou and deer;
But the plane will replace them,
In time, I have no fear.

In the mountains we find the pack horse,
Across the roadless, rocky terrain;
Which was later followed,
By that helicopter plane.

Now there is the pleasure travel,
Enjoyed by quite a few;
On the speedy motor bike,
Or the seat of a skidoo.

There also is the bicycle,
Which was invented long ago;
A lot more safe, but slower,
Than the motor bike you know.

Now we are a traveling nation,
Winter, summer, spring and fall;
Our speed it is terrific,
And our road manners full of gall.

Now transportation has advanced,
Beyond the expected goal;
Speed is the order of the day,
But in lives it claims a toll.

If only we would stop and think,
That gas and booze don't blend;
We just might be there to see,
The advancement is transportation end.

October 1976

ONWARD EVER ONWARD

Onward ever onward,
Thru the pages of life's book;
We lived and worked and worshiped,
As our tasks we undertook.

We've changed this empty country,
To a place of modern ways;
It is a lot more livable,
But I'm not sure it pays.

When the pioneer first came here,
He worked from morn to night;
He struggled to improve his lot,
With all his skill and might.

They broke the land and built a house,
And raised a family;
And the first thing that we know,
They'd formed a community.

One for all and all for one,
They helped each other out;
A neighbor was the greatest thing,
And were truly loved no doubt.

But now these sturdy pioneers,
Are fading fast away;
So may the present generation,
Think of them and say.

We salute you pioneers,
For a task so ably done;
And may we carry on the motto,
One for all and all for one."

But somehow now it seems,
This idea has ebbed away;
The local community has come and gone,
And modernization is here to stay.

October 1976

THE GOOD OLD TIMES

Fifty years have come and gone,
Since I can remember when;
Those were the days when I was young,
And much has changed since then.

A pioneer house,
Brought out from the East;
'Twas cold and paintless,
To say the least.

Of grey felt paper,
The memory still lingers;
It showed not the smears,
Of my baby fingers.

A coal oil lamp,
With base of red;
A smoky glass,
But light it shed.

The old wood stove,
Where we baked our bread;
When the oven got hot,
The top got red.

The aroma of,
The burning wood;
Made the food you ate,
Taste twice as good.

An Atwater Kent radio,
Sat on the shelf;
Had a six-volt battery,
To power itself.

Three tuning dials,
And two sets of earphones;
A big metal horn,
With a wonderful tone.

The songs of Wilf Carter,
At six in the morn;
I rose very early,
To hear thru the horn.

251

In a big barrel churn,
Our butter we made;
It wasn't worth much,
But on groceries we'd trade.

A William's sewing machine,
From ages past;
It settled itself,
In a museum at last.

There was the old telephone,
Where the crank you'd turn;
And you'd listen in,
The news to learn.

Then there was the extension,
That you hooked up to the fence;
Using radio earphones,
With very little expense.

There were eaves trough on the roof,
And the rain ran out a spout;
We'd watch our own reflection,
As into the barrel we'd shout.

A wooden pump,
Out in the house yard;
It always squeaked,
When you pumped hard.

The smoking old lantern,
Hung in the straw barn;
While you milked the cow,
With the crumpled horn.

The horses ate,
Their measure of food;
While to harness them,
On the manger I stood.

A hen walked by,
On footless legs;
But she very kindly,
Still laid eggs.

A mother cat,
Of nigh twenty years;
When Puss-in-Boots died,
I shed some tears.

A poor milk cow,
Who slipped and fell;
But in three long months,
I nursed her well.

The old water trough,
By the pump house stood;
Where we dipped many a hen,
We wished not to brood.

A pump and a jack,
To fill this tank;
But an old gas engine,
You must really crank.

A skating rink,
By the old barn well;
You worked like blazes,
And played like hell.

Boughten hockey sticks,
Cost quite a lot;
So the old scoop shovel,
The goalie got.

An old gray mare,
We drove to school;
She could bite like a dog,
And run like a fool.

Then an Indian pony,
We bought for seven bucks;
Us kids thought that we,
Had all the luck.

So ski we must,
And toboggan too;
Life was great,
I'm really telling you.

But the pony died,
In depression years;
Lack of good grass,
And I again shed tears.

In a two wheeled Eaton cart,
We traveled down the road;
To that one roomed country school,
Where we studied the teacher's code.

A high wheeled wagon,
And one of steel;
They were very useful,
But the bumps you'd feel.

Pickling grain with formaline,
So shovel it you must;
The smell of it was terrible,
And my back it nearly burst.

A half bushel measure,
For filling the drill;
You counted them carefully,
And none you dared spill.

A Van Brunt drill,
On the box we'd sit;
While four sturdy horses,
Walked straight with it.

Picking stones,
With team, chain and boat;
With a crowbar and shovel,
To dig them out.

A binder pulled,
By horses four;
While sheaves rolled thru,
The knotter for sure.

Oat bundles,
In a cone shaped stack;
With a three tined fork,
And many bends of the back.

A threshing machine,
Run by gas or steam;
With many a man,
And many a team.

An old Ford car,
With narrow wheels;
Kept right on running,
Despite the squeals.

Then a Chev sedan,
With windows made of glass;
A twenty-seven model,
We really had some class.

There were only minor changes,
In the thirties as you know;
Times were hard and money scarce,
There was no place but down to go.

But with the coming of the war,
Money flowed more free;
The farming lifestyle changed a lot,
So up it went you see.

And now we are real modern,
But are we yet more free;
For all these modern gadgets,
Must be paid for, don't you see.

November 1976

I MET A FRIEND

I met a friend the other day,
I hadn't seen for years;
'Twas very good to meet again,
But we've changed a mite I fear.

We talked a bit and laughed a bit,
And had a cup of tea;
A very delightful time you know,
For both of us you see.

We must discuss the by gone times,
When both of us were young;
Of all the tricks we used to pull,
And the things we did for fun.

We spoke of the days when times were hard,
And our money we must make;
We snared the gophers on a string,
And tails for a penny take.

Things were less expensive then,
A nickel bought a lot;
We made our fun amongst ourselves,
And hung on to what we got.

We wore our clothes with patches on,
And didn't seem to mind;
People were more friendly then,
Than in good times you'll find.

We didn't seem to mind a bit,
To eat what we could grow;
For store bought stuff was mighty scarce,
When we were young you know.

We had not time to run around,
The way the young do now;
We stayed at home to do our work,
With beads of sweat upon our brow.

We talked of school and education,
The difference twixt then and now;
Of all the advantages that we had,
That the moderns can't see somehow.

Now it was fun to reminisce,
Back to when we were young;
Although our hearts are just as gay,
I'm afraid our knees are sprung.

Our hair it needs a spot of dye,
Our figures changed a bit;
We've got a wrinkle here or there,
But our brain is very fit.

What I really wonder is,
Will the youngsters of today;
Look back with longing memories,
When fifty years have passed away?

Will they be as fit and healthy,
Or even just alive;
For in these days of progress,
It's hard just to survive.

November 1976

WHEN ITS SPRINGTIME IN SASKATCHEWAN

When its springtime in Saskatchewan,
And the fields are turning green;
It is the most delightful place,
That I have ever seen.

The little lambs are bleating,
The calves are skipping high;
Its lovely in Saskatchewan,
Beneath a bright blue sky.

The mooley cow is nibbling,
At all the tender shoots;
Enjoying springtime greatly,
I "dinna hae ma doots".

The little colts are frisking,
Near their mothers' side;
It's glad I am! Saskatchewan,
Is the place I doth reside.

The tiny yellow chickens,
Run helter skelter thru the grass;
While mother hen is watching,
To let nothing them harass.

The noble rooster stands and crows,
The gobbler, gobbles loud;
When its springtime in Saskatchewan,
Under skies without a cloud.

And then there are the kittens,
In the hay stack in a hole;
While mother cat is stalking,
The gopher on his prairie knoll.

The baby pigs are squealing,
As a lineup they doth form;
When its springtime in Saskatchewan,
It's usually nice and warm.

The frogs are croaking loudly,
As the setting sun goes down;
And many reeds are shooting up,
From out their bulbous crown.

Many little balls of fluff,
On Saskatchewan sloughs abide;
While other of their feathered friends,
In the nearby bush reside.

There's the crocus and the dandelion,
The bluebell and buttercup;
Let us know that in Saskatchewan,
Winter time has given up.

So now you see Saskatchewan,
Is a busy place in Spring;
It's not just nature in high gear,
But man too must do his thing.

November 1976

FARMERS AROUND THE WORLD

A farmer has his dignity,
That he surely must uphold;
He's the most important sector,
Of society I'm told.

He must work to earn his living,
And raise his family;
And supply a multitude of foodstuffs,
For the rest of humanity.

For what could we do without him,
In any part of the world;
He's the backbone of the nation,
Where e'er its flag is unfurled.

He's a man of many colors,
And languages quite a few;
His nationality matters not,
It's his products which we view.

Now there's the wheat from Canada,
And oranges from Japan;
Cotton from America,
Or peanuts from Siam.

There's tea from out of India,
There's coffee from Brazil;
There's sheep from down New Zealand way,
That pasture on the hill.

There's palm oil from Nigeria,
Or even little Zaire;
There's cattle from around the world,
To make one stand and stare.

There's spices from Indonesia,
Castor oil from Sudan;
Flax from out of Russia,
And sugar beets from Iran.

Turkey has its olives,
France is noted for its wine;
North America grows tobacco,
Which is really very fine.

There is hemp seed grown in India,
And feed grains in many lands;
There are date palms on the deserts,
Across the burning sands.

Now all products need caretakers,
When and where they're grown;
He may have different outlooks,
But as a farmer he is known.

Now all you city dwellers,
Look on him not with disdain;
For without the diversified farmer,
Your lives would be in vain.

December 1976

ABANDONMENT

I drove down the busy highway,
Thru the sand hills heading north;
I watched the many old abodes,
For all that I was worth.

There were many old abandoned homes,
In a state of deep decay;
Along that winding black topped road,
That we passed that summer day.

Built in the days when the west was young,
By the sturdy pioneer;
On a homestead quarter to protect,
The ones we held most dear.

Built of logs so straight and small,
And then chinked up with clay;
We look on them with distaste now,
But they were a palace in their day.

There was one I especially noted,
No doubt built with love and care;
It made me stop and wonder,
Who had resided there.

Was it a happy family,
Who lived there years ago;
Or was sadness and sorrow present,
Perhaps we'll never know.

I like to think of a man and wife,
With children two or three;
Living there in comfort,
As a happy family.

But no doubt the Great Depression,
Caused them to move elsewhere;
Leaving their beloved home,
At which others only stare.

The windows are all broken now,
The clay has all dropped out;
It makes one stop and wonder,
What the depression was about.

And then when times improved again,
The larger farms took over;
But the memories of the departed ones,
Will stay close by forever.

November 1976

BLENDED HERITAGE

They came into this new land,
This barren land, this free land;
They came from other provinces,
They came across the sea.

They settled in this new land,
They worked hard in this free land;
They brought from other countries,
Their "Heritage" you see.

They brought along their languages,
Their customs and their pride;
Many came as bachelors,
Others brought with them a bride.

Some brought equipment with them,
To break the virgin sod;
Some brought their cross and Bible,
To keep in touch with God.

They moved in by cart and wagon,
On foot, by ox or horse;
They adjusted to the hardships,
As just a matter of course.

They struggled on together,
Some made the grade we know;
But some were not so hardy,
And the hardships caused them to go.

The ones who stayed were hardy,
With gumption, guts and gall;
With brains and brawn and backbone,
And even that's not all.

They worked with horse and oxen,
Lived in shanty, house or shack;
They kept right on looking forward,
Refusing to turn back.

They progressed ever onward,
Thru winter storm and summer sun;
They shared their work and worry,
And united in their fun.

Ad there were many little children,
Whom we know were born at home;
For doctors too were very scarce,
And penicillin was unknown.

Now it is these little children,
Who are living here today;
Regardless of our race or creed,
I guess we're here to stay.

But the succeeding generations,
Are more footloose and fancy free;
They stay a bit and then move on,
To bigger things you see.

And the many little homesteads,
From those far off bygone days;
Are now big farming units,
To make modernization pay.

December 7 & 8, 1976

CHRISTMAS AT FIVE

Now what do you like about Christmas?
Was asked of a boy of five;
Being a bright little fellow,
Here was his reply.

I start looking for Christmas,
When the catalogue comes in the mail;
And I write a letter to Santa,
Knowing he'll never fail.

Then I start asking mommy,
"How far is Christmas away?"
And she very casually tells me,
December twenty-fifth is the big day.

But I will wait very patiently,
Still asking every day;
"Is Christmas getting closer?"
Or is it still far, far away.

I see the toys and goodies,
In the many stores where I go;
"Is Christmas getting closer,"
I'd really like to know.

Then the bigger boys and girls,
Are complaining of their tests;
So I know that Christmas is closer,
That big day, that is the best.

Then comes their Christmas concert,
With songs and dance and all;
With recitations for the younger ones,
Then Santa comes to call.

With jingling bells and Ho! Ho! Ho!
With a smile on every face;
A bag of candy he'll pass out,
To each child in the place.

Now this little boy inquires,
"Was that really Santa Claus?"
No! just one of his many helpers,
Mother says without a pause.

The little boy would like to know,
"How much longer must I wait?"
Just a few days now says mother,
As she starts into bake.

And of course wee Bobby,
Has many things to do;
As the older kids are home from school,
Skating and sleighing, too.

And then there's decorating,
And that sweet smelling tree;
Must all be hung and put in place,
For everyone to see.

Now at last it's Christmas eve,
And excitement is in the air;
Off to bed the children go,
And say a little prayer.

Now that little boy of five,
Can hardly go to sleep;
Santa seems to keep appearing,
While he's busy counting sheep.

At last the angel Sleep takes over,
And he nods his little head;
Then we tuck him in snugly,
In his little trundle bed.

Next morning very early,
Before the adults are awake;
Those tiny footsteps patter down,
Yet no sounds do they make.

But when he reached the parlor,
And saw the presents beneath the tree;
The yell he gave from his wee throat,
Would wake the dead you see.

For there before his very eyes,
Were parcels piled high;
To a little tyke just five years old,
They seemed to reach the sky.

The excitement and the happiness,
That spread across his face;
Was enough to restore our faith,
In all the human race.

December 1976

OUT BACK

Away out back,
In a tree lined lot;
Is a little house,
We have near forgot.

It stands so sturdy,
Straight and tall;
With no paint left,
On it at all.

The boards are weathered,
Warped and grey;
It has surely seen,
A better day.

It contains a seat,
With holes for two;
The adult size,
And one for children, too.

A box or nail,
Is located there;
An Eaton's catalogue,
For all to share.

You may study,
While you sit;
If needs must be,
You wait a bit.

But that little house,
Is feeling low;
And the catalogue,
Is gone you know.

But it waits and wonders,
About the jerks;
Who have installed,
The waterworks.

But we leave it there,
Just in case of need;
For it has been useful,
Yes! indeed.

And a swallow' s nest,
Sets above the door;
Shows it's not forgotten,
For evermore.

January 1977

268

ME, MYSELF AND I

Can I look at myself in the mirror,
And say that I like what I see;
Can I look myself straight in the eye,
And say, "I'm proud of me".

Can I look my neighbor straight in the face,
And say I've done him no wrong;
Can I rise in the morning with nary a grouch,
And give to the world a song.

Can I talk to myself of things I've done,
And would I do them the same again;
Can I look back to days gone by,
Without sadness, sorrow or pain.

Do I have a guilty conscience,
About those whom I have wronged;
Or do I feel all's right with the world,
As I follow life's pathway along.

Can I talk to myself and not feel guilty,
For things I should have done;
Can I look at how I played life's game,
And say that I have won.

Can I look ahead and see for myself,
A life free from worry and care;
If these I can do without failing myself,
Then a mansion in heaven I'll share.

December 1976 - January 1977

SUGAR IN 1974

Sugar, sugar, sugar the dear sweet stuff,
Is something that we somehow need;
First we look at the quoted price,
Then search our pocket book indeed.

In December of seventy-four,
It reached an all time high;
At eighteen-seventy for twenty-five,
It really hit the sky.

That's three quarters of a hundred bucks,
For just one hundred weight;
At this rate of rise in price,
Inflation can't be beat.

You may say just substitute,
With another form of sweet;
But somehow that gritty white stuff,
Really can't be beat.

Then there is the brown kind,
Whose price is just as high;
We cut the amount we bake with,
In hopes we don't have to buy.

And there is the icing kind,
Which we spread mighty thin;
So you can see the cake peek out,
Instead of us peek in.

Then there is the cube sugar,
Whose price is too, too high;
We drop one in our coffee cup,
And for the second give a sigh.

Cake and cookies, pies and tarts,
We used to bake full fare;
But on the sugar can is marked,
"Expensive", there's none to spare.

There's lots of sugar on the shelf,
But the price is out of reach;
Somehow it keeps on rising,
No matter how we screech.

Now what I'd really like to know,
Is why we cannot grow the beet;
Set up our own refining plant,
And make our sugar sweet.

Now we can grow that very same beet,
To feed our pigs and cows;
So why can't we extract that juice,
For human food somehow.

I know that it is readily done,
In Alberta's sunny south;
Why can't Saskatchewan do the same,
And promote industrial growth.

Besides it's full of strength and energy,
And its taste you can't excel;
It gives you vim, vigor and vitality,
And helps to keep us well.

January 1977

271

IN MEMORIAM

Here's to a school that's come and gone,
On a prairie road in the west;
A lonely little white schoolhouse,
That stood up to the test.

On the corner of section one and four,
Near the center of the east side;
Was where our little school house stood,
And some of the teachers did reside.

Now it was built in thirty-four,
When times were hard and wages low;
But it was a dire necessity,
As our children had no where else to go.

Now many nationalities,
Agreed to co-operate;
To build a learning center,
Their children to educate.

"Twas in the year of thirty-five,
She opened up her door;
For twenty-five years she stood there,
Their young minds to explore.

'Twas in the year of sixty-one,
The unit rang her death knell;
We could not keep her open,
Although we fought like hell.

Now twenty teachers sat thy throne,
Thru depression years and on;
With forty-eight pupils in they seats,
Most all of them now gone.

Oh yes! she still is useful,
As a farmer's garage and shop;
But in line of moral prestige,
It's really quite a drop.

The teacherage too was moved away,
To make a neighbor's home;
So we have but the school yard left,
All else is sold and gone.

Now weep ye not old schoolyard,
Tho everything else is gone;
No doubt fond memories linger,
In the hearts of everyone.

January 1977

'TIS SPRING, 'TIS SPRING

The other day along the road,
I saw an early sign of spring;
There stood an old pappa gopher,
Doing his best to chirp and sing.

The wind was rather chilly,
And the snow was pretty deep;
But he was doing his very best,
His spring spirits to upkeep.

He stood erect and crossed his paws,
Looking like an aggressive male;
And as we drove on down the road,
He flicked his bushy tail.

But when passing two days later,
I felt pangs of sad remorse;
For there beside his winter exit,
Lay his stiffened little corpse.

A car had done the dirty deed,
Was it an accident, is the thing?
But a brave heart had ceased to beat,
For announcing, "It was Spring".

Spring 1977

274

HIS MAJESTY

The Old Bull stood on the crest of the hill,
To survey his lowing herd;
He looked at them with love in his heart,
And thought of the tales he'd heard.

When cattle prices had gone sky high,
His harem had increased;
He had to work from morn till night,
His duties never ceased.

For the government paid a subsidy,
To keep the calves you know;
And somehow or other,
They always seem to grow.

And then of course when prices fell,
The farmer's in a bind;
He can't decide if he should sell us all,
As we're putting him behind.

But with his determination,
He'll hold on a while yet;
In hopes a decent living,
From my offspring he will get.

Now they are importing,
Some of the exotic breeds;
Trying to acquire more red meat,
For the consumer needs.

But my sleek black hide and stamina,
I'll not let them ignore;
There's a lot of little black calves yet,
As in the days of yore.

Now there's artificial insemination,
Which is really all the go;
But it's far more expensive,
And a lot more work you know.

So why not let me just run at large,
I'll do my best you know;
I'll be a lot more safe and sure,
Then the test tube kind they grow.

And then they have the transplants,
Which eliminates us guys;
But I think we'll bide our time,
As the cost is pretty high.

I used to rule the rangeland,
Like the sturdy buffalo;
But grain is taking over,
So one of us may have to go.

Now I have studied the pro's and con's,
Of my use in the prairie west;
And despite this modernization,
I'll continue to do my best.

You may talk about modern trends,
Of which these days are full;
But when it comes to propagation,
I'm still a lot of bull.

Spring 1977

PRAIRIE PICTURE

A little white house on a hillside,
A dusty trail past the door;
A little log barn and a quarter of land,
Now who could ask for more.

A team of horses, large and strong,
A well-shined walking plow;
A garden plot and a flowing well,
And a fence around the old milk cow.

A mother pig in a little pen,
Some piglets fat and pink;
A dozen hens in a house of their own,
And a mother cat as quick as a wink.

A collie dog to act as guard,
As he sleeps beneath the tree;
His eyes are closed but his ears alert,
All dangers he will see.

A healthy family inside the door,
A mother and children three;
Two little rooms both snug and warm,
Fixed up for the world to see.

The sun shines most every day,
And the rain seems to come in time;
This little house 'neath the prairie sky,
Is a dwelling that's most divine.

The winter winds are mighty fierce,
And wild are the winter storms;
But the occupants of the little white house,
Are always snug and warm.

They tend their stock with loving care,
And wait for spring to come;
They respect their neighbors, and pay their bills,
And count their blessings, one by one.

Now is not this the way to live,
Independent and carefree;
No one to dictate what you do.
Your on your own, you see.

January 1977

THE NORTHERN LIGHTS

The Northern Lights are dancing,
Across the northern dome;
Like Santa's reindeer prancing,
On their journey back home.

I stood and watched in wonderment,
As they kept marching by;
Ribbons of silver, green and red,
Across the northern sky.

They stopped not a single moment,
Vibrating as they went;
Far greater then the works of man,
Their beauty was Heaven sent.

We know not when they'll come there,
Nor how long they'll stay;
But like a flash of lightning,
They quickly pass away.

One moment their exploding,
Like fireworks at the fair;
Then only seconds later,
There is nothing there.

Many shades and tints and hues,
Flit rapidly across the sky;
Twisting like a serpent's tail,
While stars twinkle up on high.

We stand there feeling pretty small,
And gaze at the array;
Marveling at how they disappear,
Yet wishing they would stay.

January 1977

PARENTS

Parents are only children,
Who have older grown;
Who now reside as man and wife,
With children of their own.

Now none of them are perfect,
And no doubt they ever were;
Just because they want you to be,
Just shows that they care.

Now you think that they are grouchy,
And abuse you, yes you do;
But if you only stop and think,
It shows they care for you.

And then there are the times,
That neglected, you think you are;
But if they gave you everything,
Your later life they mar.

They will not give you everything,
That your buddies have you know;
They think that if you do without,
It will help you morals grow.

That if you learn to bank your pennies,
When you are very small;
That when you've become an adult,
Into a savings plan you'll fall.

Now you must learn some manners,
Be not greedy, vulgar or impolite;
Learn to resist when others pick,
But don't be the one to start the fight.

Wear not a chip upon your shoulder,
Nor yellow down your back;
Learn to pull your weight with others,
And be not accused of being slack.

Be not lazy at your small tasks,
And what you do, do well;
Hold up your end in the way of work,
But take time to play a spell.

Be honest with those about you,
And to yourself be true;
Trust those who prove trustworthy,
And your friends will believe in you.

These are the basic principles,
Your parents try to teach;
And if you'll only listen,
The stars you'll surely reach.

March 1977

HISTORY OF WHEAT

Now Canada has an industry,
Considered one of the best;
And much of it is grown,
Out in the prairie west.

If we look back to times gone by,
When with a stick they tilled the sod;
Thus wheat was grown by the hands of man,
And with the help of God.

For the Apostle in the Bible said,
"As you sow; so shall you reap";
And this applies in many ways,
As well as growing wheat.

Now man cannot live by meat alone,
And so he needs his bread;
Thus Canada's grain growing industry,
It's now world wide, it's said.

But wheat itself has been harvested,
For nigh six thousand years;
Neolithic man did grow it,
To quell his hunger fears.

Then to Egypt, Palestine and China,
The use of flour spread;
For too these hungry nations,
Liked to have their bread.

We hear it mentioned in the Bible,
As the basic food of man;
Jesus used it along with fish,
To feed a mighty clan.

And when the hungry Caananites,
Out from Egypt went;
It was wheat as well as corn,
That Joseph with his brothers sent.

They found some in Egyptian tombs,
Placed there to aid the dead;
For no matter where he went,
The pharaoh must have his bread.

It traveled to the Indies,
When Columbus came from Spain;
And in the year of fourteen ninety-four,
They grew a crop of grain.

Then on into old Mexico,
In the year of fifteen ten;
It stayed there for a while,
Then it spread on again.

The first wheat grown in Canada,
Was in the year of sixteen ought five;
At Port Royal, Nova Scotia,
The project came alive.

Then it spread into Quebec,
And eastern parts of the U.S.A.;
But it was quite awhile,
Before westward it came to stay.

They tried growing wheat at Selkirk,
For many and many a year;
Suffering from warriors, frost and locusts,
Also pigeons, floods and mice, I fear.

But with Scotch determination,
They tried and tried again;
And in the end succeeded,
In growing a fair amount of grain.

Now it became a permanent project,
To improve the breeds of wheat;
Scientists met with disappointments,
But would not admit defeat.

And David Fife a farmer,
Down in old Ontario;
Was testing grain for milling,
And how good that it would grow.

And when he needed breeding seed,
A friend in Glasgow he wrote;
Who in the lining of his hat,
Pilfered some from a Danzig boat.

He mailed them here to Canada,
As foundation seed;
And it became the grandparents of,
The widespread Red Fife breed.

It was from a single seed,
Originating from these few;
After many, many setbacks,
An outstanding breed he grew.

For there were many breeds of wheat,
From which they had to choose;
But Saunders struck the jackpot,
And found he couldn't lose.

A plant of Hard Red Calcutta,
He crossed with one of Red Fife;
The resulting plant named Marquis,
A boon to the farmer's life.

They kept the milling qualities,
Of the Red Fife as you know;
The Calcutta cut the season,
But ten days for it to grow.

So in the year of nineteen-ten,
The new breed was released;
And with this new wheat called Marquis,
The threat of frost was beat.

There were many other varieties,
As Prelude, Ruby and Pioneer;
Red Bobs, Garnet and Reward,
But Marquis topped them all I fear.

But Marquis had a failing too,
As rust it could not stand;
So now they must develop,
A new grain for this land.

In thirty-five they licensed Thatcher,
Which came from the U.S.A.;
Followed by Apex, Regent, Renown and Redman,
Canadian contributions here to stay.

But the rust was mighty ornery,
And a cousin rust moved in you see;
So they must find a counter actant,
To the strain of 15B.

They needs must go to work again.
At the plant breeding game;
They found the answer at Winnipeg,
And Selkirk was its name.

And other breeds have been developed,
With improvements quite a few;
As Pempia, Napayo and Sinton,
Neepawa and Manitor, too.

So things have changed immensely,
Since the first wheat plant came up;
In fact it might have been here,
When Adam was a pup.

But the farmer like the scientist,
Never knows when to give in;
So he will keep on trying,
And leading with his chin.

But now these prairie provinces,
In Canada's mid-west,
Grow many thousand bushels,
And its quality is the best.

For Saskatchewan is the center part,
Of the "Bread Basket" of the west;
With acres and acres of grain growing land,
And soil that's the very best.

We send many kinds of grain,
To our ports both east and west;
Of the highest milling quality,
And grades that stand the test.

But to grow this world needed foodstuff,
We must have sunshine and rain;
So let us say unto the Lord,
"Help us grow this needed grain".

But when we get those bumper crops,
We can't sell it as you know;
There's millions starving in the world,
But we have quotas to stay below.

So our grain it lies in piles,
Or else sits in the bin;
While our expenses pile up,
With no income coming in.

But this is just one problem
Of wheat growing in the west;
And some how we will survive it,
As we have all the rest.

Fall 1977

PUNISHMENT

Times have changed an awful lot,
Since the days when I was young;
For on a nail, behind the door,
Was where the Razor Strap was hung.

Now each mischievous boy or girl,
With mischief, went so far;
Then father deftly walked across,
And pulled the door ajar.

A few well laid swats across,
Their little plump behind;
Would change their line of reasoning,
Within this mischievous mind.

And somehow or other,
As on that strap, I do reflect;
It made children treat their elders,
With all care and due respect.

But now, somehow or other,
That strap has passed away;
And many naughty children,
Go merrily on their way.

And then, we had the woodshed,
A little ways outback;
Of wood to pile, and switches,
There wasn't any lack.

But this too, has passed away,
With the advent of the power;
Father has no weapons now,
To make their boyhood flower.

The hairbrush also played a part,
To keep the young in line;
But it too is losing out,
With the inflation climb.

For father's hair, is thinning,
So a brush he doesn't need;
So many a wayward youngster,
Has taken to using weed.

Now if we had sufficient work,
To keep these boys and girls in line;
They'd grow up big and strong,
With morals mighty fine.

But with less work, for them to do,
And punishment, near extinct;
How can we correct their faults,
Or make them stop and think.

January 1978

GOOD-BYE EDMONTON -HELLO BUFFALO

Along the bus route heading out,
Not far from the city lights;
Right along the black top road,
I saw a wonderous sight.

A herd of noble animals,
Large, small and in-between;
It was the greatest wildlife,
That I have ever seen.

I would say nigh two hundred,
Beasts of this noble breed;
Stood there, peacefully grazing,
What a wonderous sight indeed.

They stood contentedly in the snow,
Behind a fence of wire;
Just as if the "Good Lord" meant,
That they should peacefully retire.

It's hard to believe these noble beasts,
Roamed the plains at will;
That they were a common sight,
But an easy prey to kill.

They served the native peoples for,
Their food and clothing needs;
For without this noble beasty,
Life would have been hard indeed.

But then the buffalo hunter,
Moved in to slaughter free;
Taking only hides for sale,
Wasting a lot you see.

And with the advance of civilization,
The buffalo became quite rare;
They were in danger of extinction,
And no one seemed to care.

But the government took over,
When they became too few;
Setting up the game preserve,
Their numbers to renew.

As the leader stood in watchful silence,
Observing the world go by;
I saw him shake his massive head,
With a tear-drop in his eye.

For that large land, that free land,
Of which they were the peers;
But brought his near extinction,
In just two hundred years.

So now this wild animal,
Lives in partial domestication;
I wonder if his mind returns,
To that far-off civilization.

February 1978

FROM ON THE SIDE OF THE ROAD

I sat by the side of the dusty road,
And I watched the world go by;
The hill was high, and the sun was hot,
And I heaved a sleepy sigh.
Like a picture before my very eyes,
I saw each one's life go by,
There were visions of loving and giving,
And some of sadness and fury.

I saw a lonely trucker,
Wishing he were home;
Awaiting him was a lovely bride,
Very much alone.
She was hoping and praying,
As she had always done;
That he would make it safe and sound,
As this was his last run.
But somehow or other,
Fate took a hand they say;
And on this lonely mountain road,
He lost his life that day.

Next there came a bus load,
Of children full of fun;
On their way to the sunny beach,
I visioned, I was one.
We dove, we swan, we walked and ran,
Then rested while we ate;
It took me back, to days long gone,
When I was near their age.
How great it was to be young again,
With never a worry or care;
So for their health and happiness,
I said a silent prayer.

Next there came a cadallac,
All shined up in great array;
I visioned therein a wealthy man,
Who's hair was turning gray.
He was just a passing stranger,
Who lived no-where around;
I hoped he had a happy home,
At wherever he was bound.

Soon a half ton came in view,
Driving at full speed;
I knew that by the risks he took,
It was a time of need.
Now the lady was in labor,
And his nerves were mighty bare;
So while they sped quickly onward,
For them I said a prayer.
And years later when I saw them,
Their children numbered four;
So my prayers must have been answered,
"To keep happiness in store".

Then over the brink of the hill,
Came a roadster at full speed;
He was taking many risks,
A dangerous life indeed.
But then I saw the reason,
It was flight he had in mind;
With siren screaming shrilly,
The cop car came behind.
And there before my very eyes,
A wanted man was taken;
I know it is a way of life,
But it left me a little shaken.

There was that monster transport,
Which took the hill too fast;
And when he reached the bottom,
It was to be his last.
For far and wide beyond the curve,
His contents were thrown out;
But the van went down the canyon,
And the driver died no doubt.

And next came that little car,
With tin cans on behind;
The latest local bride and groom,
With happiness in mind.
I saw ahead nigh twenty years,
And a family large they had;
Their finances were not very great,
But what a lovely Mom and Dad.
Six children blessed their happy home,
All well and fair of face;
A lad and lass of great respect,
A credit to our race.

And of course there was the farmer,
In his greasy overall;
Driving quickly down the road,
As if he had no time at all.
He needs must get a quick repair,
And get right back to work;
For the farmer is a busy man,
And his duties must not shirk.
But I envisioned as he passed,
His rush was all in vain;
For by the time fall rolled around,
He'd be in debt again.

Next around the upper curve,
Came an ambulance full speed;
There had been an accident,
A dreadful thing indeed.
They were rushing three survivors,
To the hospital you know;
I prayed they'd make it safely,
As they had not far to go.
But of those who still remain,
On that curve not far away;
Two would never rise again,
Mangled to death they lay.

Now across the road stood a little house,
I know it wasn't grand;
But it housed a pair of loving hearts,
Some of the best, in this hilly land.
They had pioneered the area,
Where now the roadway ran;
It was but then a wilderness,
Uninhabited by man.
Now they watched, as the world went by,
And somehow it made them glum;
They often wished that they were back,
As in the days when they were young.

They liked it when their little haven,
Lay in the sunshine bright;
Where quietness and peace remained,
Throughout both day and night.
There was none of this hurry-scurry,
Nor all this rush and speed;
If they could but turn back the clock,
And forget this modern creed.
And live a life of quietness,
Relaxation, love and care;
Then their happiness would be complete,
Knowing God was in charge up there.

Now I awoke from my daytime dream,
Glad that everything was fine;
And saw the traffic driving by,
In a straight and narrow line.
I heaved a sigh, and rose to go,
But I glanced across the way;
The little house stood in solitude,
For its folks had moved away.

You see I had been dreaming of,
The happiness a few years back;
For now the hill had been removed,
And the road was, straight and wide and black.
There are traffic signs along the road,
And policemen on patrol;
Speed limits have been cut a bit,
To help drivers reach their goal.

June 1979

GRANDPARENTS

Grandparents are just parents,
Who have older grown;
Their hair is gray and their step has slowed,
For, they've raised children of their own.

They are a great connecting link,
T'wixt the present and the past;
And always have a tale to tell,
If only they are asked.

If one would just sit and discuss,
The times when they were young;
Of how they worked to raise their kids,
And what they did for fun.

Of what a nickel bought back then,
And what they did without;
Of how they spent their leisure time,
They lacked of it no doubt.

Of how they had to change their plans,
When children came along;
Of how they had to scrimp and save,
Whenever things went wrong.

For there was hail and frost and drought,
In those days, same as now;
And no insurance to cover it,
But they made out somehow.

For they were made of sterner stuff,
That knew not the word give in;
If one walked out, on wife or kids,
It was a cardinal sin.

Of how they lived a rugged life,
Respecting the Lord I vow;
I think they led more moral lives,
Than even we do now.

How they watch their children's children,
And relive when they were small;
Times may have changed an awful lot,
But that matters not at all.

As long as love abides within,
Those hearts both young and old;
It is a blessing for them both,
And a treasure to behold.

So let us respect these older folk,
And listen to what they tell;
For when we have older grown,
Will we do near as well?

June 1979

TO A COUNTRY GRAVEYARD

I wandered down the lonely road,
On a sunny day in June;
My thoughts were reaching back in time,
And then I heard a tune.

It took me back still further,
To when the west was young;
Of how our forefathers, lived and died,
And of how our inheritance begun.

T'was then I saw the graveyard,
On a flat-top, gravel knoll;
Had any of its inhabitants,
Ever reached their goal.

Beneath that time worn wooden cross,
Lies a mother and her twins;
The "Good Lord" took them to his home,
When diphtheria had set in.

And then there was the pioneer,
Who died, drug by a horse;
The gophers have his grave invaded,
Just as a matter of course.

Not far away is a hand carved stone,
Taken from a near-by field;
To a loving husband and father,
Who by an accident was killed.

Nearby we see a tiny grave,
Of a babe who died at birth;
His parents never really knew him,
As he had so little time on earth.

And of course there are the head stones,
Of those older folk that died,
From overwork and under care,
But with a lot of pride.

And if we look a little closer,
Many plots, no name doth bear;
Some were never known,
And some folks, just don't care.

Some markers vandals have destroyed,
Desecrating a sacred plot;
Destroying the back bone of our heritage,
Which we should respect, a lot.

Some graves are sinking downward,
Some crosses stand awry;
Is this the way to treat our forefathers,
Who for us, so bravely lived and died.

Now there are some artistic works,
Within these acreage's small;
Which show all were not thoughtless,
And our relatives to recall.

So present generation,
Think your thoughts a few;
T'is not that many "swiftly passing" years,
Till you'll reside there too.

Summer 1981

FALL

The hoar frost glistens on the grass,
As the morning sun doth rise;
Soon, it too will pass away,
Before my very eyes.

The mallard ducks and wild geese,
You know, are feeding in the grain;
To fatten up, and wend their way,
To the south again.

And the chippy little gopher,
His appearance, is more rare;
For he is busy storing food;
For his winter fare.

The trees have turned a russet brown,
After last week's green and gold;
The sap is slowly settling down,
As each daylight hour unfolds.

The fall winds too are rising,
And brisk breezes fill the air;
Pine and spruce are all that's left,
For the wildlife to share.

Most of the songbirds left us,
A week or so ago;
For seeds are all that doth remain,
For bill of fare you know.

The ants and bugs and butterflies,
Have vanished with the frost;
Some have crawled beneath the dirt,
But many lives were lost.

The green grass too has ripened up,
In shades of brown and tan;
And all the little flowers,
Have completed their life span.

But if you watch very carefully,
You'll see the odd cocoon;
The funny little caterpillar,
Has set up his winter room.

The muskrat and the beaver,
Are busy as can be;
For one must work, so one can live,
Nothing in this world is free.

Now this is mating season,
For many of the mammal clan;
They are alert and watchful,
For any sign of man.

As much of their protection,
Has fallen with the wind;
Then comes hibernation,
Before the cold winter sets in.

The world around looks barren,
Fog rolls in, then snow;
But mother nature, guides her children,
So some may survive you know.

October 1981

TO A MOUNTAIN

I stood and stared at the mountain,
How near it seemed to be;
Yet it was miles distant,
As it is so immense, you see.

T'was in the long lost era,
That upheaval, came to pass;
When there were only bugs and worms,
A crawling through the grass.

For when Mother Nature takes the notion,
To change her face a bit;
You don't know when, or where,
She will leave a mount or pit.

And then the glacial age moved in,
To rip and cut and tear;
To destroy much of the wildlife,
And stir up some land, for sure.

But then perhaps a dinosaur,
Was standing somewhere near;
But just the same as you or I,
He fled in abject fear.

Wild animals watched the change,
Down thru the years you know;
And grazed along your timberline,
When grass commenced to grow.

And of course, man followed,
With trap line, pack horse and canoe;
And behind came the surveyor,
With his tools and crew.

It was not long until the rails,
Had bridged your wide expanse;
But yet you stand unconquered,
Nature's beauty to enhance.

Many are your glaciers,
Which still rest away up high;
Looking like white floating clouds,
Just below the sky.

But I stand down here and stare at you,
You make one feel so small;
I don't feel I'm any larger then,
The bugs, who in the grass do crawl.

And I realize that you,
Will live on and on and on;
While that in decades very few,
I well be dead and gone.

December 1981

SAILING

The sun was slowly settling,
Across the silvery sea;
As the ship was slowly sailing,
Which sends you, safely south to me.

Softly settled the snow flakes,
Down from the star studded sky;
There'll still be several sad partings,
To separate you and I.

For you are a swanky sailor,
And I'm still, a sailor's lass;
Tho' you are sailing the seven seas,
Your safe return, is all that I ask.

So sail on, my swanky sailor,
Your seven silvery seas;
But be sure my trusty sailor,
You soon sail back to me.

November 1980

I SMILE AND CARRY ON

Years have come, and years have gone,
Since I was young and gay;
I thought not then, that all would change,
And youth be swept away.

But my speed has slowed with passing time,
As I have older grown;
I look not back with discontent,
But I smile and carry on.

My back is bent, my step is slow,
My hair has turned to gray;
No one could guess the aches I feel,
As I smile on today.

My heart, it sometimes skips a beat,
My pressure's getting low;
Sometimes I have to stop and rest,
But I smile as I go.

My legs they ache, my feet they swell,
There are creaks in both my knees;
But still I just keep plodding on,
And smile as I wheeze.

Arthritis is a bug I've got,
My joints are sore and bent;
I try not to let the people know,
That my smile is Heaven sent.

My sight is growing dimmer,
No soft sounds do I hear;
My waist isn't any slimmer;
But a smile, I try to wear.

My skin is getting wrinkled,
My hair becoming thin;
But it's the feeling in my heart,
That lets that smile in.

There's days that I would rather sleep,
Than do the work you know;
But somehow one feels better,
When you smile as you go.

For if you sit and ponder,
About your aches and pains;
That smile soon will disappear,
And what really have you gained.

So take the bit between your teeth,
Lose not from life all fun;
Grab those precious moments,
And just smile and carry on.

August 1980

GAVEL - 1980

Now we the ladies of 234,
To St. Walburg came today;
With the best of Christmas wishes,
We this gavel to give away.

We'd like to send this little gavel,
On its very merry way;
To help it to complete the circuit,
And come back to us someday.

Now the year of 1980,
Is coming to its end;
To your Honored Royal Lady,
This gavel we do send.

Our ladies are like Santa,
To bring you friendship dear;
And may we with God's blessing,
See you again next year.

As we wish you Season's Greetings,
Of friendship, hope and cheer;
And may your Lodge grow stronger,
In the new and prosperous year.

November 1980

ONLY A GRANDMOTHER

"Your only a grandmother", so they say;
But you know you've seen the better days.

Years have passed since you were young,
Times have changed, but you still have fun.

You once were a girl, free from care;
Romping and playing everywhere.

You grew to a day, with style and grace;
A credit to the human race.

Then you were a mother young and gay;
Raising your family, day by day.

But time has a way of traveling on;
Until one's youth has come and gone.

Your hair has turned from brown to gray;
And you travel slower, you often say.

You sometimes think the young don't know;
How much their heart and soul must grow.

To love and learn and carry on;
When you older folk have passed along.

Will they have the guts, the will and pride;
To stand united side by side.

To show their offspring, as you showed them;
How to be graceful ladies, and noble men.

Or will they in this "rat race" of life;
Struggle only for greed and strife.

Climb to the top on souls of friends;
And live for gold to the very end.

Or take the advice of an elder who knows;
It's only love that grows and grows.

March 1981

THE RESCUE

The billowing sea, was like drifting snow,
As it struck the rockbound coast;
The rescue party, had given up hope,
As they feared all lives were lost.

But seven shipwrecked sailors,
Were out in the raging hell;
Struggling to hold onto the wreckage,
As the white-caps rose and fell.

Go out they must, and take the risk,
To save those loved ones dear;
They knew not what lay just ahead,
And their hearts were full of fear.

So the five who took to the sea again,
Were robust, brave and strong;
If "they had not faith" in God above,
They could not last for long.

But faith was strong in each ones heart,
And their boat was strong also;
Their muscles taut, as iron bands,
As the boat bobbed to and for.

Their strength had taken them far enough,
That they saw the wreckage clear;
And when they saw their friends alive,
They overcame their fear.

Ply your oars, with all your might,
Yelled the master of the clan;
We'll make it yet, my sailor boys,
We'll save them every man.

They inched their was across the foam,
Out to that storm doomed boat;
They watched, yet worked with all their might,
And hoped it would stay afloat.

They were very near exhaustion,
When hull met hull you know;
And the seven shipwrecked sailors,
Their death holds, could let go.

They helped them into the small boat,
And headed back for shore;
Where the cheers that greeted them,
Have been recalled, from days of yore.

June 1981

307

CHANGES

The old hawk swooped across the land,
As the evening sun went down;
She looked aghast, at the change there was,
And across her brow a frown.

It was not many years ago,
That she hatched here, young and brave;
Many were the trees then,
The wild life to save.

But both have disappeared now,
And the flowers too have gone;
All is black and barren now,
Which once was soft and green.

She swooped and soared, then rose again,
But she could not understand;
Why all the natural vegetation,
Had been taken from this land.

It seemed to her a dead land,
With no splash or chirp or song;
Where were the birds and animals,
They to were also gone.

The robin and the meadow lark,
The partridge and the wren;
The "squeaky bird", and mallard duck,
Had left the slough and fen.

The sly old fox that we had known,
Had also left his den;
The wily coyote, now where was he,
Not in his usual glen.

The squirrel, the mink and rabbit,
Were as scarce as they could be;
And behold! the beaver dams were gone,
As far as one could see.

The silver brush and willow,
The smell of new mown hay;
Were buried in the blackened sod,
To make modernization pay.

The buttercup and crocus,
The dandelion too;
The old man's beard, and violet,
Were gone to name a few.

But nature's silence was the hardest,
For her to comprehend;
And the noise of modernization,
She did not understand.

1981

DUFFERIN COMMUNITY CLUB

Now we have a little Club,
In number if not size;
As middle age is creeping up,
And some of us, it has passed by.

Most of us have stoutened out,
Since we saw sweet sixteen;
But lets consider all the children,
We've raised in the "in between".

But as we have grown stouter,
Our hearts have grown too;
That's why we do our little thing,
To help others as we do.

They always say give a helping hand,
To help our fellow man;
That's why you see us reaching out,
To do, the little things we can.

We have our monthly meetings,
Do our business, have a chat;
Have a lovely cup of tea,
And converse on this and that.

And by the time the meeting's over,
Some new project has a start;
This year an afghan and a quilt,
Is on what we've set our hearts.

Now we discussed the many patterns,
For our projects as you know;
And with each passing minute,
Our ambition seemed to grow.

So we appointed a committee,
To organize each one;
To sorta boss the others,
And tell them how it should be done.

For we're at the knitting, sewing age,
And try a project every year;
Donate a little here and there,
To bring someone a bit of cheer.

We may be neither young or spry,
But we hold our friends most dear;
And we'd rather sit to do our work,
Than run around I fear.

February, March 1981

310

THRU THE EYES OF A PINE

A pine tree stood by the side of the road,
And it watched the cars go by;
Tall and straight, and very tall,
It gave an ominous sigh.

I started as a little seed,
Before the white man came;
Thru winter storm, and summer heat,
I somehow lived on the same.

I watched the changes come and go,
Since I was a sapling small;
Tall and straight, I grew and grew,
Thru seasons, one and all.

My trunk extends towards Heaven,
My limbs are for the birds;
The rustle of the prairie wind,
Is the sweetest thing I've heard.

I saw the Red men multiply,
And fight against the white;
I saw the buffalo come and go,
It was a terrific sight.

I watched those early settlers,
Hue out their homestead yard;
I was just a little pine tree then,
Who faithfully stood guard.

The highway was not always there,
Of this I know for sure;
For a narrow little prairie trail,
Wandered from door to door.

And with the passing of the years,
I straight and taller grew;
Shading many little children,
And adults quite a few.

But some of those older settlers,'
Left for greater things;
Some reside not far away,
And some have Heavenly wings.

But here I stand, as time moves on,
And pavement runs along my feet;
I look and marvel at the change,
As trucks and cars and buses meet.

There's airplanes, and jets and 'copters,
Flying high up in the air;
I was part of this scenic view,
Before all this was there.

I've stood for years twixt earth and sky,
As a guide, to the race called man;
I'll try my best to carry on,
And the era's of time to span.

November 1981

WINTER'S COMING

October now has rolled around,
And I'm sure that fall's at hand;
The turnips are in the cellar,
And the carrots are in the sand.

The summer fallow blackened,
The fertilizer is spread;
The garden is all cultivated,
And all the plants are dead.

The leaves are falling swiftly,
In shades of red and yellow;
The pumpkin's turned to deepest orange,
And the apples ripe and mellow.

The fruit is in the sealer,
The pickles in there too;
The meat is in the freezer,
So there's not much left to do.

The bales are in the yard,
The sheaves are in the stack;
Everyone is worrying,
When cold weather is coming back.

The cattle are collected,
The corrals are tight and strong;
So we are all waiting,
For winter to come along.

We've hunted out our toque and mitts,
And our coat and boots;
And we've ordered our "Red Flannels",
From a place called "Simpson Sears".

Now that we are well-prepared,
For the winter blast;
It's November on the calendar,
And winter's here at last.

The clouds are growing darker,
And snowflakes fill the air;
The wind is blowing briskly,
So we know that winter's here.

So we suffer thru the winter,
Of blowing winds and drifting snow;
But we have faith in God,
Spring will come again, you know.

December 1981

EVENING EVENTS

As darkness slowly settles down,
And evening falls in place;
It is a time to sit a bit,
For all the human race.

It is the time to stop and think,
Have I accomplished, what I should;
Can I now with conscience clear,
Watch mother nature's mood.

Observe the little things that happen,
At the closing of the day;
How mother hen so carefully,
Tucks her little chicks away.

How many flowers close up tight,
To sleep the dark away;
And little stars come peeping out,
To guide the travelers way.

Then there are the little songbirds,
Who sleep with head beneath their wing;
And the frogs come out at evening,
And with lusty voices sing.

Now Pussy Cat is on the prowl;
In search of a midnight meal;
And the old hound dog is speaking,
To express the way he feels.

How many little butterflies,
Hide away their colors bright;
Before the dusk of evening,
Has faded into night.

The busy little honey bees,
Who come from yonder hive;
Have returned as dusk was falling,
In danger of their lives.

But those pesky wee mosquitoes,
Have flocked out in full force;
And the damage they are doing,
Is hard on man and horse.

Now momma cow lies peacefully,
As darkness closes in;
Resting from a hard days work,
As woman-like she wags her chin.

The sun has sank away, way down,
An hour or so ago;
And twilight too has slowly vanished,
I'd like to have you know.

January 1982

DRIVING

I stood out in the moonlight,
To watch the traveler pass;
I could not hear his motor,
But I certainly smelt his gas.

I waited very quietly,
Until he passed from sight;
Then I walked into the house,
And bid my fears good night.

His car was bright and shiny,
With chrome and fancy paint;
But all those fancy fixtures,
Don't make you what you ain't.

Next morning as I listened,
To the local radio station;
I heard he never made it,
To his destination.

His speed, it was excessive,
And the curve, too sharp you see;
So he had taken a quick way,
To reach eternity.

He was not a careful driver,
This I'm sure, that all could tell;
For he, woke up for breakfast,
In a Precinct, known as "Hell".

It's not him that I feel sorry for,
But those he left behind;
So "please" you reckless drivers,
Keep your "loved ones" all in mind.

January 1982

THANK YOU LORD

It's such a pretty world today,
Look at the sunshine all around;
Look at the rain as it falls to the ground;
Look at the rainbow up in the sky;
And thank the good Lord up on high.

It's such a beautiful world today,
Look at the green trees all around;
Look at the grass upon the ground;
Look at the clouds up in the sky;
And thank the good Lord up on high.

It's such a pretty world today,
Look at the wild flowers all around;
Observe the rocks upon the ground;
Look at the lightning up in the sky;
And thank the good Lord up on high.

It's such a pretty world today,
Look at the animals all around;
Look at the water on the ground;
Look at the mountains up in the sky;
And thank the good Lord up on high.

It's such a beautiful world today,
Look at the birds flying all around;
Look at the insects on the ground;
Look at the stars up in the sky;
And thank the good Lord up on high.

It's such a wonderous world today,
Look at the snowflakes all around;
Look at the snow banks on the ground;
Look at the snow floating down from the sky;
And thank the good Lord up on high -- Amen.

January 1982

INSOMNIA

I lay awake so late at night,
I count the seconds as they fly;
I watch the clock so carefully,
As the minutes slowly, pass me by.

I cannot somehow seem to reach,
That friendly land of Nod;
And as I toss, and turn, and stretch,
I send out a prayer to God.

May those peaceful bonds of life,
Which hold day and night, together;
Always come when needed most,
In times of life's stormy weather.

May I have a conscience clear,
As water in the nearby stream;
May I sleep, the sleep of babes,
And have a very pleasant dream.

January 1982

SASKATCHEWAN

It's a white land, a bright lad,
As far as one can see;
It's a good land, a hard land,
Yet Saskatchewan is for me.

It's a cold land, a bitter land,
A land of ice and snow;
It's a clear land, a windy land,
No matter where you go.

It's a ski doers land, a skaters land,
With lots of ice and snow;
It's a fishing land, a hunting land,
Almost everywhere you go.

It's a winter land, a summer land,
With two seasons poles apart;
It's a good land, a true land,
For those who are brave of heart.

It's a stony land, a sandy land,
A land where rivers flow;'
It's an open land, a wide land,
Most anywhere you go.

It's a grain land, a cattle land,
With lots of space for both;
It's a farming land, a grazing land,
Yet you must work for all your worth.

It's a rich land, a poor land,
Where taxes take your shirt;
But a free land, a pretty land,
If for a living, you must work.

It's an oil land, a gas land,
With minerals to burn;
It's a tractor land, a car land,
For which many people yearn.

It's a rough land, a tough land,
For those afraid of chills;
But a bright land, a warm land,
For those wanting summer thrills.

It's a green land, a growing land,
Where boys, men must become.
But a brown land, a dry land,
Beneath a rainless, summer sun.

It's a happy land, a sporting land,
Beneath a prairie sky;
It's a good land, with good people,
Where I'll live until I die.

January 1982

SEXES

There are two sexes in this world,
In every generation;
Both are needed, I would say,
For future propagation.

Of course it's said before we're born,
The male, has chromosomes x and y;
The baby girl has double x,
Which both carry till they die.

Now this one tiny chromosome,
Is where the difference lies,
Otherwise we're all the same,
From feet right up to eyes.

Now statistics tell us,
That the extra "x" is great;
It's not determined by the lady,
But by her ardent mate.

And that double "x" is stronger,
And more babes, with it survive;
Thus the female population,
Is very much alive.

But man develops, his muscle and brawn,
From the time he's a growing boy;
But the lady develops, her beauty and figure,
To that same man's pride and joy.

They claim the male the stronger sex,
This I do not know;
For the female is more flexible,
No matter where you go.

Now she can wear pantsuit or dress,
Whichever she doth choose;
But if father wore a silken gown,
His prestige he would lose.

And papa, when he takes a swim,
His trunks he must put on;
If you saw him, in a bikini,
He would never live it down.

A male, who lets his hair grow long,
Does look rather silly;
But long blonde locks, look rather nice,
On a pretty little filly.

Now ladies suits are another thing,
It can be one piece or two;
As long as it is short enough,
She gets a big woo---woo---.

But let the male half of the people,
Wear his pants too short;
And when he goes a walking by,
He'll make the ladies snort.

But when we go for lunch or drinks,
The male it seems must pay;
So the female is on top again,
We will have to say.

Now men somehow can sit around,
While the housework doth get done;
It's nice for him he got the "y",
The lucky son of a gun.

Now whether it be x or y,
It seems to matter not;
We have to take what we are given,
And live with what we got.

So the war goes on and on,
Between that little x and y;
But somehow they get together,
To create, for the sweet by and by.

January 1982

WHAT IS FEAR?

Fear is waking in the night,
Feeling things are not alright.

Fear for family, fear for friends,
Is a fear that never ends.

Fear for those who are traveling far,
Fear for those in a motor car.

Fear of illness, fear of death,
Fear of running out of breath.

Fear of fire, fear of cold,
Is a fear, we all behold.

Fear of poison, fear of pills,
Fear of imaginary ills.

Fear for children on the street,
Fear of falling off you feet.

Fear of robbery, fear of theft,
Fear for those, who have just left.

Fear of violence, fear of guns,
Fear of those who are on the run.

Fear of trouble, fear of speed,
A very common fear indeed.

Fear of bulls, fear of bees,
Both can give us shaky knees.

Fear of lightning, fear of thunder,
When the Heaven's are torn asunder.

Fear of earthquake, fear of flood,
Fear of the Devil in one's blood.

But regardless of the fears we have,
Our life on earth is grand;

So put all these fears aside,
And enjoy it while you can.

January 1982

DIARY OF AN UNBORN CHILD

Today my little life began,
Although my parents do not know;
The union of an egg and sperm,
And I began to grow.

I'm just a tiny speck of life,
But I'm to be a girl;
Blue eyes, and blonde hair,
Which mom will love to curl.

Two weeks more have passed,
Still mom don't know I'm here;
I'm still just considered part of her,
But I'm really me, I fear.

It's next week -- my mouth will open now,
Soon I'll eat, and laugh just so;
Then this little mouth will learn to speak,
And I'll call "momma" as you know.

My heart is beating now, all by itself,
And gently it will continue on;
Rest it cannot now, this I know,
Or I well have passed, to the great beyond.

Last week to, has come and gone,
And arms and legs, I'm getting now;
But many months will have to pass,
Before I can reach up to mom--somehow.

Again a week has passed away,
And tiny fingers have shown up now;
Someday I'll use them for work or play,
When mother show me how.

Six weeks have passed away,
Since life for me began;
But my folks only learned today,
That here I really am.

I hope your happy mom and dad,
I know that you must be;
I'm looking forward to see you both,
My name is Kathy, don't you see.

Two more weeks have come and gone,
And my hair is growing now;
It is smooth and bright and shiny,
Like my mother's, I know somehow.

A few more days, have passed away,
And I can almost see;
It's dark in here, but all is bright,
Out where my parents live, you see.

'Tis Christmas Eve, and my heart is strong,
I'm praying that naught to me, will go wrong;
And that on Christmas Eve from now on,
I'll be able to hear those Christmas songs.

Christmas now has come and gone,
And I'm looking forward to next year;
And in July I'll be myself,
I'm strong and healthy, do not fear.

The last day of my life began today,
I've found I'm unwanted, don't you see;
But I hope there is a place in Heaven,
For murdered children just like me.

I know I'll make a lovely angel,
With soft, pink skin, and shiny hair;
And somehow, I'll try to forgive them,
And maybe meet them there.

November 1981 - January 1982

I'M GETTING OLDER

I found I'm growing older,
And lost my magic touch;
I can't stand up to all the gaff,
Although I'd like to, much.

It used to be I ran a lot,
And I puffed a little bit;
Now, if I only walk a lot,
I puff until I sit.

It used to be, I worked a lot,
And slept a little bit;
Now it is, I sit a lot,
And sleep, part time, I sit.

It used to be an ache or pain,
Left while I slept at night;
Now I rub and stretch a lot,
And still the pain's a fright.

It used to be, I'd carry things,
Lift and climb at ease;
Now the steps they trouble me,
My old joints, almost freeze.

It used to be my hair was brown,
With bits of gray mixed in;
Now my hair is almost white,
And a bit more sparse or thin.

But with the aging of the body,
The mind to must progress;
Both become much wider,
Is a truth, I must confess.

But we do not mind the wider part,
As it gives us more, to sit on;
And makes our smile broader,
To be remembered, when we're gone.

Our chin has got the double look,
Our waist line follows thru;
We no longer have the willow look,
No mater what we do.

Now we might get absent minded,
But, not really stupid, as you know;
We've still got some mental gumption,
Although we've lost our "get up and go".

So keep right on living ladies,
Although your step be slow;
Your loved and honored for yourself,
Not for your speed, you know.

So pass on your words of wisdom,
In a gentle sort of way;
So that the youth can benefit,
And make your experience pay.

January 1982

AS SEEN IN A BUS DEPOT

I sat in the crowded bus depot,
And watched the crowd pass thru;
Knowing not, from where they came,
Or where they were going to.

There was every age and color,
That one would ever see;
I know not a single soul there,
Nor did any of them know me.

There sat a dapper business man,
Looking bored and stiff;
White shirt, and tie, and mustache,
And a forty-six midriff.

And next to him an Indian,
In moccasins and jeans;
Long black braids, down his back,
And a T-shirt, just for teens.

Along the middle of the bench,
Sat a lady, large and stout;
Well over three hundred pounds,
I really have no doubt.

And next to her a trim young Miss,
A steno or a teacher;
And right near by a gentleman,
By his garb, an active preacher.

Next to him an elderly couple,
Gently holding hands;
Showing they were going double,
Right to the promised land.

Right by them a Negro lady,
With her daughter by her side;
Their beauty was outstanding,
Let me to you confide.

And then a lad in plaster cast,
Where his leg had been broken;
With the names of friends engraved,
Just as a friendly token.

Two nuns sat across the aisle,
In their religious garb;
Their smile was so sweet and helpful,
As they worked hard for the Lord.

And then a troop of young cadets,
Wandered here and there;
Impatiently waiting for their bus,
To take them, only they knew where.

On the next bench sat a teacher,
With all her thoughts asunder;
Returning her class from a nature trip,
Of seeing nature's wonders.

A pair of corporals entered then,
With quick and steady stride;
To check if all was well within,
And passed out the other side.

Just then an older man rushed in,
With repairs beneath his arm;
One glance at him, and we all knew,
He lived upon a farm.

Now a mother and her baby,
Back in the corner sat;
So the tiny one could nurse awhile,
I'm very sure of that.

Then there were two ladies,
In furs and fancy hats;
And by the looks upon their faces,
A pair of snobbish cats.

Then there wandered in a man,
In a state of sad repair;
Beneath his arm a six-pack,
And in his eye a stare.

Then an airman, home on leave,
Strode up to the ticket stand;'
He was leaving for the front,
In a war torn foreign land.

Now did you ever sit on a depot seat,
And see these selfsame throngs,
Studying all these walks of Life,
Wondering where they're going, after they'd gone.

February 1982

PUPPY LOVE

A lonely little puppy,
Sat on the cold cement;
He knew not where he'd come from,
Or why he had been sent.

The evening was dusk and chilly,
The sun was going down;
He could not see why he was here,
Within this little town.

He patiently watched and waited,
For someone to come near;
But no familiar scent arrived,
Of those he held most dear.

He'd been dropped here just this morning,
By a stranger in a car;
Who had quickly snatched him up,
Down the highway very far.

Still he sat and whimpered,
As hungrier he had grown;
He was thinking of his family,
And the kennel known as home.

Then down the lonely walkway,
Came a girl, not yet grown up;
Her hand reached out to fondle,
The lonely little pup.

Love sprang up between them,
As head and hand did meet;
And as she knelt before him,
Pink tongue brushed pinker cheek.

So a lost and lonely puppy,
Had found a new made home;
Love and care was what he sought,
And this he would return.

February 1982

TO BECOME A MAN

You must venture into the bigger world,
And learn more of the golden rule;
Learn to be a stable man,
And not to act the fool.

Learn with others, to play the game,
And for honors to compete;
Learn to follow the rules of life,
And above all, not to cheat.

Learn to fight, for your place in the World,
And to separate, wrong from right;
Learn to stand on your own two feet,
Whether it be day or night.

Learn to cope when things go wrong,
And exchange this plan, for that;
And when this don't work out just right,
Not on your face fall flat.

Learn to climb life's ladder,
And place each foot just right;
And not to tramp on the backs of friends,
To reach that ultimate height.

Treat your friends, with care and respect,
To the underdog lend a hand;
Be a leader in your group,
But not with a heavy hand.

Learn to take advice of others,
And not a smart aleck become;
Learn to judge between truth and lies,
And in this world have some fun.

Learn to accept responsibility,
And in money matters be a sage;
Learn how to select your closest friends,
And always act your age.

Share your smiles with the world around you,
But leave your sorrows far behind;
Be kind to those in need of help,
And try to keep an open mind.

If these things you can accomplish,
And from trouble making can refrain;
I'm sure you'll be a successful man,
And a happy life will maintain.

February 1982

331

THE OAK TREE

There's an old oak tree in the garden,
Where a swing has hung for years;
It brings back many memories,
And many hopes and fears.

It's a place of solace and beauty,
A place where flowers grow;
It's a place for sitting and thinking,
Where anyone may go.

The lilacs bloom in the springtime,
And the roses bloom in the fall;
It's a place of peace and contentment,
At any time at all.

You can watch the bees and butterflies,
Throughout the summer time;
And hear the little songbirds sing,
Whenever the weathers fine.

'Tis a place of color and comfort,
When fall has rolled around;
The brilliant leaves from that old oak,
Almost cover the ground.

And when winter time has come again,
And all is white with snow;
The old oak still stands straight and sturdy,
Whether the wind be high or low.

And the old oak tree keeps listening,
To everyone's hopes and fears;
And the swing has been replaced now,
But it saw many smiles and tears.

So when you are worried and weary,
Go sit on the new made swing;
Talk to that old oak tree,
And listen to the birdies' sing.

February 1982

GONE BUT NOT FORGOTTEN

I drove down the vacant road,
Little used now by man;
Till I came to a lone hedge row,
Where once many children ran.

I saw a cairn of cement,
And a brass plaque there upon;
I stopped, I stood, and looked fondly back,
Upon those who had come and gone.

My parents, and my parents' parents,
Nearby did reside;
And all their friends and neighbors,
Had lived here side by side.

They pioneered the prairie,
When they were young and strong;
They grew, and learnt the hardships,
As time passed ever on.

They got their education,
From experience first hand;
They learnt things the hard way,
In this new and bitter land.

They worked to break the soil,
Build their house and made a home;
Took themselves a loving wife,
As life was to dreary all alone.

Most raised themselves a family,
Despite their troubles and strife;
Lived in a close community,
Through happiness and grief.

They populated the prairie,
Some stayed and some moved on;
But time we know moves rapidly,
And now they all are gone.

Neighborliness is a thing of the past,
And acres belong to one;
There is no one living on many roads,
And the country schools are gone.

The land has passed to larger farmers,
And larger houses are the fad;
All the little homesteads,
Are gone, which makes me very sad.

All we have is memories,
And perhaps a tree or two;
To remind us of those bygone days,
When yards were quite a few.

The struggle is for greater things,
And its push, push, push;
But we take not time to live no more,
As we must always rush.

December 1982

LEARNING

I stood by the side of Life's narrow road,
And looked each way with a smile;
I thought back to times, long ago,
And retread many a weary mile.

I looked at my life as carefree and gay,
Before I attended school;
Of love freely given by parents young,
If I followed the golden rule.

Then came the time of learning,
To walk, to talk, and to run;
Learning to read, and then to write,
Even that was considered fun.

But responsibility came with growth,
When I reached the age of school;
For I now must leave parental care,
And obey the teachers rules.

I must shoulder my books, and alert my mind,
And still follow those same golden rules;
For life's narrow path led to the door,
Of that little, old, white school.

And one must make new friends you know,
Learn to work, and with others play;
Learn to share and co-operate,
And gain some knowledge every day.

Now you must take grades one to twelve,
And take it in your stride;
Learn to stand on your own two feet,
And within the law abide.

One must learn to do the things.
By which you can a living make;
Not to fritter away your time,
And to learn by your mistakes.

So lets pass on our words of wisdom,
In a gentle sort of way;
So that future youth can benefit from,
And make your experience pay.

December 1982

TO A LAYING HEN

Oh noble bird of the poultry race,
Small and quick and full of grace;
Eating lots and jogging much,
A fowl with the human touch.

You may be brown, black, white or grey,
It matters not, so some folks say;
With beady eye and bright red head,
You will work and work, till you drop dead.

Working harder than some folks do,
Laying eggs for me and you;
Production limits you must attain,
To pay us for our milk and grain.

But you are not fussy what you eat,
Perhaps it's worm or bug or meat;
As long as there's enough you say,
Another egg appears each day.

Now they are smooth and round and long,
And with each one you sing a song;
It's advertising so they say,
And you also know that it doth pay.

Your eggs are mostly white or brown,
But on other shades we never frown;
White and gold are held inside,
Where all the calories there reside.

You lay an egg most every day,
With no time out for holidays;
For if production should ever stop,
That's the time, you hit the pot.

But at twelve days work for just a dollar,
I would not say, you were white collar;
If man could do but half so well,
The economy wouldn't be shot to hell.

January 1983

VALUE OF A CREAM CHEQUE

I'm looking back with fond memories,
At a scrap of paper in my hand;
I'ts known as a cream cheque,
The backbone of the land.

It was mother's meager pittance,
For her many hours of labor of love;
And we all knew, she'd spend it wisely,
With the help of God above.

It helped us in the twenties,
When things got tough you know;
Giving us many little chores to do.
Which helped to make us grow.

And when the thirties came along,
And things were mighty bad;
That meager little cream cheque,
Was all the cash we had.

But we had our cream and butter,
And milk for on our oats;
We made ice cream, for our desert,
And cheese for on our toast.

It bought our shoes and clothing,
Kept food upon the table;
Put a little gas in the old Chev,
To run when it was able.

It helped us buy a battery,
For an old fashioned radio;
And sometimes got a little treat,
For the kids, who helped you know.

It kept us off the government dole,
Which my parents were too proud to take;
We kept right on milking cows,
That same ten bucks to make.

And then as we grew older,
And off to school we went;
It was often those little cream cheques,
That to us were sent.

It bought our small necessities,
Put bread upon our table;
Paid ten cents for a film,
Which is not a money fable.

We watched for the mailman every week,
Waiting for our cream cheque to appear;
It was the cheque that bought our shoes,
And most other things I fear.

It brought us home for Christmas,
Paid our books, and pens and shorts;
Induced us into working hard,
For good marks on our reports.

Gave us graduation,
And then a ticket home;
Set me up in teaching,
But I could not leave it alone.

As having started milking,
When I was only four;
And all through school I practiced,
And enjoyed it all the more.

So I kept right on trying,
Helping others milk their cows;
I never did forget it,
And went back again somehow.

Then t'was in the forties,
To that task I did return;
But I was the mother then,
And for that extra cash I yearned.

Of course there were the problems,
Of milking with "little one" you see;
But at times it was accomplished,
With one upon my knee.

And tiny calves, and little kids,
Mix very well as they grow;
When you put them in a box stall,
It's a circus, as you know.

But to keep these cream cheques coming,
And make the business pay;
You must do things very regular,
And in a business sort of way.

So you organized your family,
Around your cows you know;
But no way, you could sit back,
To watch your money grow.

For did you ever try to milk ten cows,
And keep six kids in line;
It keeps one rather busy,
But those cream cheques looked just fine.

But as the children grew up,
You taught them to help you out;
It made your work some easier,
But often made them pout.

It helped to send them off to school,
For their higher education;
Bought them clothes and books and pens,
And helped on their tuition.

But about this time of need,
The government stepped in;
And put us on a quota system,
Which really was a sin.

It cut out many little shippers,
Who needed those extra bucks;
But it benefitted the big guys,
Who were shipping milk by bulk.

Then they started shutting down,
Your outlets close at home;
And charging you more transportation,
To truck out all your cans.

Sure they paid you higher prices,
But your expense went up "tout suite";
So they put on a subsidy,
To help you make ends meet.

But the government sure buggared things,
With all their quota play;
For one could never organize,
To make their hard work pay.

So many shoppers quit the job,
And left it to a few;
So bulk milk, and the big guy,
Have the upper hand you know.

They won't give you any more quota now,
And if you over ship a can;
They snatch away your subsidy,
And claim part value on your can.

Subsidizing powdered milk,
For export so they say;
Another slap for the farmer's wife,
For working hard every day.

But if they'd put the penalty,
On milk shippers instead of cream;
Their the ones, that glut the market,
With powdered milk, t'would seem,

So I sit here studying,
A cream cheque, from days gone bye;
Thinking how much better off we were,
When the government, kept its fingers from our pie.

January 1983

MEAT, NOW AND THEN

I walked down the spotless aisle,
To where the meat counter stood;
It looked so very appetizing,
That I know it must be good.

I stood there and thought back,
To the many years ago;
When the beef ring was in operation,
Before the freezer days you know.

They used to butcher every week,
A beef you hoped was good;
And shared up the cuts of meat,
So each got the piece they should.

They had a local secretary,
Who kept books of all the parts;
Of who had supplied the animal,
All the weights, and refund charts,

Of course there were the times,
It didn't work this way;
But you had to take, just what you got,
And look forward to another day.

Then you took it home and cooked it,
Or put it in an old fashioned ice box inside the door;
Packed it well and snapped the lid,
Hoping no water leaked upon the floor.

In winter time it was quite different,
As you butchered your own meat;
You froze it solid in the great outdoors,
And packed it deep in wheat.

They had no fancy wrapping paper,
But the grain it done no harm;
For we brought it in and washed it,
In water nice and warm.

As the weed seeds away back then,
Were buckwheat, stinkweed and thistle;
If they remained on the roast of meat,
They'd likely make you whistle.

But mice were another thing,
Which sometimes, the bin, invaded;
That's why we had to pack it deep,
For we liked not their tracks they traded.

But when it started thawing,
In the warmer days of early spring;
You hurried up and canned it,
To preserve the precious thing.

Of course at times you made corned beef,
Or salted it in brine;
Then regardless of the weather,
It tasted mighty fine.

Then there were some that fried their pork,
Packing it in crocks,
Covering it with lots of lard,
And topping it with salt.

There also was the dry salting,
Where you rubbed it very well;
Then left it set for several days,
To dry as hard as hell.

So when the summer rolled around,
You were glad to beat the heat;
You could rejoin the beef ring,
And get yourself fresh meat.

Now the present generation,
Know not these ways of life;
So they march up to the meat counter,
And pick out the things they like.

January 1983

PEOPLE WITH BONES

There are many kinds of people,
In this old world of ours;
Those that give out stinkweed,
And those that pass out flowers.

They are like the body's bones,
On which we build our society;,
Some are good, some are bad,
There is quite a variety.

Now there are the wishbones,
No doubt of whom you've heard;
They are always wishing for someone else,
To do the work they should.

They wish for this and wish for that,
But make no effort to acquire;
Thinking it should be handed them,
Because they so desire.

Then there are the funny bones,
Who sometimes are okay;
But they make sly fun of others,
That is not right I'd say.

They get awful tiresome,
If they do not pull their load;
And they don't think it is funny,
If it's them, that someone goads.

Then there are the knuckle bones,
Which knock that which others do;
They cannot see others better them,
And in society, number quite a few.

One must ignore the things they say,
And work on with a will;
Proceed to do the things you want,
And try to improve your skill.

Then there are the people,
Who belong to the jawbone class;
They talk and talk, of what they do,
But do little of anything else.

They tell all their friends and neighbors,
What they should do and how;
But when they are asked to help,
They are not willing to somehow.

But in most circumstances,
Talk is very cheap;
No doubt that is why,
Bull shit comes in heaps.

Then there are the prayer bones,
Which many people use;
I hope they are straight and sincere,
And not meant to abuse.

Some people seem to pray for things,
To take the place of honest toil;
But why should one shirk from work,
Until he becomes old or ill.

Then there are the backbones,
Of every job, or club or troop;
Who get their shoulders beneath the load,
And work until they're pooped.

If it was not for the backbones,
Of our body, and of our society;
There'd be a lot less accomplished,
And we know the reason why.

So try to be a backbone,
Hold up your end and do your share;
Speak not ill of others,
Or ask for everything in prayer.

Do not depend on wishing,
Or others ridicule in fun;
Do not knock the other fellow,
But get the necessary done.

February 1983

344

SLEEP WORRY

I lay in my bed,
In the dark of the night;
I listen for sounds,
With all my might.

I hear the clock tick,
Loud and clear;
And a tiny mouse,
That brings me fear.

The creak of a board,
The furnaces' roar;
Then I fall asleep,
And hear no more.

I wake with a start,
And all is still;
But I hear a tapping,
On my window sill.

The wind has risen,
And a nearby tree;
Is knocking gently,
For only me.

The silent board,
The quiet mouse;
Gives an eerie feeling,
To this old house.

Where lack of all noise,
Somehow don't do;
So I lay awake,
Tensed up and blue.

Waiting to hear,
A creak, squeak or roar;
So I can again pass through,
Sleeps welcome door.

I worry and fret,
What I should do tomorrow;
Seeing life pass so quickly,
Much to my sorrow.

How can one find time,
To accomplish their quota;
And a life unfulfilled,
Is not worth one iota.

So sleep while you should,
Get up bright and gay;
You have so much to do,
On the coming day.

So clear your conscience,
Relax your hand;
And you'll slowly slip,
Into sheep counting land.

February 1983

SASKATCHEWAN - GOD'S COUNTRY

I'm glad I live in Canada,
Especially the prairie west;
For I think that all in all,
It's the region that is the best.

I'll admit it's cold in winter,
And sometimes there's lots of snow;
But it's a healthy climate,
No matter where you go.

I've never seen an earthquake here,
Like they have in other lands;
Where your house falls down around you,
Which I would not say was grand.

Then there are the floods,
Which inundate so many parts;
The don't happen in Saskatchewan,
There's no place for them to start.

Yes, we have our run-offs,
In Saskatchewan in the spring;
But that's what makes Saskatchewan,
Do its production thing.

And when the springtime rolls around,
The sun is bright and strong;
The snow, soaks into the soil,
And the grass is green, before too long.

The flowers soon are blooming,
And birds are here again;
And the nicest thing to ever see,
Are the effects of a springtime rain.

The farmer's working in his fields,
The housewife in her garden;
Everyone is working hard,
To get all the little seed in.

Somehow we seem to get the rain,
Perhaps it's a little late or not;
But if we do our work well,
We most always get a crop.

There were the days of the dust storms,
But they seem to have passed away;
But then we need some minor trouble,
If everything else is "all okay".

Oh, sure we get a hailstorm,
Most every year or so;
It's always safer to insure,
As we know not where it will go.

Yes, we have the grasshoppers,
Flea beetles, army worms, and the rest;
But no one has seen volcanoes,
Out in the prairie west.

We never see an avalanche,
Out on our western plains;
Just one more advantage to,
Our place of life again.

Tornadoes show up very seldom,
And their strength is not as great;
As in other locales of the world,
This I'd like to state.

And to see all our fertile farmland,
As a sea of green and gold;
Makes one realize Saskatchewan,
Is a heavenly sight to behold.

So let's enjoy our life here,
And not complain of what we get;
For many parts of this world,
Are much worse off yet.

February 1983

THOUGH I AM BLIND

What do I see,
Though I am blind;
I see not with my eyes,
But only my mind.

I see with my fingers,
I see with my nose;
My ears help too,
Don't you suppose,

I see the wind,
As it gives a sigh;
I see the train,
As it passes by.

I see the flowers,
On bush and vine;
I see the food,
On which we dine.

I see the love,
In a child's heart;
As from his mother,
He's forced to part.

And with the coming,
Of the spring;
I see a lot,
Of little things.

The grass sprouts up,
The rain doth fall;
The sun shines bright,
Over it all.

I see a bird,
In a nearby tree;
As the sound of his music,
Floats down to me.

I feel the sun,
As it goes to bed;
And sense the stars,
Up overhead,

I feel the passing,
Of the seasons;
And know by heart,
All the reasons.

Feeling the snowflakes,
As they fall;
Making a blanket of white,
Over it all.

Going to bed,
And thus to sleep,
Shutting out darkness,
That I somehow must keep.

September 1983

TIME GOES ON

We are slowly growing older,
No matter how we try;
To stay strong and flexible,
Alert, alive and spry.

Growing older's getting tougher,
Somehow we can't keep up;
Although everyone's been trying it,
Since Caesar was a pup.

Our eyes are growing dimmer,
And our glasses getting thick;
We cannot step along too good,
Unless, accompanied by a stick.

But we were only given,
Two feet on which to stand;
And if God is only willing,
They'll get us, to the promised land.

Our hearing is getting fainter,
Very garbled and unclear;
For it too is aging,
So I'm getting deaf, I fear.

Our sex drive too is failing us,
As do all things with age;
But one cannot live forever,
As in life's book we're just a page.

Now may we keep our faculties,
Be bright and free from pain;
Keep ourselves quite mobile,
Although we need a cane.

Have our friends about us,
Chat, o'er a cup of tea;
And do a bit of knitting,
While we watch T.V.

Play a hand of cards,
And hear the daily news;
Read the local paper,
And express our personal views.

Take a little bit of time,
To just sit and reconstruct;
Recall those days when we were young,
When living was not, all luck.

November 1983

UP! UP! UP!

Inflation's got us by the neck,
And to death, it's choking us;
I don't know anything that we can do,
Except make an awful fuss.

Coffee is going higher,
And sugar has hit the sky;
Meat's away up in the clouds,
Until we can't afford to buy.

But peanut butter it's on top,
At eight-ten for three pounds;
Yet Trudeau, still keeps telling us,
Our economy is sound.

Interest rates keep rising,
Until it's twenty past;
We can't afford to borrow,
And our credit's gone at last.

So we draw our belt in tighter,
And try to find what it's about;
Weigh the pros against the cons,
And decide to do without.

Cook a little plainer,
Wear a little less;
Phone not quite so often,
And burn yourself less gas.

Get a job to earn a little,
Raise a family of one;
Cut out cigarettes and alcohol,
And all your other fun.

This way you pay the taxes,
And the rent when it falls due;
The power, water, and telephone,
Are only just a few!

But sometimes I wonder,
What we're living for;
But then, <u>there's the cost of dying</u>,
Which we can't afford.

1983

COUNT YOUR CALORIES CAREFULLY

We like the stand up straight and tall,
And hold our tummies in;
When Tuesday night has rolled around,
We hope we're still as thin.

Now seven is your weigh-in time,
And our chart is carefully signed;
For "Taking Off the Pounds" you know,
It's our motto you will find.

When we've ceased to pop the buttons,
And most of the bulge has gone;
The zippers they slide easily,
And your old clothes can be worn.

That's when we get advanced you know,
To join the League called K.O.P.S.;
It is a badge of honor,
For us ever slimming T.O.P.S.

So count your calories carefully,
As on fruit and vegetables you eat;
Let's not expand the waist line,
Nor bulge out on the seat.

Push aside the fatty foods,
Turn up your nose at cake;
Drink not high calorie alcohol,
And let sweets stay on the plate.

With all these little tricks you know,
You'll change from T to K;
So count your calories carefully,
I know you'll find it pays.

October 5, 1986

HISTORY OF COMMUNICATION

Now communication is far different,
From what it used to be;
How have things in era's past,
Affected you and me.

It used to be our forefathers,
Lived in clans, or tribes or bands;
And had no communication,
With folks in other lands.

The tom-tom drum or bagpipe,
Would sound out their challenge fair;
Or the smoke signal of the enemy,
Would tell us he was there.

Then works of art or drawings,
Were used to communicate;
To show us what we should know,
Of someone's plans or fate.

From these sign languages developed,
Which could be written down;
And extended to an alphabet,
Of credit and renown.

We know each separate area had,
A dialect of its own;
And could only partially understand,
Those tribes away from home.

'Twas because of poor communication,
That the Tower of Babel fell;
A language change by God himself,
To spread people for a spell.

So those that could communicate,
Went each their separate ways;
To set the roots of countries,
That, we still have today.

But time and progress moved along,
And populations expanded too;
They mixed with other cultures,
And communications grew.

In the early days of man,
Messages were sent by foot;
A relay runner traveled fast,
Sometimes running till he dropped.

Then they used a horse and rider,
To communicate they say;
But accidents befell them,
As they sped on their way.

Then there was the one time,
In our Canadian History;
That Laura Secord used her cow,
To communicate, thru the enemy.

Pigeons too were often tried,
In time of war or need;
But it was too precarious,
And undependable indeed.

But word of mouth was not enough,
So helpers must be found;
To extend and speed up,
The range of human sound.

In the middle seventeen hundreds,
The idea of the telegraph was heard;
Twenty-six letters for the alphabet,
And a current, to spell out the word.

But by the year of eighteen thirty-five,
The Morse Code came into style;
And by the year of forty-four,
He sent a message forty miles.

In the year of eighteen fifty,
A Trans-Atlantic Cable they tried to lay;
But the project was abandoned,
Until a future day.

But in the year of fifty-seven,
The project came to pass;
Ireland and Newfoundland,
Could communicate, at last.

In the following sixty years,
They laid over twenty more;
So communication was sped up,
From our eastern shore.

Let us not forget the telephone,
Which most of us have on the wall;
It lets us talk to friend and neighbor,
Or place a long distance call.

Now Alexander Graham Bell,
A Canadian of great fame;
In the year of seventy-six,
Invented the phone, that bore his name.

In the century, that's come and gone,
Since o'er the wires, his voice came;
There have been may improvements,
But the principle is the same.

The old crank phone, we had for years,
And the dial phone is here to stay;
Now there's the desk phone, and button phone,
And the view phone is on its way.

And then there is the Royal Mail,
Which always must go thru;
It can travel across the country,
In days numbering very few.

We've seen the days of the post-rider,
The post chaise, stagecoach and train;
But now they use the mail truck,
And some by airplane.

It used to be that two cents,
Saw a letter on its way;
But now it costs you twelve cents,
And that's not enough they say.

We also have the newspaper,
Which comes every week or day;
To give us ads, the news, or social,
And the politics, so to say.

We see the latest farm facts,
And the gossip of Trudeau;
You can read the little comic strip,
Or your horoscope you know.

Then there are the magazines,
To which one subscribes by mail;
And blind communication,
In the form of Braille.

Of course there is the shorthand,
Used in office work;
A form of communication,
The user cannot shirk.

The radio, was first thought of,
Well over a hundred years ago;
But component parts must be made,
Before this new project could grow.

'Twas in the early nineteen hundreds,
The system came alive;
And in the following fifty years,
For perfection, they did strive.

Now radio is an industry,
Of basic mass communication;
Employing many thousands,
In the field, and in the station.

We can get the worldwide news,
And the weather before it's here;
We can listen to our favorite song,
Or hear politics quite clear.

We can tune in on short wave,
Or have a C.B. close at hand;
So you see we are communicating,
All across the land.

Twas in the year of twenty-six,
That T.V. was first found;
A new way of communication,
Synchronizing both pictures and sound.

And in the early thirties,
They began broadcasting to the World;
And another flag of communication,
At this time was unfurled.

And we have had improvements,
Numbering quite a few;
In color, and cable programs,
And reception too.

Now global communication,
Has been amplified by far;
It's a T.V. and telephone satellite,
Officially named Tel-Star.

And then there's telemetry,
Which maps the world below;
Records it on a tape,
And broadcasts it, to us you know.

So you see communication,
Has thus advanced by far;
From runners, and smoke signals,
To talking to a star.

May 1977

MORNING ON THE LAKE

I woke up very early,
As the fog, was hanging low;
The wind was soft and lazy,
So it had no where to go.

It drifted very gently,
Across the little bay,
Until the daylight, and the breeze,
Frightened it away.

It rolled across the surface,
Of the water, as it went;
Like smoke rising from a fire,
Whose life was nearly spent.

And as it softly disappeared,
The wildlife came in view;
They were waiting for the clearing,
As many fishermen, were too.

The little ducks were diving,
For their food, you may be sure;
And the gulls, were flying overhead,
In feathers white and pure.

And then there were the pelicans,
Who floated on the waves;
Looking for their breakfast,
Like a band of errant knaves.

The noisy crow, soared overhead,
In feathers black as ink;
And every time one moved a bit,
He set up quite a stink.

The saucy little red squirrel,
Looked on with great disgust;
And shook his bushy little tail,
When running was a must.

And then there was his cousin,
Large and quick, and gray;
Begging for the tidbits,
From not too far away.

And soon the human fishermen,
Were out in forces full;
To break the silence of the lake,
And disturb the early gull.

The roaring of the motorboats,
And the waves, upon the shore;
Broke the eerie silence,
As the fog became, "No More"!

Now let us admire nature,
In a respective sort of way;
And leave things as we found them,
When we silently steal away.

July 1981

A GLIMPSE OF BLENDED HERITAGE

"Twas in the year of seventy-five,
Our project came to birth;
The aim was "Blended Heritage",
We worked, for all we were worth.

We struggled ever onward,
Our promise to fulfill;
To record the work, of those long gone,
And those, still climbing life's steep hill.

'Twas a group of simple soldiers,
With our tools of mind and pen;
We thought it but an easy task,
To record the deeds of men.

But somehow, we got more involved,
As our project came to fore;
The snowball kept on growing,
Which caused our thoughts to soar.

From five school districts at the start,
In our own location;
It expanded up to nineteen,
Then we showed our hesitation.

With officers and committees,
We met every little while,
We worked, and talked, and phoned each other,
Like words, were going out of style.

We wrote many little letters,
To friends and strangers too;
And each time a note we got,
We read it thru and thru.

Lots of times we got no answer,
So we took pen in hand again;
And by yet another go around,
We felt like using words profane.

And carefully we collected,
Each epistle from the mail;
To read, and check and edit,
Until our eyesight almost failed.

Now all this time our officers,
Must legalize a deal;
And the folks called "Friesen Printers",
Was the one who stamped their seal.

Now there were may questions,
We must agree upon, you know;
The number of publications,
And a cover, designed just so.

The kind of paper most suited,
To our personal enterprise;
And the kind of type, and size of print,
Most suited to the readers' eyes.

Then there was the layout,
The format and the rest;
The index and the pictures;
To make our book the best.

Now all we representatives,
Corrected stories every week;
Had coffee with our associate,
As each mistake we'd seek.

These corrected stories, to Mrs. Keay did go,
For her mark of approval, and the final check;
For we didn't want a single 'boo boo',
In our History Book by heck.

Then off to Friesen Printers,
Went our stories, ream by ream;
For we must have our galley sheets,
To realize our dream.

Then back came those sheets from Friesen,
For each of us to check again;
And the selecting of the pictures,
Drove some almost insane.

Of course there were the arguments,
Over the minor, this and that;
But it was very seldom,
That it ended in a spat!

Of course all this must be financed,
In a business sort of way;
To ascertain the pros and cons,
And to make the project pay.

We set our price at 25, (dollars that is),
For a thousand pages strong;
For even a sturdy Scotsman,
How could that price be wrong.

So we pushed ourselves nigh onto death,
For three long arduous years;
Our grey hairs got slightly greyer,
Especially around the ears.

'Twas in the year of seventy-eight,
The momentous task was done;
And the books, rolled off the press,
Three thousand, one by one.

Then our work began all over,
In a different sort of way;
Because each copy must be checked,
Before the consumer had to pay.

Now the duds went back to Friesen,
And the goodies, were for sale;
To recompense the Credit Union,
So our credit didn't fail.

But still finances ran too short,
And interest seemed to climb;
So from our committee members,
We borrowed, many a dollar and dime.

Then we paid off the Credit Union,
As our friends and members shared the load;
We again became a working group,
To sell where ever we could.

Now we have worked for five more years,
Our debts to settle for;
We banked our assets for interests sake,
So perhaps we may pay you more.

But let us stop a moment,
To give thanks to those who worked;
Giving time, and thought and money,
And very few have shirked.

Now there was Ada and Maurine,
Who worked away out west;
To search out the Ada pioneers,
They done their very best.

From Alada we had Atelio,
Who alone the job did fill;
His energy was great,
And his time spent, greater still.

Now Baldwinton and Irene,
They worked hand in hand;
Jack and Lil were good at finding,
The past history of that land.

Blue Bell was represented,
By Pearl and Carl Ackerlund you know;
They sought our many histories,
That helped our book to grow.

Now Eddingfields were members,
Aided by Kitty Groskoff too;
Their work was much appreciated,
They came from Cairnsview.

Dufferin was represented,
By ladies numbering three;
A lot of material was gathered by,
Hazel, Jo and Dorothy.

Now Eastbank was the district,
Where Ted Guggamus did dwell;
He was a great supporter,
And done his work real well.

Happyland was represented,
By Groskoff and DeRoo;
Aided by the Lloyd brothers,
Who were a great help too.

Langmark, Thule and Wasteena were joined,
Under the Keay regime;
With Anna, Alex and Ron the leg men,
And Margaret, our "Book Club Queen".

Now Madawaska had two Muriels,
To collect its History;
They were ardent workers,
I'm sure that you can see.

Mount Ethel had Martha Chisan,
Who traveled from afar;
Who with the aid of Atelio,
Brought her district up to par.

In Ruth we had a pair of Mary's,
By the name of Watt and DeRoo;
And with the aid of Marcel,
They carried their workload thru.

Seagram and Winter worked together,
With Audrey and Muriel Barnett doing their thing;
And with some help from far off Clarence,
Made their area more interesting.

Wilbert had three willing ladies,
To record its picturesque history;
Florence Grant, Gladys Hewson and Edith Wismer,
Were the selected workers three.

Then there was Rene, who aided them,
And helped the Wilbert ladies too;
He was a very willing worker,
And a helper to quite a few.

Vance was the central area,
From which Blended Heritage sprung up;
From here came Louie and Harold,
Who's idea kept right on growing up.

So lets take off our hats to them,
And all the others who got "History Fever";
Our project was a great success,
And may "Blended Heritage" be around forever.

On the mild sixth of February,
In the year of eighty-four;
Our Book Club had a meeting,
And finally closed its door.

We think our book one of the best,
And financially, we're in the black;
We've made a lot of very dear friends,
And parting makes us sad by heck.

But no doubt in another decade,
Our Club should re-convene;
And update a successful project,
But by then we'd be the elderly, it would seem.

December 1983 - February 1984

CHRISTMAS AS IT WAS

Again the Christmas season,
Has come and almost gone;
But somehow it is not the same,
As in the times long gone.

It used to be we worked for love,
To create whatever we gave;
Now they see, how much they can buy,
As to money, they are a slave.

It's spend the bucks regardless,
Of whether you can pay;
The day of reckoning can always wait,
Until a later day.

Christmas has gone commercial,
In many more ways then one;
Most must have their alcohol,
Before they can have their fun.

There's turkey and the trimmings,
There's candy, nuts and mistletoe;
How far it's came, from that first Christmas,
Is a great deal you know.

For when Christ was born in Bethlehem,
Beneath a shining star;
Much of the world was primitive,
And no one heard of a car.

Travel was by camel then,
By donkey or on foot;
Slavery was predominant,
And Herod got all the loot.

Times were very hard then,
Laws were unfair and cruel;
Spending is in excess now,
And the excess is the rule.

But still we look on Christmas,
As the holiday time of the year
And we lay aside our differences,
To bring all others cheer.

367

But could we not be less commercial,
And give a bit more of ourselves;
Make it a season of loving,
Sharing with Santa and his elves.

The singing of the carols,
And the manger scene;
The "Little Baby Jesus",
And Mary was the queen.

All the Kings and Wise Men,
The angels from afar;
And many, many common people,
Praying to a star.

So let us remove "Commerce from Christmas",
Give a little more just of ourselves;
Make it a time of living and giving,
And personify "Santa and the Elves".

February 1984

INTO THE PAST

A little old lady sat knitting,
As she gently rocked to and fro;
Her fingers performed the stitches,
But her thoughts were of long ago.

She chose not, to think of the present,
With a body full of pain;
But looked back to many years ago,
When she was young again.

Her mind dwelt in her girlhood days,
When she was straight and strong;
Of how she ran and skipped a lot,
And her hair was blond and long.

Of how she grew to womanhood,
Fair in figure and face;
A blessing to her parents,
And a credit to the human race.

Then the sickness struck her,
Carrying her nigh to death's door;
Tormenting her mind and body,
Till she'd hark for the heavenly shore.

She'd been a wheelchair patient,
For nigh onto forty years;
But she still remained a lovely lady,
And of death she had no fears.

She complained not to those around her,
Nor had she ire for her fate;
She wore a smile wherever she went,
As a friend she stood first rate.

And as a pillar of strength, she sat there,
Tho frail of body and limb;
She was soon to join her maker,
To live in peace with him.

February 1984

WHAT IS A GRANDMOTHER?

She is the parent of your parents,
On each side of the family tree;
But that's not all she really is,
Nor what a grandmother means to me.

She's a body who really cares,
And has time for all my woes;
She speaks to me, firm but gentle,
And of what she says she knows.

She has time for hugs and kisses,
And can brush my hair just so;
She knows when to hold me tight,
And when to me go.

Her experience has taught her much,
Of what life is all about;
She knows when to ask for help,
And when to kick us out.

Don't forget she raised your mother,
And also your daddy too;
So she has learnt by practice,
What to do for you.

So listen to her carefully,
Tho you think her old and worn;
For she became a grandmother,
The minute you were born.

She knows when to dust your britches,
Or take you by an ear;
But she's had lots of experience loving,
Of that you need not fear.

For if you'll only listen,
By her experience, you may gain;
She has a lot of knowledge,
On keeping this old world so sane.

One day you'll be a grandmother,
In the years to come;
And if you've listened carefully,
It can be a lot of fun.

February 1984

ADVICE TO A FATHER

To become a father,
Is not so very hard;
But to be a true one,
You must trust in the Lord.

You must be a wise man,
To choose a loving mate;
If you wish to provide your child,
With affection and not hate.

You must be a good provider,
And protect him from all harm;
Show him true affection,
Be decisive, strong, yet warm.

Love him and his mother,
Teach him to love you back,
Just don't dole out the money,
While his morals run off track.

Take part in all his projects,
Show interest in his work;
Show him how to be a man,
And not a hoodlum or a jerk.

And do not let your faith desert you,
If at listening he doth fail;
Just guide his spunk and fire,
Some day your trust, will prevail.

Inside every father's heart,
There is a playful child;
So join with them in their adventures,
But let them not run too wild.

Spend not too much to spoil him,
Make him earn, what he doth desire;
Supply him not with all you missed,
Or his ambition will loose fire.

In the eyes of your little son,
You're the greatest that can be;
You can scale the highest mountain,
Or swim the deepest sea.

You can catch the largest fish,
Or be a prince in Spain;
As long as you doth show him love,
He cares not, your work is plain.

In the eyes of your little boy,
Santa Claus, Superman and father are one;
Just keep him thinking that way dad,
And life will be so full of fun.

Now you as a loving father,
May have stature large, or small;
As long as you're a good father,
Size matters not at all.

And when your son gets older,
You'll have differences a few;
But then don't you really hope that,
He'll make a better man than you.

He'll absorb lots of your knowledge,
If you have taught him right;
He'll also gain from other sources,
So help him win his moral fight.

As he gets a little older,
He'll think you are all wrong;
"Old fashioned" is what he'll call you,
But your patience must be strong.

He will fall back on his "Grandpas",
As a source of knowledge and love;
As they are full of jokes and riddles,
And not bossy in the advice they give.

And if you're a proper father,
You'll do some listening too;
To accept the younger generation,
Is a thing that you must do.

You must gain their confidence,
Treat them both fair and square;
Do not insult them, before their friends,
But, when they seek advice be there.

Do not check on them too closely,
But advise them, to within the law abide;
For if they join the outlaw group,
You can't stick by their side.

So just be a helpful part,
Of your child's life and love;
Help him grow in mind and statue,
And respect the Lord above.

Teach him to wear a smile,
Although his heart be sad;
Dark clouds do have silver linings,
If he knows how to find them, dad.

Let him follow in the footsteps,
Of a father good you see;
And let his roots surpass your own,
On that momentous family tree.

And when he still is older grown,
And became a father too;
He'll realize how right you were,
And say, "Dad! I love you, too".

March 1984

TO THE GRADUATES

Life is a "hill" before us,
Which we must work to climb;
Let us move steadily upward,
To reach the crest in time.

For if we falter, or loiter,
Along our path thru life;
The plan that God has set for us,
Will end in sadness and strife.

We will not have accomplished,
The mission, we set out to do;
We will have failed, our inner self,
And failed our parents, too.

Life's path may be strewn with roses,
But some thorns, also there may abide;
It is for us to select the good things,
And put the wrong ones aside.

So take a tight grip on the future,
And pull with all your might;
If you are a willing student,
Things will work out alright.

So the "Best of Everything" to you,
And may God lend a helping hand;
May your life be a bed of roses,
Until you reach the "Promised Land".

March 8, 1984

BREAKFAST -- LONG AGO

I stand in front of an electric stove,
And turn a button with ease;
I stop and think of long ago,
When to get my breakfast, I'd freeze.

I rose in the morning early,
To light the old cook stove;
Shook the kettle gently,
To find that it had froze.

Took out the dusty shaker,
To rattle clean the grates;
Or your stove would only smolder,
And your breakfast would be late.

Then with chips, and old newspaper,
Soon had the stove alight;
But shivered for a little while,
Till the top got red and bright.

It took most half an hour,
Till heat was flowing free;
And your kettle, was on the boil,
To brew your pot of coffee.

Then you made the porridge,
While the big, old kitchen got hot;
For you then must call the family,
From father down to tot.

Tucked beneath the woolly blankets,
The air so frosty clear;
It gave all, a great big appetite,
Of that we had no fear.

But by the time they've risen,
The stove is cherry red;
And for the aroma of burning wood,
There is something to be said.

The oats were hot and steaming,
The milk as cold as ice;
And every little pair of hands,
Were eating in a thrice.

There was no artificial heat,
I'm sure you're well aware;
Unless you kept on poking wood,
Into that stove with care.

Now all you modern ladies,
Who think yourselves, so posh and fair;
Think how your parents, and grandparents lived,
And show them, you really care.

June - July 1984

ADVICE TO A YOUNG MAN

I'm looking down the railway track,
At a switch box standing there;
It's much like our future life,
At which we stand and stare.

With our hand upon that switch,
Or the throttle of our life;
We know not, which track to follow,
Will it be happiness, or strife.

Should we ease the throttle gently,
Of take right off on high;
But no matter how we do it,
We'll live until we die.

Perhaps we'll take the right lane,
Down that straight and narrow line;
Or perhaps it will be the other one,
With low spots and hills divine.

The one may be smooth sailing,
With a mediocre end;
While the ups and downs of the other route,
Will us to glory send.

The straight and narrow track no doubt,
From potholes or stones be free;
But dull and drab and on even keel,
Is not the route for me.

But I like those hills and valleys,
I'd like you to comprehend;
So I'll take the high road,
Until the bitter end.

But no matter, which the path,
Be faithful, to a friend;
Give out love and kindness,
And the underdog defend.

And to those in need of help,
Your good right hand extend;
And to those aged, and lonely hearts,
Try to be a friend.

If the road becomes too narrow,
And the incline too rough and steep;
You can always use the switch box,
If faith, will all you keep.

You almost always get a chance,
To put life, on another track;
But like the mighty railroad,
There's no way to turn it back.

July 1984

TO A WORM

Did you ever bite an apple,
And then peek in;
To see a little green worm,
And on his face a grin.

He looked at me, and caught my eye,
And this is what he said;
"If your mouth was any bigger,
I'm sure that I'd be dead".

Please remove your grimy hand,
And do not squeeze me so;
For "I am just a little worm,
And I would like to grow".

Now I see you watching me,
With that large and glittering eye;
Does that stare of disbelief,
Mean that I must die.

Oh Please! you great big human,
"I'm sorry that I'm here";
Tho "I fill your mind with shock,
You fill my life with fear".

I know that you are horrified,
That somehow I got here;
Although I'm just a baby worm,
Whom my mommy thought quite dear.

I am deep within the core,
Which you do not need;
So toss me out quite gently,
As I've only ate one seed.

Now I know you're human,
But I hope you'll treat me fair;
So finish up your apple,
As if I wasn't here.

So with a twinkle in his eye,
He quickly crawled back in;
So I took my last tasty bite,
And responded with a grin.

I walked over to a black spot,
Planting my core with care;
In hope that I could grow a tree,
Or at least to that worm play fair.

July 1984

THE DRIFTER

I sat by the side of the burning embers,
As the fire sank down low;
I hurried not, to put it out,
As I had no where else to go.

I sat and stared at the glowing coals,
As before me passed my life;
I'd like to be able to live it again,
With a little less trouble and strife.

I'd like to say I'd fulfilled the purpose,
For which to this earth, I came;
And done my part, not to break the hearts,
Of those I loved in vain.

Now my mother dear, I greatly fear,
Was saddened by my disrespect;
For my lack of interest in learning,
She'd sought for me by heck.

And then of course, like many others,
I pulled those childhood pranks;
None too bad, but some not good,
But it was no way to show my thanks.

I had my drinks with others,
And sometimes I drank alone;
But time just drifted on ward,
Till all my friends were gone.

The cigarette became my crutch,
On which I must depend;
I sit here with it in my hand,
And it's causing my bitter end.

Oh Yes! I made some very dear friends,
Male and female alike;
But somehow I was the quitter,
Drifting aimlessly thru life.

I married a beautiful lady,
And we had children three;
But because, I was a drifter,
She walked out on me.

Not that I really blame her,
For stability means a lot;
One must keep on working up,
And hang on to what you've got.

Yes I became a drifter,
And a drifter I will remain;
But if I had my life to live over,
I'd make some drastic change.

I'd pull myself up by my bootstraps,
To the rung at the top, that's right;
I'd consider advice of those gone before,
And hang on with all my might.

July 1984

LOST - A GOOD FARMER

Oh! What has become of the farmer?
Who lived in the days gone by;
Who worked 'til it hurt,
To save his shirt,
And respected the Lord on High.

Oh! What has become of the farmer?
Who lived in the long ago;
Who planted his land,
With a steady hand,
And lived in hope it would grow.

Oh! What has become of the farmer?
Who attended church each week;
Who worked with a will,
His duties to fill,
And on Sunday the Good Lord did seek.

Oh! What has become of the farmer?
Who paid his bills with cash;
He's gone from the earth,
Regardless of worth,
He cannot afford to be rash.

Oh! What has become of the farmer?
Who was a neighbor to all;
He gave a hand,
Across the land,
Whether it be spring or fall.

Oh! What has become of the farmer?
Who loved both his family and friends;
And with great pain,
I'll say it again,
His kind, have come to an end.

Oh! What has become of the farmer?
Who for food raised grain so clean;
It's now filled with spray,
I know you'll say,
Yet we eat it sight unseen.

Oh! What has become of the farmer?
Where the family was supreme;
It's gone down the drain,
To produce more grain,
And be a slave to the big machine.

July 1984

EVENING AT THE LAKE

Throw another log in the fire,
So the coffee pot doth boil;
Keep that fire burning,
For just another little while.

The smoke is rising slowly,
And the wind has left the bay;
The fishermen, are fishing,
To complete another day.

Children too are playing,
With a lack of zest and vim;
And many are the tired ones,
As daylight slowly dims.

But the mosquitoes, they take over,
For yet another spell;
You swat them very ardently,
And then you scratch like hell.

You hear a distant ball game,
The big time league, by the very sound;
But its just a pickup game,
Between friends newly found.

The gulls are circling overhead,
And dive, like a bullet sent;
A little splat, and rise again,
A minnows life is spent.

The trucks and cars move slowly by,
With due respect and care;
For most of the cautious drivers,
Realize that children will be there.

There are marshmallows roasting,
At the fire on a stick;
And the little children stuffing,
Till you'd think they would be sick.

But soon the darkness settles,
And all is quiet then;
A mingling of the many people,
Who have the fishing yen.

July 1984

ALCOHOLIC EFFECTS

It is an age of "sipping saints",
I'd like to have you know;
No matter who, or what they are,
It's to the pub, that they must go.

It's lady-like to "drink it up",
And the gents they "slurp it down";
All seem to afford it now,
Tho some still on it frown.

But you know there is a saying,
On what alcohol does to man;
It can be his ruination,
So control it if you can.

It's broken more wedding rings,
Than either axe or hammer;
It can make you lose your self-respect,
And put you in the slammer.

More homes are destroyed by firewater,
Than ever burnt by fire;
You may not believe all this,
But try and prove that I'm a liar.

And then there are the children,
Who also suffer, quite a few;
Due to money spent on alcohol,
Neglect and beatings too.

Homes have been wiped out, of course,
In an emotional sort of way;
But regardless of the degradation,
It seems alcohol is here to stay.

It has emptied out more purses,
Than society will admit;
So if your going to buy it,
Stop!! and think a little bit.

Can I pay all those I Owe,
And have a small bit left;
Can I lay aside for my old age,
And not drink myself to death.

Have I got a driver's license,
That I'm proud to show around,
Or am I paying extra penalties,
As under alcohol, I was found.

Have I wrecked a lot of vehicles,
Causing damage, injury or death;
Or let another person drive,
When I had alcohol, on my breath.

Have I been responsible,
On each job, that I have done;
Or have I lost my perspective,
And went off to have some fun.

Some say that mostly money,
Is the root of evil in this land;
But things would be a whole lot better,
If drugs and booze were banned.

July - August 1985

385

RETIRED FARMER

I quit the job of farming,
To retire into town;
For somehow or other,
The work began to get me down.

I could not get in motion,
With the rising of the sun;
And keep up the necessary speed,
Until the day was done.

Tho I retired from that farming,
A number of years ago;
Somehow one don't forget it,
I'd like to have you know.

And when the harvest rolls around,
The old spark still is there;
The gathering of the grain and sheaves,
One must in this excitement share.

For as I ride down the busy highway,
I look from left to right;
To see who's oats, are greenest,
And who's barley is getting ripe.

I observe the herds of cattle,
It they are fat or thin;
And how the pasture is standing up,
In spite of a drying wind.

I see the little calves, and colts,
As they frolic on the hill;
It takes me back those many years,
To when I was farming still.

I make note of the hay crops,
If it be thick or thin;
Or if the ripening grain crops,
Have a growth of weeds within.

For with these modern chemicals,
A farmer can help control his lot;
But in the end he has to take,
Whatever he has got.

He can rearrange his plans,
And try to improve next year;
But Nature too can change her mind,
And put things out of gear.

So do not invest too heavily,
Make the bucks, before you spend;
For farming is very unpredictable,
And a "deep hole" may be your end.

August 1985

ODE TO A DISHWASHER

I stand before my kitchen sink,
With water hot and cold;
Thinking back to days gone by,
How we did it, in times of old.

We carried water from an outdoor well,
To heat on an old black stove;
Its contents were as hard as rocks,
Softened only with our love.

We split the wood for this old stove,
With muscles brown, and axe;
It used up those excess calories,
That now, our figure, seems to tax.

We got our fingers nice and black,
Before the stove was lit;
As we struggled with the kindling,
We had to cuss a little bit.

Sometimes the wood was soggy,
And the paper hard to light;
Often the head snapped off the match,
As it we tried to strike.

So then we'd add a drop of fat,
Coal oil or diesel fuel;
To get that damp wood burning,
And keep our tempers cool.

But it's so different now,
With water hot and cold;
But still no one likes doing dishes,
As in the days of old.

Now some have automatic washers,
But to use you first must rinse;
Now doing everything twice,
Don't to me make any sense.

But you may take a shortcut,
By acquiring a four-legged friend,
It matters not the color,
Whether he be black or sand.

As long as he likes licking plates,
Before the dishwasher gets its turn;
This makes a housewife's paradise,
Where the most dreaded job is concerned.

August 1985

POWER-OFF

Now times have changed an awful lot,
Since forty years ago;
I found that out the other night,
I'd like to have you know.

And then very suddenly,
Our power disappeared;
The change it was terrific,
Even worse than I had feared.

I had to sit me down and think,
What it was that I could do;
For I could not use the oven,
And the stove top was out too.

The freezers, they quit working,
With no power in their line;
So you kept them tightly shut,
So the food would keep just fine.

You could not use your sewing machine,
As its one that you plug in;
You could not wash your dirty clothes,
If that was your planned out whim.

A can you could not open,
Or the microwave turn on;
The clocks all cease their ticking,
Since our power was all gone.

The furnace it quit working,
No power, the controls to operate;
"Twas light the backup heater,
Or suffer a chilly fate.

We could not get drinking water,
Or brew a cup of tea;
The electric knife failed to function,
So no sandwiches for me.

We could not watch our soaps,
Or turn on the radio;
But we could sit and talk a bit,
Which we seldom do you know.

Many things we had to improvise,
While our power was not there;
Showing we'd become dependent,
For our daily fare and care.

And as darkness was soon coming,
We rushed to do our chores;
As we had no old-fashioned lantern,
To work with out-of-doors.

Now we could light a candle,
Or an oil lamp at best;
We could not see the weather,
Or hear any of the rest.

It made the children wonder,
How we lived those years ago;
They could not see how we survived,
Thinking us very primitive and slow.

But in those so-called backward days,
We got along just fine;
We earned our bread with honest toil,
And for family life had some time.

We were not always on the road,
Running here and there;
But we loved our families just as much,
Showing we had time to care.

We did not have a lot of cash,
But we paid as we went along;
We did not have a guilty conscience,
Owing money was considered wrong.

We did not have the gadgets,
That many have today;
We just worked a little harder,
Is what the old folks say.

As I could not run the vacuum,
Or make some coffee brew;
So I ate an apple,
And went to bed to have a snooze.

But snoozing was not natural,
At that time of day;
So I sat up to write this poem,
To drive my cares away.

August - September 1985

HARVEST TIME

It's clear as a bell,
And wet as hell,
But harvest must go on.
You wonder and wait,
And curse the fate,
That brought the rain along.
You stand and stare,
Then offer a prayer,
That the rain won't last too long.
But then towards night,
The skies are bright,
And you break into a song.
But as in the past,
It didn't last,
How could the Lord be so wrong.
Then the stars came out,
And twinkled about,
As tho the rain was gone.
But do not fear,
It was so clear,
The ice became quite strong.
And before morning light,
The ground was white,
And <u>Harvest Time</u> was gone.

October 1985

391

"MOTHERS"

What would we do without mothers,
They're the most needed thing in the world;
Ever since the beginning of time,
When "nature's flag" was unfurled.

Yes, Jesus needed a mother,
Although his father was Divine;
And so does every little tadpole,
Tho her species be different than mine.

Now who would create the offspring,
Of man and animals very rare;
Of birds and tiny fishes,
If their mother wasn't there.

Now who would have the patience,
To cuddle a baby small;
With tummy ache at midnight,
If there were no moms at all.

Now mother must know nursery rhymes,
And read aloud to girls and boys;
Show them how to wind a top,
And repair the broken toys.

They must bathe the tiny bodies,
Take snarls from their hair;
Cuddle them, and kiss them,
To show they really care.

There's clothes to patch and floors to scrub,
And meals to cook you know;
But moms are meant for children,
No matter where you go.

Now who can find a missing sock,
Or kiss a scrape or bruise;
Fathers may be very nice,
Somehow it's mom they choose.

Now I'm not downgrading fathers,
For their much needed too;
But when God created mother,
He knew what he had to do.

November 1985

392

ADVICE ON AGING

My brain is full of zest,
And my body has some fire;
But I'm afraid my ambition,
Has two flat tires.

My beauty got the wrinkles,
My hair has turned to grey;
I have to admit to you,
That I've seen better days.

The starch is in my spine,
And the sense is in my head;
If they become addled,
Then I might as well be dead.

But I keep my nose down,
Not up in the air;
And I speak to my friends,
When I meet them anywhere.

I spend more time a talking,
Than I sometimes do admit;
And if things aren't pressing,
I just like to sit.

I keep my hands busy,
And my brain on "Red Alert'";
It keeps one happy,
And it isn't hard work.

But do not sit idle and pout,
Enjoy life while you can;
For we were put upon this earth,
For the good of our fellow man.

December 1, 1985

AFTERTHOUGHTS OF CHRISTMAS

What do we know about Christmas,
Not very much I fear;
'Tis a season for living and giving,
It should be the best time of the year.

But Christmas has become so commercial,
With parents spoiling their young;
That many of the old Christmas songs,
Are hardly ever sung.

How often do family and friends,
Collect for an old-fashioned due;
Most are hitting the fast lane,
For Hawaii or Timbuktu.

How many mothers and fathers,
In the cities large and bright;
Think to stay home on Christmas Eve,
Declaring it a family night.

How many children hang a stocking,
To be filled with goodies and cheer;
To be tasted and played with later,
Well into the forthcoming year.

How many mothers and fathers,
Give the simpler things of life;
A book, a pencil and candy cane,
Causing Joy instead of strife.

Many invest very unwisely,
To keep up with the Christmas season;
Needing to pay for a long time to come,
Without a very good reason.

All these things must be paid for,
Causing worry and hardship great;
So why not do some soul searching,
Before it has got too late.

Enjoy the Christmas season,
In a small conscientious way;
Give love and cheer and happiness,
For which, with big bucks, you don't have to pay.

Teach your children the value of Christmas,
Do not spoil them thru to the core;
Explain the value of Santa,
The Babe, the hymns and the star.

'Tis a season of living and giving,
But give from your heart, not your purse;
Be free with your love and affection,
And don't make their morals worse.

January 1986

SEAGRAM

I stand before this rustic rock,
Letting my thoughts drift back to the past;
To when this was a pioneer land,
Of hills and flowers and grass.

But the pioneers were a sturdy lot,
And decided they should stay;
Regardless of the hardships and toil;
Not many went away.

But as nature took its course,
Some children came along;
And they had to be taught,
The three R's, along with history and song.

So 'twas in the year of 1913,
A ratepayers meeting took place;
To establish a seat of learning,
On this very place.

The south west corner of the south east quarter,
Was the site the department chose;
Of twenty-eight, forty-two, twenty-four,
That's where we are standing now.

Now three trustees were elected,
Mr. McGonigle, Prongua and Bush;
With Ed Barnett as Sec. Treasurer,
Things went ahead in a rush.

Two acres were to be bought,
At the price of forty dollars;
To set up a place of learning,
For these promising scholars.

Then fifteen hundred dollars was set aside,
To build and equip this place you know;
Suitable to educate and train,
These children's minds to grow.

Thus in the year of fourteen,
With Reverend Baird on the throne;
Nineteen anxious children,
Made Seagram, No. 227, their part time home.

Now Seagram Lake was christened,
In around about ship-shape way;
As an empty Seagram's bottle was found,
On the shore of an unnamed lake one day.

So to his surveyor partner, He jokingly spoke up,
Saying "Seagram Lake" is as good as any;
Tossing it far out from shore,
Creating a situation that was rather funny.

For the Seagram name was passed along,
To the district and the school;
To some of the people there about,
It was against their etiquette rules.

Forth-five teachers graced thy throne,
In a period of fifty-three years,
A few were old, most were young,
But they taught you much I fear.

In the year of 1930 - 31,
Seagram's population became very great;
Like sardines they were closely packed,
With Edna Beaudty as head of state.

Now fifty-two pupils in one classroom,
In grades from one to ten;
My what a difference between education,
As it is now; and was then,

Over 180 pupils sat thy seats,
Of many religions, creeds and races,
Many educated children,
Left to take, their "grown up" places.

For over twenty years, the school was church also,
Providing for our morals too;
Catholics had the morning service,
The United in the afternoon.

Then along came the war torn years,
And Seagram, joined with the rest;
To fight for King and Country,
They done their very best.

Over a dozen boys and men,
Took part in that sad affair;
Most of them returned to us,
But a few remained out there.

Now Seagram had its highlights,
Which numbered quite a few;
Look ye back with me now,
While I name you just a few.

There were the Christmas concerts,
Where all children had a part;
Drama, drills, verse and song,
Performed with all their heart.

The candy bags, and Santa Claus,
Sometimes his tummy fell;
But the goodies in that paper bag,
Really tasted swell.

There were the Sunday afternoons,
With skating on Prongua's slough;
And the hockey games you often played,
Against Winter, Ruth and Manitou.

Then there were those wild old shivarees,
That lasted all night long;
But somehow we survived the stories,
The music, alcohol and song.

Then there were the dances,
When the school was generally packed;
The local orchestra, played peppy tunes,
And of alcohol no lack.

Some of the local young stuff,
Had a "banty rooster" scrap;
But when the next dance rolled around,
Everyone was back.

Also there were the "drama plays",
That the community club put on;
With the work and fuss and practicing,
Winter never got too long.

Of course there were the picnics,
Which took place every year;
Where you met your friends and neighbors,
And enjoyed a bit of cheer.

There were ball games and pillow fights,
Foot races and a booth;
The horseshoe pits were busy,
And at times the language was uncouth.

But we enjoyed ourselves to the fullest,
While we waited for supper time;
The meal it was delicious,
And the pie it tasted fine.

For the cooks in that hilly country,
Were far beyond compare;
That's why so many healthy people,
Originated there.

May 3, 1986

THE PAST

There's memories that linger,
Down thru the years;
Memories of <u>Hope</u>,
And memories of <u>Fears</u>.

Memories of <u>Joy</u>,
Memories of <u>Sorrow</u>;
Memories of the past,
And a by-gone "tomorrow".

Memories of <u>Work</u>,
Memories of <u>Play</u>;
And of looking forward,
To a better "today".

Memories of <u>Sickness</u>,
Memories of <u>Health</u>;
Memories of <u>Poverty</u>,
Memories of <u>Wealth</u>.

Memories of <u>Taking</u>,
Memories of <u>Giving</u>;
Memories of how,
To make a good living.

Memories of <u>Sunshine</u>,
Memories of <u>Rain</u>;
Memories of <u>Pleasure</u>,
Memories of <u>Pain</u>.

Memories of <u>Diapers</u>,
And little Dresses of silk;
Memories of <u>Pablum</u>,
And many bottles of milk.

Then came the boys,
With fond memories too;
Harder to raise,
And with problems a few.

Memories of Winter,
Memories of Spring;
Memories of Summer,
When heat is the thing.

Memories of Fall,
As the years roll around;
Of Harvest and Hope,
For the next go-around.

Memories of Friends,
Memories of Foes;
Wondering how they made out.
And where did they go.

If we could but live over,
Those days long ago;
Would those memories be sweeter,
I really don't know.

So why not enjoy the memories,
Use them while we can;
For these too will fade away,
As it does to every man.

May - June 1986

WINNERS NEVER QUIT

Now all you young and restless,
Who wish to become a success;
Set yourself a goal in life,
And strive on your very best.

First you need a desire to learn,
To become, what you set out to do;
You cannot change your mind,
And drop it, half way through.

You must keep your mind and body,
As healthy as you can;
For it is harder to succeed,
If you're only half a man.

You are only what you eat,
So judge your intake as you go;
Health can be ruined very easy,
And then what can you do.

Do not smoke the cigarette,
Or with alcohol be too free;
For a ruined constitution,
You do not want to see.

Of course there is the drive you need,
To keep your goal in sight;
So don't let your desire lapse,
Or you'll find success in flight.

Wishful thinking will not make,
A profitable career;
So put your forward in "Bull Low",
And do not shift your gears.

Be resourceful in your attitude,
And when success seems in vain;
Work out your problems carefully,
But always try and try again.

Persevere regardless of,
The times you've lost before;
Come forth with every effort,
Some hardships you must endure.

There is that old time saying,
And I'm sure it's full of grit;
That the quitters never win,
And the winners never quit.

Put your trust in the Lord above,
And carry on the best you can;
If your determination lasts,
You'll be your own top man.

So!--think things thru and not be careless,
Do not risk your life in vain;
Be honest with your fellow man,
And treat the Good Lord just the same.

June 15, 1986

TO A TAIL

All little pigs have tails you see,
But really I don't know why;
Unless to cover up your bum,
To make them less exposed or shy.

I have not found a use for it,
As by it you cannot hold him;
If they had put a knot in it,
A hand hold it could have been.

Now try to load a market pig,
And by his tail, hold him straight;
To ease him up the loading chute,
Or thru the pig fence gate.

That tail seems to control his mind,
And ornery he becomes;
His forward seems to be reverse,
And the loaders hands are thumbs.

Now with an ardent cuss word,
You stumble, trip, or fall;
It's then you wish that gall-darn pig,
Had no tail at all.

Really its only use is, to monitor his health,
A tight curled pinkish little tail;
Shows his health is good,
But if its straight and white, he's needing better food.

Now many breeders cut them off,
To stop tail-biting later;
Deeming not how queer they look,
Like a four-legged po-tatter.

But that little finger sticking out,
At the joining of two hams;
He cannot even swat a fly,
And for his owner, can show he gives a damn.

And when that ornery pig,
Reaches his bitter end;
I know not what we can make from it,
Except to designate his other end.

July 1986

404

A POCKET OF NATURE

A lonely winding country road,
That we used in years gone by;
A narrow grade, a sloping hill,
That seemed to reach the sky.

Green grass grows on either side,
With wild roses here and there;
With tiger lilies further back,
Where there was room to spare.

Cattails standing straight and tall,
In the slough where water lies;
The tadpoles and the wigglers fled,
As we went driving by.

The badger brush and willow,
Vie on either side;
To make a protective haven,
For the wildlife to hide.

The partridge and the prairie chicken,
Still in this sanctum abound;
While now in most all places,
They are never found.

A timid deer stands watching,
Wondering what to do;
No doubt in a few years time,
Her kind will be threatened too.

The gopher stretches tall,
From upon his pock-marked knoll;
But he too is growing less,
Due to poison I am told.

Of course there is dear cousin skunk,
To admire from afar;
But don't let him, get too close,
To your motor car.

Now clover grows along the ditch,
And wild insects here doth feed;
One feels close to nature's ways,
If one takes time to see.

Two birds nests hang in yonder tree,
So we know the hatch is on;
For mother's nestled snugly down,
While pappa bird gives forth with song.

Sir Hawk swoops slowly overhead,
In search of food they say;
But I wonder if he's thinking,
Those bygone's were the better days.

It's nice to know there are some spots,
Where nature still exists,
Where one can reach back to earthly things,
If one has time and the desire to insist.

But then we leave this Holy spot,
Where God still reigns supreme;
To hit the highway smooth and wide,
Controlled by speed and gasoline.

The country roads have disappeared,
The wildlife too has gone;
It's graveled grids and highways now,
That all motorists travel on.

June 13, 1986

SUCCESSFUL MOTHERHOOD

That little hen so brave and quick,
Will stand her ground to protect her chicks;
A nest she hid, in grasses tall,
And thirteen eggs she laid in all.

Small and round and creamy brown,
In a hollow of grass, upon the ground;
Predators she held at bay,
Whether it be night or day.

A mothering spirit, she did hold,
Her tactics were both brave and bold;
A bundle of nerves, in a grassy nest,
Showed motherhood at its very best.

Twelve chicks hatched, from those marbles of gold,
Twelve "Little Peepers" for mother to scold;
And mother being both determined and able,
Those twelve little chicks all reached the table.

December 1, 1986

THE TORNADO

I sat by the side of the slumbering stream,
As it slowly sailed thru the sand;
I sat and stared, when I knew I cared,
For life seemed to me so grand.

The song of the birds fell silent,
And the sun sailed under a cloud;
The shadows suddenly closed in on me,
And darkness settled like a shroud.

The sudden chill soon reminded me,
That life is a two way street;
The sun, the sand, and the silvery fish,
Or shadows, and sadness, and defeat.

The western sky darkened instantly,
As the twister came into sight;
I understood, why nature then,
Was silent, and dark as night.

I stood in awe, and wonderment,
At the strength of nature's forces;
Glad that I was not in line,
Of nature's uncontrolled resources.

Moments passed and the sun came out,
And the slumbering stream sailed on;
But the trail of destruction was eminent,
Where the twister had come and gone.

February 1987

COFFEE

I'm a coffee-aholic,
And a television fan;
I sit before the picture tube,
And drink it while I can.

It is the spice of life,
To the elderly as you know;
It gives your mental laziness,
Some more get up and go.

It makes you feel like rising early,
To make that precious drink;
Then you can sit and sip a bit,
While you plan and think.

After about the fourth cup,
I'm ready for my work;
But while I'm in action,
Don't expect me to stop or shirk.

I drink it in the bathtub,
I drink it at the sink;
I drink it while I work,
And when I stop to think.

I drink it very early,
I drink it very late;
It's the times I must resist,
That I have learned to hate.

I drink it while I visit,
In cupfuls, one, two, three;
And when I sit and meditate,
It's the coffee cup for me.

You can take your tea and crumpets,
Your alcohol and coke;
But if you take my coffee,
I'll not find that a joke.

I sip when I am studying,
I drink as I write a verse;
For I'm a coffee-aholic,
But God knows, I could be worse.

There are those that take to beer or wine,
To whiskey, rye or gin;
But I'll stick to my coffee,
Until I'm all done in.

And when I reach that Pearly Gate,
And the Good Lord invites me in;
I sure hope that up in Heaven,
Drinking coffee ain't a <u>Sin.</u>

March 1987

TO A SQUIRREL

Oh little squirrel, so quick and fast,
Why do you whistle so;
With body brown and bushy tail,
You're always on the go.

Long and sleek and full of fire,
You scoot up the highest tree;
You jump, you run and flip your tail,
Always floating free.

A little mite, with heart so brave,
As quick as the eye can see;
Looking out for tidbits rare,
And as saucy as can be.

He wakes you in the morning,
And teases you all day;
His chatter still goes on and on,
Till night chases day away.

Where do you get your energy,
Your speed, your timing gear;
If you were not so synchronized,
You'd be dead, I fear.

Your enemies are many,
As you quickly flit about;
Your eyes are very watchful,
And no doubt your heart is stout.

And if one treats you kindly,
Friendly you'll become;
But I hope you stay within the bush,
You little son of a gun.

For when you move to yard sites,
Your damage is severe;
You make many people,
Shed a regretful tear.

So be a jolly fellow,
And stay where you belong;
Out among the campsites,
Whistling nature's song.

Spring 1987

411

MAKING FRIENDS

Don't put off until tomorrow,
What you can do today;
For you never know, but that tomorrow,
Will be a bit too far away.

To accomplish what you want to do,
You must set to with a will;
Put your heart in what your doing,
Keep climbing life's steep hill.

Don't give in to temptation,
Seeking out the easy trail;
Or let laziness over come you,
And your determination fail.

Set your goals, but not too high,
So disappointment, rules the roost;
Keep your eye on the guiding star,
Don't refuse a little boost.

Accept with grace, a helping hand,
From those who wish to serve;
You'll both feel better for it,
It may help you make the curve.

For life's road is often rocky,
But a slight push is all we need;
Just a smile and shake of the hand.
Makes life much easier indeed.

So try and do your very best,
And when you can, give aid;
Accept the clasp of a helping hand,
For that's how friends are made.

June 1987

"DIGNITY"

Somehow I'm growing older,
Of this I'm well aware,
But it's not really all that bad,
For I now have time to spare.

It used to be, one rose very early,
Working from morn till late;
Now you can sleep till any time,
As we've reached the retired state.

Now my eyes are failing me,
And glasses I must wear;
But at least I have the time to read,
Instead of "rare and tare".

My ears too, are getting weaker,
I don't hear every little word;
But I can still get by you know,
And there's lots I've already heard.

My joints are just a trifle stiffer,
They tire, ache or break;
So I've slowed up a little bit,
And less exercise I seek.

My feet too are showing signs,
Of the walking they have done;
So I sit me down, and put them up,
Watching others run.

My face shows wrinkles, tho I'm fine,
They say age is what it's all about;
I tell them that it's just the knowledge,
From my brain reflecting out.

My back too, can't stand lifting,
The way it used to do;
But age lets you ask for help,
So do it; I'm advising you.

Independence is just fine,
But don't push your luck too far;
Accept some help, with pride and grace,
For your friends like you as you are.

Do not let your will power,
Cause you any pain of grief;
Accept your age most gracefully,
Your still noble beyond belief.

July 1987

413

THANKS FOR EVERYTHING

Thank you Lord, for what I have,
And that I'm sickness free;
Thank you Lord for what I am,
And that I belong to me.

Thank you Lord for a healthy mind,
That can think and work and do;
A right to hold my head up high,
I thank you for that too.

Thank you for two pair of limbs,
That function as they should;
Thank you for the privilege too,
Be strong, and kind and good.

Thank you for the friends I have,
And that they call me friend;
I'll do the best I can for them,
Until the very end.

Thank you Lord for a family large,
Who can manage on their own;
And lead me not to interfere,
And cause dissension to be sown.

Thank you Lord for the generation,
As grandchildren, they are known;
May their lives be long and happy,
And not with sadness overgrown.

Thank you for my eyes that see,
Myself and all my friends I meet;
Thank you for the guts I have,
To stand on my own two feet.

May I distinguish right from wrong,
And stand up for the right;
Not putting up with domination,
Without a mighty fight.

Thank you Lord, for a body strong,
And a mind that speaks out free;
Thank you Lord, for life and hope,
And for letting me be ME.

August 1987

ADVICE TO TEENAGERS

Now all you young wise acres,
Take advice when it is given;
If you do not work, to earn your shirt,
You'll never reach you goal of Heaven.

This world owes you nothing,
You came into it without a stitch;
You must work to grow, and grow to work,
It's not up to it, to make you rich.

No doubt you can be wealthy,
In many ways you know;
Physically, mentally, morally or financially,
Are some of the ways to go.

Do not believe your parents,
Owe your livelihood to you;
It cost them a lot, to get you here,
And troubles quite a few.

Then there is the government,
And friends no doubt a few;
Who don't mind helping out a bit,
But it is really up to you.

So stand up with a willing heart,
Take Labor by the hand;
He's not such a bad companion,
To walk with to the promised land.

For, if you're not a willing worker,
Some say you're going to find;
You'll have to work, for the lad that Was,
And left laziness behind.

So face the world with your head held high,
Your back held straight and strong,
A smile on your determined Jaw,
And the task won't seem so long.

Thus you'll climb those many hills of life,
And coast down those places smooth;
You'll make it to the promised end,
And have time for fun and love.

September 1987

OUR PARADE 1987

'Twas in the year of 1912,
Our town obtained a site;
Our streets were surveyed and named,
Our town had acquired its rights.

So in the year of Eighty-seven,
Our town is now extended;
And seventy-five years of growth,
Are in this parade well blended.

With much work and planning,
Our committees struggled on;
To try and share with others,
Those days that are now long gone.

The parade it was terrific,
With entries quite a few;
Things back to the beginning,
And modern entries, too.

The Shriner's band led the parade,
With music loud and clear;
Bringing back fond memories,
From the days of yesteryear.

Mayor Manegre and Ron Kelly,
Followed the marching band;
At organizing the parade,
They had a very big hand.

An old gas pump by Benny Paron,
Brings back memories of old;
Really quite a difference from,
The place where his gas is now sold.

There were several outside floats,
As the Legion pipes and drums;
The Energy Doctor from Battleford way,
Down the street did come.

The Champions of Law and Order,
Was a float from Battleford;
They kept the Peace in those good old days,
For this you may take my word.

The big machines by Novakl,
Cement and all the rest;
Have helped upgrade our community,
And they are the very best.

Finley too, has big machines,
That are used on the farm today;
A far cry from those horse machines,
But wow! What one must pay.

Then Cargill also had a float,
A new company that came to town;
With products, chemicals and such,
To help the farmer carry on.

The Pool they had a half-ton,
Stating "to help is why we're here";
And God only knows the farmer,
Will surely need it all I fear.

I.G.A. had a flower decorated float,
Drawn by a half-ton;
Yvette Dupuis as representative,
Of the largest store in town.

Now the Cut Knife Credit Union float,
Was done up in colors royal;
Balloons and streamers of white and purple,
Showed it had taken lots of toil.

The Country Roads were serving lunch,
As its float traveled round the town;
Bed, and tub and stove,
They provided for everyone.

The stove was rather shaky,
The bed and tub were full;
But they have rooms for everyone,
And good highballs as a rule.

The S.G.I. float came next along,
With a balloon so big and fair;
Later it was floated high,
In honor of our Mayor.

Our local Royal Bank, also had a float,
Personal Touch banking the Idea;
And how to save your money,
Was what it was all about.

The Co-op under Jim Cruikshank,
Yours for Service is it's plan;
They are very obliging fellows,
So support them when you can.

Brown's Imagery had a creative float,
A big camera on four wheels;
Shows that their new found business,
Is rolling right along we feel.

The hospital and the nursing home,
Displayed their work and care;
To show that when they are needed,
They will certainly be there.

The Lucerne also had a float,
With a rider known as Sam;
The Black Hole -- A keg of beer,
A bucket of chicken, good enough for any man.

A unique and different project,
Next caught   our eagle eye;
When the Dells and Bells went touring,
They were looking mighty spry.

Half a dozen peddlers,
In unison you see;
Bringing back the old days,
In the minds of you and me.

The museum had a float,
With costumes old and rare;
Many seniors were aboard,
And the manager was there.

In fact she won the prize that day,
As the best dressed senior in town;
So let's take off our hats to,
The costumes in old days found.

The ministers had a very nice float,
To unite them all as one;
We are all one in Christ Jesus,
Mothers, fathers, daughters, sons.

The Royal Purple had a float,
Depicting its work you know;
Justice, Fidelity, Hope and Charity,
For others as they go.

An old time band was playing well,
On a flat deck as we've seen;
They made ones thoughts in time rollback,
As Achermans' music was supreme.

Now Orval Ens with Martha,
Sitting sedately by his side;
His Model A, keeps putt-putting on,
Taking them for an old-fashioned ride.

The Athletic Recreation float,
Was by Jack Ovens drawn;
A lively group of sportsmen,
Were transported there upon.

The Town float wished a Happy Birthday,
To our friendly little town;
May we try to keep it so,
And not turn friendship upside down.

The Wednesday Girls had a unique float,
With a barn dance and music grand;
An old time box social,
That in years gone by was grand.

And a team of little goats,
With Parker kids in control;
Represented the by-gone days,
When animals and children shared carefree souls.

A little boy was close behind,
With his best friend a pup;
Only small in a big parade,
But somehow, he still kept up.

The Dufferin float carried many elders,
From that old time district clan;
One wearing the neighbors overall,
To represent a farmer man.

The ladies wore old time costumes,
Done hand work as they went;
Considering all the fun we had,
It was time well spent.

A well broke ox and river cart,
Sponsored by a local man;
Brought back the days of the pioneer,
When work began at dawn.

A stationary engine,
Brought in from Tatsfield Pool;
Showed us how in old times,
Man was a working fool.

Traveling right along the Route,
With Lloyd Howe in seat of State;
Was an old time combine,
Manufactured in the year of thirty-eight.

Bob Duncan had a horse and buggy,
Like in old time courting days;
Sometimes cars get flats or stuck,
But the horse always knew his way.

The fire engine joined the parade,
With Mel Sawatsky at the wheel;
To see that we have one on hand,
Makes us lots safer feel.

The Oddfellows float pulled by super D9,
Portrayed their circles three;
Friendship, Love and Truth,
And help for youth you see.

Gordon Blackstock's '24 Model T,
Came touring down the street;
To show us that those good old cars,
Are very hard to beat.

In among this vast parade,
A lone lad rode free and unafraid;
Mark Erickson, the uni-cyclist,
His balance and maneuvers were top grade.

A number of covered wagons,
And riders dressed in style;
Brought up the end of the parade,
Having traveled many a mile.

Wright, Goulette and Millhouse,
McCallum, Jamieson and Grier;
Also a pair of Ramseys,
All with appropriate gear.

There were many riders,
On animals beautiful and bold;
Trained and decked in beauty,
Brushed like burnished gold.

We also see Mr. Walter Bonnaise,
An Indian rider in full dress;
He won the native trophy,
A pride to Canada's West.

The streets were lined with people,
Old and young, rich and poor;
Local folks and strangers,
Who all came to stand and stare.

From all across our country,
And from down in U.S,A,;
All said 'twas Cut Knife's greatest,
A very Historical Day.

The meals they were delicious,
The cooks deserve medals, too;
But that last enormous breakfast,
It was tops for me and you.

Winter 1987 - 1988

CHRISTMAS THEN AND NOW
(For Senior's Party)

Christmas time has changed a lot,
Since the day when we were young;
But I can guarantee you that,
It hasn't gained in fun.

We used to get a natural spruce,
That grew out in the wood;
And let children of all ages,
Help decorate, the best they could.

For decorations were homemade,
By many little folks, you know;
This was half the fun of Christmas,
To see their faces all aglow.

But now those self same Christmas trees,
Are bought at prices high;
And somehow their aroma,
Is not like in days gone bye.

Many use the artificial trees,
There are many kinds they sell;
They will last for a long, long time,
Without any mess or smell.

But the love of those old trees,
The aroma was just great;
Enhanced by turkey cooking,
And pudding on the make.

The smell of the wood stove burning,
And the sight of popcorn balls;
And little children laughed with glee,
As many folks, came to call.

Then there was the Christmas stocking,
Which hung upon our bed;
We ate from it so carefully,
To make it last 'tis said.

But now there are so many treats,
Throughout the whole long year;
Kids don't enjoy their Christmas,
Half as much I fear.

The fudge it was delicious,
Made with nuts and dates;
But you got up very early,
And stayed up very late.

Many of the toys and games,
Were homemade, with love and care;
And all of your invited relatives,
Put in an appearance there.

For much work was necessary,
To prepare for all the fun;
But father was secretive,
And mother on the run.

But the excitement of the little ones,
When old Santa had been here;
Made all the work worthwhile,
For their beliefs were sincere.

But it was a time of happiness,
Talked about throughout the year;
And one felt serene and loving,
Because the Lord was near.

And when the day was over,
We were tired out I fear;
But gave our thanks quite readily,
Looking forward to another year.

But things are so different,
With not much thought, of the Lord;
The presents are all bought,
With cash some can't afford.

The presents are not Christmas like,
As they want cars to wreck or race;
Everything must be computerized,
To portray mostly war and space.

There are all these little robots,
To which one cannot show affection;
And cars and trucks and army games,
Which don't pass loves inspection.

The dolls they make so homely,
And animals much the same;
And the colors are ridiculous,
But the children aren't to blame.

But Christmas has gone commercial,
I'd like to have you see;
It has become a money game,
Too rich for you and me.

If we could only show them,
And help them to understand;
Christmas is a time to love and give,
And not, from others to demand.

And before the day is over,
Many little hearts are sad;
And many toys lie broken,
To the sorrow of Mom and Dad.

For by the time the season is over,
Many parents are in debt;
And many things have fell apart,
And the children are upset.

So how can they be merry,
And show true respect and care;
If there is deep worry, on their mind,
Happiness cannot be there.

So I look back with deep respect,
On the Christmases of old;
When the season was for family,
Not for spending all your gold.

So try to use your common sense,
And spend as you see reason;
Keep a lid on intoxication,
And due respect for the season.

May we have a Merry Christmas,
With not too much worry or fear;
Enjoy our friends and relatives,
And be back again next year.

December 1986

Local poet published in National Anthology

Maurine Becotte, poet

Maurine Becotte of Cut Knife, Sask., has just had original poetry published in "Wind in the Night Sky", a treasury of today's poetry compiled by The National Library of Poetry. The poem is entitled "Out Back", and the main subject is a memoriam to the outhouse of yesteryear.

The National Library of Poetry seeks to discover and encourage poets like Maurine by sponsoring contests that are open to the public and by publishing poems in widely distributed hardback volumes.

Maurine has been writing for fifty years and her favorite subjects and ideas are anything from a butter cup to farming to toasts to brides, politics, and war and history. A real variety of topics.

Maurine has also been nominated for distinguished membership in the Society. She also will receive a "Poet of Merit" Award plaque. As a gift to Maurine, The National Library of Poetry is presenting a recorded cassette album of poetry written by five award-winning poets - including Maurine's works. Maurine will also see a poem published in The National Library's "The Coming of Dawn", scheduled for printing in the Winter of 1993.

Maurine has self-published her works, with the help of her family, in 6 volumes of "Housewife Harmony". These volumes are available at $5 per copy or $30 for a complete set of 6.

Out Back

Away out back, in a tree lined lot
Is a little house, we have near forgot.
It stands so sturdy, straight and tall;
With no paint left on it at all.
The boards were weathered, warped and grey;
It's surely seen, a better day.
It contains a seat, with holes for two;
The adult size, and for children, too.
A box or nail is located there;
An Eaton's catalogue, for all to share.
You may study, while you sit;
If needs must be, you wait a bit.
But that little house, is feeling low;
And the catalogue, is gone you know.
But it waits and wonders, about the jerk;
Who installed, the water works.
But we leave it there just in case of need;
For it has been useful, yes! indeed.
And swallows nest, sets above the door;
Shows it's not forgotten, forever more.

- Maurine Becotte

Poets interested in publication may send one original poem, any subject or style, 20 lines or less, to The National Library of Poetry, 11419 Cronridge Drive #10, P.O. Box 704NR, Owings Mills, Maryland 21117. Please be sure to include your name and address with your poem.

All poems received are also entered in The National Library Poetry's North American Open Poetry Contest, which awards over $12,000 in prizes annually.

Wednesday, June 23, 1993

Printed in the United States
141631LV00002BC/2/P